TROUBLE IN THE CHURCHYARD

Churchill and Pemberley Mystery Book 4

EMILY ORGAN

Trouble in the Churchyard

Emily Organ

Chapter 1

"NEVER MIND, Mrs Churchill. Better luck next time."

"That's the third time you've said that to me, Mrs Thonnings."

"Nine balls thrown," added Doris Pemberley, "and not a single coconut."

"Thank you for that, my trusty assistant," responded Annabel Churchill, "but I didn't really need it spelled out. Come on then, Mrs Thonnings, let's have another go. I'm feeling lucky this time."

"It's a penny for three throws."

"I know that. I've already paid for three rounds, haven't I?"

Churchill handed Mrs Thonnings another penny and received three wooden balls in return. Then she took several paces back, squinted hard at the coconut directly in front of her and hurled the first ball at it with a sweeping overarm action. The ball sailed past the coconut and ended its journey in the striped curtain beyond it.

"Nearly!" shouted a voice in Churchill's ear, making her jump.

She turned to see a man in a straw boater hat standing right behind her. He had ruddy cheeks, heavy jowls and a mischievous twinkle in his eye.

"Do you mind?" she exclaimed. "You'll put me off my stride!"

"Oops, sorry!" He took a sip from the tankard in his hand.

Churchill quickly palmed the next ball and hurled it at the coconut. Once again, she missed.

"One ball left!" crowed the man.

"Thank you. I can count quite well by myself."

"Try using underarm," he advised.

"I prefer overarm."

"Oh, go on. Just try it."

"You might as well, Mrs Churchill," added Pemberley. "You've already had eleven misses, after all."

"If you say so," replied Churchill through clenched teeth. All she wanted was to be left alone to throw the balls whichever way she liked.

"Give it a bit of welly!" the man in the boater hat said encouragingly.

Churchill leaned forward, gently tossed the ball underarm and knocked a coconut off its stand.

"Hooray!" cheered the man in the boater. "You did it!"

"I did, didn't I?" replied Churchill with a grin. She smoothed her helmet of lacquered hair proudly.

"Told you it'd be better to bowl underarm," said the man.

"You did indeed. Thank you."

"And it worked!"

"It did."

"Well done, Mrs Churchill," said Mrs Thonnings, stepping forward to present her with the coconut. She wore a floral tea dress and the strong sunlight made her red hair look even more artificial than usual.

"Have another go, Mrs Churchill!" the man in the boater said persuasively, offering her a shiny coin.

"An entire shilling?" she replied incredulously.

"That's thirty-six balls in total," said Pemberley.

"I don't really have the appetite to throw that many balls at coconuts. My arm aches enough as it is after twelve."

"Have a go at something else, then," suggested the man, still holding the coin in his outstretched hand. "Throwing hoops, perhaps? Or skittles for a leg of lamb?"

"A leg of lamb?"

"That's the prize."

"Why are you offering me money?" Churchill asked. "Do I appear to be in need of charity?"

"This is Mr Butterfork," said Pemberley. "He's extremely generous."

"Is he indeed? Well, it's nice to meet you, Mr Butterfork."

"Likewise, Mrs Churchill. The sun is shining, the scrumpy is flowing and I intend to enjoy myself as much as is humanly possible at the Compton Poppleford Summer Fete. Every penny spent ends up in the coffers for the poor and needy. You can't ask for more than that, can you?"

"Indeed not."

"So, go and have some fun spending my shilling. And here's one for you, Miss Pemberley."

"Thank you, Mr Butterfork," said Pemberley.

"Now, spend, spend, spend!" he said with a grin, flinging his arms wide to demonstrate the expanse of the fete.

The field was filled with colourful awnings and marquees. A gentle breeze fluttered among the flags and bunting, playfully lifting the edges of gingham tablecloths. Lively chatter, children's laughter and the strains of a trumpet filled the air. A loud thwack sounded across the field at regular intervals as someone hammered the high striker in an attempt to send a toy mouse up a pole to hit the bell.

"Just right there would be perfect," an authoritative voice announced.

Churchill turned to see a gangly, dark-suited man pointing a camera at her.

"I beg your pardon?" she replied.

"Gather together, the four of you," he ordered.

They did as he asked.

"Closer!" he barked.

"What a bossy man," muttered Churchill as Mr Butterfork put one arm around her and one around Mrs Thonnings for the photograph.

"And... smile!"

The photographer clicked the shutter before Churchill had time to adjust her pearls and twinset.

"Just a moment. Who are you?" she asked.

"And smile again!" He took another photograph. "Lovely! Keep an eye on the *Compton Poppleford Gazette* this week. Your picture might make it in there."

Churchill was about to remonstrate when the jangle and chime of countless little bells reached her ears.

"Oh look, the Morris dancers are coming on," said Mr Butterfork as a dozen men dressed in white clothing took up their positions at the centre of the field. Their trousers were tucked into long red socks, and they had ribbons and bells tied around their arms and legs. Their hats were covered in flowers and they carried an assortment of sticks adorned with more bells and ribbons.

A hook-nosed man with a long grey beard struck up a

jaunty tune on his accordion and the men began to skip about and hit their sticks together in time to the music.

Mr Butterfork cackled and slapped his thigh, the scrumpy slopping out of his tankard as he did so.

"Isn't it a lovely tradition?" remarked Mrs Thonnings to Churchill, her own tankard of scrumpy in danger of doing the same as she bobbed her head in time to the music.

"It is indeed."

"There's nothing more English than a Morris dance, is there?"

"I should think there are a fair few things that are equally English."

"Like what?"

"Oh, I don't know. Tea, I suppose."

"That's Chinese," said Pemberley.

"Roses, then," suggested Churchill.

"Many of them originally came from China, too."

"You do get *some* English roses, Miss Pemberley."

"Yes, but they're those underwhelming dog roses, aren't they? The really nice ones come from China."

"Talking of dogs... where's Oswald, Miss Pemberley?"

The three ladies looked about them.

"I think I saw him in the parade earlier," said Mrs Thonnings.

"Are you sure?"

"Yes, he was on the lorry with the flower fairies. Didn't you see him? I assumed you'd given Miss Pauling from the orphanage permission to have him on their lorry."

"How sweet of Oswald to want to help the orphans," said Pemberley.

"Did you give Miss Pauling permission to have him on the orphanage lorry, Miss Pemberley?" asked Churchill.

"No."

"What if he's caused a lot of mischief or bitten one of the children?"

"Oswald wouldn't do anything of the kind! He would never bite an orphan or a fairy, and especially not an orphan dressed as a fairy!"

"I sincerely hope not, otherwise we'll be in big trouble. Or I should say, *you'd* be in big trouble, Miss Pemberley, for losing control of your dog."

"Oh look, here he comes now," said Mrs Thonnings, draining her tankard.

Churchill followed her gaze to see the scruffy little dog with a garland of flowers around his neck being carried under the arm of a smartly dressed man with a neat grey moustache. The man kept pausing to speak to people, presumably to make enquiries as to the identity of the animal's owner.

"Go and fetch him, Pembers," hissed Churchill. "I do hope he hasn't done anything to embarrass us."

Pemberley did as Churchill said while her employer and Mrs Thonnings continued to watch the dancers.

"I wonder what the meaning behind all these old traditional dances is," mused Churchill.

"Fertility," replied Mrs Thonnings. "That's usually the reason for dancing, isn't it? It's a celebration of fertility and of the reproductive abilities of a species."

"Is it?"

"Yes. The maidens would traditionally admire the men as they went about their dance and choose the one they considered most virile as their mate."

"I see."

"The dance provides an opportunity for the men to display their strength, good looks, prowess and well-turned legs."

"Really?" Churchill's eyes rested on a red-faced Morris dancer with a pot belly and a large, carbuncled nose.

"Yes. The maiden is fertile and looking for a mate, and the man is fertile and—"

"I'd better go and see how Miss Pemberley's getting on with Oswald," interrupted Churchill, suddenly desperate to leave the conversation behind. "I'll allow you to admire the Morris dancers in peace, Mrs Thonnings."

Churchill walked over to where Pemberley and the smartly dressed man holding Oswald were standing. She arrived just in time to hear her secretary apologising.

"What has that wretched dog done now?" asked Churchill with a sigh.

"Oh, nothing too terrible," replied the man. "Just the small matter of having eaten my sandwiches."

His voice was soft and he was well-spoken with intelligent blue eyes. He gave her a charming smile and she found herself returning it.

"Mr Pickwick doesn't mind about the sandwiches," Pemberley explained. "He said he can easily make some more."

"That sounds extremely understanding given the circumstances," commented Churchill. "It's a delight to meet you, Mr Pickwick," she added. "I'm Mrs Churchill."

"It's a pleasure to meet you, Mrs Churchill."

"And I do apologise again that Miss Pemberley's naughty dog has eaten your sandwiches. I can't for the life of me think why he doesn't have a lead attached to his collar today."

"Oh, it's here in my handbag," replied Pemberley, quickly retrieving it.

"I like the flowers round his collar," commented Mr Pickwick.

"The orphans must have decorated him," said Pemberley. "Apparently, he took part in the parade earlier."

Mr Pickwick laughed. "How delightful!"

"For goodness' sake, Miss Pemberley, put a lead on that dog so we can keep a close eye on him," said Churchill. "There's really no need for you to hang on to him any longer, Mr Pickwick. Your arm must be quite tired by now."

"Oh, righty-ho." He carefully handed Oswald over to Pemberley and dusted the dog hairs from his jacket.

"Oh heavens, what a mess your jacket's in!" said Churchill. "Do allow me to pay your dry-cleaning bill."

"I won't hear of it," he said, holding up a palm. "It's quite all right, most of it will brush off. In fact, I have a nice stiff clothes brush at home that'll do the job nicely. I'll be on my way, then. Nice to meet you both."

"And lovely to meet you, Mr Pickwick. If only it could have been under better circumstances."

"Please don't worry about the circumstances for a moment longer, Mrs Churchill. It was a great pleasure to meet your mischievous little dog, and what can there possibly be to complain about on a day like today?" He gestured toward the cloudless blue sky. "It's a lovely afternoon, it really is. I do hope you ladies enjoy the rest of the fete."

"You too, Mr Pickwick."

Chapter 2

"YOU WERE EXTREMELY lucky that Oswald's latest victim was a true gentleman, Pembers," muttered Churchill once Mr Pickwick had gone on his way. "That dog could have got us into a nasty scrape there."

"Most people are very understanding when it comes to dogs," replied Pemberley.

"Well-behaved dogs, perhaps, but not many people would have been so accommodating if a scruffy little mongrel had gobbled up their lunch."

"He's not a mongrel! He's a Spanish water dog."

"With a few other breeds mixed in."

"A touch of terrier and a splash of spaniel."

"And a gallon of mischief." Churchill patted the little dog's head affectionately. "Now then, I suppose we'd better go and spend the shillings Mr Butterfork gave us. Why on earth is the man so generous, Pembers? It makes me rather suspicious, if truth be told."

"There's no need to be suspicious of dear old Mr Butterfork. He's a lovely man."

"You do realise when you describe him as '*dear old*' that he's about twenty years younger than us."

"Isn't everyone?"

"It certainly seems that way. Still, I've always been a little suspicious of people who like to splash their money around. It's as though they have something to prove."

"Perhaps they're simply trying to prove they're generous people."

"There's generous and then there's *generous*, Pembers."

"What does that mean exactly?"

"I'm not sure, but I do feel sure that Mr Butterfork is a bit of a funny one."

The pair began to peruse the nearby stalls with Oswald safely tethered to his lead.

"I'd like to buy some of Mrs Roseball's damson jam while we're here," said Pemberley.

"You do that. It sounds delightful."

The two ladies walked up to a stall showcasing numerous jars of jam topped with patterned fabric tied in place with colourful ribbon.

"Well, these do look quite splendid," said Churchill.

A small, round lady with oval spectacles and a large straw hat stood behind the table.

"Hello, Mrs Roseball," said Pemberley. "I don't believe you've met Mrs Churchill, have you?"

"No, I haven't," replied Mrs Roseball, squinting at Churchill through her thick lenses. Pemberley introduced the two ladies and they all exchanged pleasantries.

"The afternoon's turned out nicely, hasn't it?" said Mrs Roseball, squinting up at the sky.

"It certainly has," replied Churchill.

"It wasn't supposed to be this nice, according to the forecast," continued Mrs Roseball. "It suggested a slight northerly breeze, and a northerly breeze is always rather chilly, isn't it?"

"I believe so," Churchill replied.

"But there's nothing northerly about this breeze at all; in fact, I think it's south-westerly, which can be a little fresh and damp at times. But it's quite pleasant today, don't you think?"

"It certainly is pleasant. May we buy some of your damson jam, Mrs Roseball?"

"Of course. If the breeze were any brisker then I suppose we'd feel the chill," she continued. "But it's quite light, isn't it? Much lighter than they said it would be. And from a completely different direction, too! You can't trust what they tell you in the forecast these days. It's thruppence a jar, ladies."

Churchill and Pemberley each picked up a jar of jam.

"Have a shilling, Mrs Roseball," said Churchill.

"Really? How very kind of you. A whole shilling? Goodness!"

"It's Mr Butterfork's money."

"Is it? I don't know what's wrong with that man, he's always showing off. Perhaps he's trying to impress us all, but it doesn't wash with me, I can tell you that much."

"Nor me, Mrs Roseball."

"Nor me," added Pemberley.

"They say he doesn't trust the banks and keeps all his money in a large tea chest in his bedroom. That's just asking for trouble, that is. One of these days someone'll just march in there and steal the lot. Then he'll be sorry."

"He will indeed," said Churchill.

"All he needs to do is deposit it with Mr Burbage at the bank. I've known Mr Burbage for many years and trust him as if he were my own brother."

"That's good to hear, Mrs Roseball."

"My late husband trusted him like a brother, too."

"Lovely."

"Both Freemasons," she added with a whisper, "but you didn't hear it from me."

"Indeed not, Mrs Roseball."

Churchill and Pemberley thanked her for the jam and went on their way.

"Where's Oswald, Pembers?"

"Oh!"

The two ladies glanced around but there was no sign of the decorated dog.

"I thought you just put him on his lead," said Churchill.

"I did, but then I let go of it to pay for the jam."

"Oh, good gracious, Pembers! Are you incapable of keeping him by your side for more than three minutes?"

"It does seem that way."

"Let's just hope he isn't eating someone else's lunch."

"Careful where you're walking, Mrs Churchill."

"What do you mean?" said Churchill, looking down at her feet.

"You strayed a little too close to the flower stall just then."

"What's wrong with that?" Churchill asked, surveying the colourful, scented blooms. "Such lovely flowers, aren't they?"

"They certainly are," replied Pemberley, "but Mrs Crackleby is very good at selling them. On the few occasions I've been snared by her I've ended up with more bunches of flowers than I could carry. Mrs Crackleby could sell tea to the Chinese."

"I thought you said tea came from China."

"Exactly."

The two ladies bought a couple of indulgences from the cake stall, then sauntered past the rifle range.

A blonde lady with protruding teeth called out to them. "Fancy a pop at a tin can, Mrs Churchill? Miss Pemberley?"

"No thank you, Mrs Harris. We're both a hopeless shot. It might prove a little dangerous!"

They found a couple of chairs beside the bandstand and decided to rest their legs.

"I wonder how many tankards of scrumpy Mrs Thonnings has consumed by now," said Churchill, biting into an iced lemon slice. "She likes to knock it back a bit, doesn't she?"

"Yes, she's always enjoyed a drink."

"She told me a joke about a butler, a cook and a pumpkin while I was paying for the first three balls at the coconut shy earlier, and to be quite frank it was unrepeatable."

"There's no need to repeat it, I've heard it before."

"Rather shocking, isn't it? I've never understood why alcohol causes some people to be vulgar. I can only imagine that crudeness is an underlying trait the individual generally manages to paper over with a layer of respectability while sober. A few drinks often serve to reveal a person's true character, don't they? Anyway, it's really quite pleasant sitting here with the sun warming our faces as we eat our cake. If we sit here long enough, we might see that dog of yours trot by."

"I hope so. I miss him."

The ringing of a bell brought Churchill back to her senses. It took her a moment to realise she had nodded off in the afternoon sunshine.

"Goodness! Fire!"

"Where?" replied a panicked Pemberley.

"Isn't that what the bell means?"

"No!"

"Oh, gosh." Churchill patted her ample bosom. "I thought it was the fire bell."

"No, it only means the mayor is about to address us."

"Oh, right. Shall we go and hear what he has to say?"

"Yes, let's. Look who's joined us just in time."

Pemberley pointed down at her feet where Oswald sat, poking his tongue out and panting a little.

"How lovely. Isn't he a good boy? Let's go and listen to the mayor, and then I think I'll head home. Funny how a little nap makes you feel more tired, isn't it?"

Chapter 3

Everyone's attention was focused on a small podium at the centre of the field with various flower arrangements surrounding it.

"Looks like Mrs Crackleby flogged some of her wares to the fete committee," Churchill muttered.

A table had been placed on the podium and a small, wizened man clambered up next to it, appearing to be weighed down by the heavy gold chain around his neck.

A young man laid out rosettes on the table as the mayor began his slow, languid speech. He commented on the weather and expressed gratitude for the hard work of the fete's organisers. Then he thanked everyone for attending and announced he would be awarding prizes for the various events of the afternoon.

Churchill was just about to inform Pemberley that she was heading home to put her feet up when an elegant elderly lady approached the stage. She wore a smart dusky-pink dress with pleated skirts and a matching hat. A brooch worn just below her left shoulder glittered in the sunshine, and her overall demeanour emanated excellent breeding.

"Who's that?" Churchill asked Pemberley.

"Lady Darby."

"I've never heard of her."

"She and Lord Darby live at Gollendale Hall."

"Never heard of that either, let's move a little closer so we can hear what she has to say."

The mayor continued. "We are joined by Lady Darby, who is attending today in place of her husband, Lord Darby, who sadly suffered an accidental shot to the foot at a shooting party in the Highlands this week. I'm sure you will all join me in wishing him a speedy recovery. Lady Darby will present the prizes."

Lady Darby stepped onto the stage and took up her position next to the mayor. She adjusted the brim of her hat so that it shielded her face from the sun.

The mayor scrutinised a piece of paper in his hand before reading out the results. "The winner of the tombola is... Mr Jones Sloanes." A smattering of applause followed as a slender, stooped man stepped onto the stage to be presented with a rosette by Lady Darby.

"The winner of the coconut shy with twenty-four points..." announced the mayor.

"Not me," muttered Churchill.

"Mrs Higginbath."

Another round of applause rang out.

"How well do you know Lady Darby, Pembers?"

"Not very well. Were you hoping for an introduction?"

Churchill gave a self-conscious laugh. "There's no need to assume that I wish to become *au fait* with every member of the landed gentry, you know."

"Isn't there?"

"No, although I must admit it can be terribly useful to have friends in high places. Wouldn't you agree?"

"I don't know. I've never had any."

"Oh, but you must have met some while you were a companion to your lady of international travel."

"Oh yes, plenty. But they weren't really friends; they were merely acquaintances."

"That's all these people ever are, Pembers! We call them dear friends to appear well connected."

"Do we?"

"Don't you?"

"No."

"Never mind. What do you know about Lady Darby?"

"She's been married to Lord Darby for about forty years, possibly even fifty. Her father was an American tycoon and I believe her mother was one of the Habsburgs."

"Very nice."

"Winner of the rifle range with an impressive forty-eight points…" the mayor called out. "Mrs Roseball."

"What else do you know about her, Pembers?"

"Much of her girlhood was spent in Switzerland, as I understand it. She boarded at a school over here, and as a young woman she lived in Paris."

"How wonderful."

"She speaks four languages fluently."

"Simply marvellous." Churchill watched Lady Darby hand out the prizes and wished she shared the elegant woman's status.

"And now for the results of the dog show…" announced the mayor.

"Was there a dog show?" Churchill asked Pemberley. "We should have entered Oswald for something!"

"He wouldn't have cooperated, you know that. He's too mischievous."

"You must do more to train him, Pembers."

"The best-behaved puppy..." announced the mayor. "Douglas."

A wide-eyed little white dog with large paws was carried onto the podium by its proud owner. Lady Darby patted the dog on the head, presented the owner with a rosette and engaged in some brief small talk.

"Best-behaved veteran dog..." continued the mayor. "Primrose."

Churchill watched enviously as a succession of dog owners stepped up onto the podium to collect their prizes and exchange pleasantries with Lady Darby.

"Best adult handler... Mrs Thonnings with Oswald."

"What?" exclaimed Churchill with a start.

"I don't understand!" said Pemberley.

"Your dog's been up to something else, with Mrs Thonnings this time. Come on, let's go and fetch our prize."

Pemberley scooped Oswald up and the two ladies hurried over to the podium.

"But what's Mrs Thonnings doing handling Oswald?" said Pemberley. "I didn't even know she'd entered him for the competition."

"It was probably after he wandered off while we were buying the jam. It's just as well she did as we'll get to speak to Lady Darby now."

Just as they reached the foot of the podium Mrs Thonnings sprang onto it ahead of them.

"I hope you don't mind that I borrowed Oswald!" she called out, her face flushed from the scrumpy. "I saw him running about and there was no sign of you, so I thought I'd keep him occupied and enter him for the dog show. I had no idea we'd win!"

Pemberley climbed up onto the podium with Oswald in her arms, leaving little room for Churchill. Worried she was about to miss out on an opportunity to speak to Lady Darby, the elderly detective did her best to step up and join the others.

"Room for a small one?" she chimed, pushing her large frame up against them.

Mrs Thonnings and Pemberley shuffled a little closer to Lady Darby as Churchill teetered perilously close to the edge.

"Goodness!" exclaimed Lady Darby. "This is a tight squeeze, isn't it? Which one of you is the handler?" She spoke with rounded vowels and clipped consonants.

"I am!" announced Mrs Thonnings proudly.

"And we are the dog's owners," Churchill chipped in, peering at Lady Darby over Pemberley's shoulder. "It's a pleasure to meet you, Lady Darby, and please do pass on my best wishes to your husband. I hope his foot makes a swift recovery."

"Thank you, that's very kind."

"I'm Mrs Churchill, the proprietor of Churchill's Detective Agency."

"Are you indeed? How very interesting. Now, to whom should I present the prize?"

"Me!" Mrs Thonnings piped up. "I did all the handling."

"Well done to you," said Lady Darby, presenting her with a red rosette.

"Don't I get a prize?" asked Pemberley. "I'm Oswald's owner."

"Oh, well... I'm not sure," replied Lady Darby. She turned to ask the mayor, who shook his head in reply. "I'm afraid we only have a rosette for the handler," continued Lady Darby with an apologetic expression on her face. "You do have the better prize of owning a lovely dog, however. Isn't he simply adorable?"

"We like to think so," replied Churchill proudly.

"Are you also his owner, Mrs Churchill?" asked Lady Darby.

"Of sorts. I help look after him."

"He is actually mine, though," added Pemberley, glaring at the red rosette in Mrs Thonnings's hand.

"Well, Oswald gets a lovely little rosette as well," said Lady Darby, pinning the red ribbon to his collar. "There, doesn't he look delightful?"

"He does indeed," said Churchill. "Thank you so much, Lady Darby. I sincerely hope that our paths cross again in the not too distant future. And I must add that if you are ever in need of a private detective agency, I do hope that you will consider us. We pride ourselves on utter thoroughness and professionalism."

No sooner had she finished her sentence than Churchill slipped off the podium and twisted her ankle. She managed to stifle an expletive as she sank to the ground, nursing the sharp pain in her foot.

"Good Lord! Are you all right, Mrs Churchill?" asked a concerned Lady Darby, peering over the edge of the podium. "Not hurt, I hope?"

"I'm quite all right, thank you," lied Churchill, forcing a grin through clenched teeth.

"I imagine the only real injury is to her pride, Lady Darby," added Mrs Thonnings.

Chapter 4

"I MANAGED to hobble here this morning," Churchill said to Pemberley the following day as the two ladies sat in their office, "but I'm not sure it was wise. You should have seen my ankle yesterday evening. It had swollen to the size of a balloon!"

"I think it was a mistake trying to squeeze yourself onto that podium," replied Pemberley. "There really wasn't room for us all."

"They should make the podiums for these things a bit bigger."

"They weren't expecting three people to collect a single prize."

"If you ask me it was Mrs Thonnings who shouldn't have been there. Oswald isn't even her dog!"

"I'd like to know which handling skills she employed to win the competition. I've never known Oswald listen to anyone before."

"Can I hear someone ascending the stairs to our eyrie, Pembers?"

"I believe so."

There was a knock at the door.

"Enter!" trilled Churchill.

She felt an odd shiver as a tall, thin man dressed in black entered the room. He wore a wide-brimmed hat with a black shabby coat over an even shabbier suit. His cheeks were gaunt and he fixed her with a pair of icy, steel-grey eyes.

"Oh, good morning," Churchill said reticently. "Do excuse the fact that my foot is up on my desk. I gave my ankle a rather nasty twist yesterday while conversing with Lady Darby."

The man registered this comment with barely a nod. He removed his hat to reveal a completely bald head, save for a handful of wiry grey hairs.

"I'm Grieves," he said in a deep, quiet voice. "The sexton."

"Are you indeed? Well, it's nice to meet you, Mr Grieves. You'll have to excuse me for not getting up. It's the ankle, you see. But do please take a seat."

Churchill detected an odour of damp earth as Mr Grieves seated himself opposite her with his hat on his lap.

"May we have some tea, Miss Pemberley?" she asked brightly.

Pemberley nodded and dashed into the room at the back of the office with Oswald following close behind her.

"What brings you here today, Mr Grieves?" asked Churchill.

"Something's amiss in St Swithun's churchyard." His eyes were unblinking.

"Oh goodness, is it?" Churchill felt another shiver. Although not a believer in the supernatural, she dearly hoped Grieves wasn't about to relate a ghost story to her. "What exactly is amiss?"

"I've noticed a fair few things."

"Such as?"

"I didn't hold much stock by them to begin with, but after the first couple happened I began to wonder."

"I see. And what are these things you noticed, exactly?"

"They're not much to speak of when considered individual-like, but when they're all added up together there's no doubt something's awry. Inspector Mappin wasn't the least bit interested, mind you."

"Why doesn't that surprise me?" said Churchill with a nervous laugh.

The sexton's gaze was so intense she found it a struggle to maintain eye contact. She fervently hoped Pemberley would walk in with the tea tray just to shift his focus for a moment. "Well, we're always happy to help here at Churchill's Detective Agency," she said. "Perhaps we could begin by discussing what these *individual-like* incidents actually are."

Churchill leaned forward to find a fresh sheet of paper, but immediately found she was unable to do so with her foot up on the desk. She gripped her leg and slowly eased it down onto the floor. "Ouch. I really didn't expect conversing with Lady Darby to be so perilous! Do you know her at all?"

"I know the family tomb."

"I see. Yes, I suppose you would."

Churchill noticed her hand shaking slightly as she dipped her pen into the inkpot. Mr Grieves's presence was making her feel more than a little uncomfortable.

"First of all, I found a rose on old Arthur Brimble's grave," said Mr Grieves.

Churchill wrote this down. "And that's unusual, is it?"

"Very." He stared pointedly at her.

"Has no one ever left a rose, or a flower of any other sort, on Arthur Brimble's grave before?"

"Never. He died in 1842 and had no known relatives."

"Is it possible that a long-lost descendant of some sort discovered his final resting place and came to pay their respects?"

"No. And anyway, the rose was placed there at some point during the night."

"Really?" Churchill felt a prickle at the back of her neck. "Can you be absolutely sure of that?"

"I always check the graveyard at dusk and dawn."

"And at dusk it wasn't there, but by dawn it was?"

"That's correct."

"Gosh! Oh, thank you, Pemberley. Tea! Tea, Mr Grieves?"

"No thank you."

"Cherry bun?"

"No thank you."

"I see. Now, where were we? Ah yes, the rose on Arthur Brimble's grave. What else is there, Mr Grieves?"

"Some lichen was removed from the headstone of old Sally Fletcher."

"Lichen?"

"Yes, and a bit of moss too, I suspect. You can see her name quite clearly now."

"Again, one might presume that the headstone was cleaned up by a family member."

"Old Sally Fletcher had no family. She was a spinster of this parish."

"Then perhaps a friend of hers did it."

"Her friends would all be dead now. She died in 1882."

"I see." Churchill made some notes on her piece of paper, unsure as to what she could do about any of this. She took a sip of tea, then asked, "Anything else?"

"A small hole beside the final resting place of Benjamin

Grunchen. I noticed it this morning while I was digging a grave."

"A hole? What sort of hole?"

"Just what I say. A hole."

"How big?"

"So big." He circled both hands.

"Could it possibly have been made by a rodent?"

"I wouldn't have said so. The only rodents I see in the graveyard are rats the size of your dog here, and I shoot them. There was no little pile of soil like you get with a rodent hole. You know how they dig away with their paws and create a small mound behind them?"

"I can picture that, yes."

"There was none of that. This was more of an exploratory hole. Made with a trowel, I'd say."

"You mean to say the hole is there as a result of human activity?"

"I'd say so."

"And it appeared overnight?"

"Possibly. I haven't seen anyone digging around with a trowel there in the daytime. I'd have told them to sling their hook if I had."

"Why would someone dig an exploratory hole in the grave of Benjamin Grunchen?"

"You tell me, Mrs Churchill."

"I don't suppose there are any Grunchen family members about to explain themselves?"

"There are plenty of them, but I haven't got round to asking yet because I only noticed the hole this morning. I don't see why any of them would dig a hole in his grave, though. It seems a most singular thing to do."

"It certainly does. Any other suspicious antics in the graveyard?"

"Some grass has grown on Saul Mollikin's grave."

"Isn't that supposed to happen?"

"Not to Saul Mollikin's grave it's not. Grass has never grown on it."

"Goodness, why ever not?"

Grieves lowered his voice and leaned forward a little. "Not a single blade of grass has ever grown on Saul Mollikin's grave for two hundred years."

Churchill shuddered. "Well, that is unusual. I wonder why that might be."

"They say he was cursed by the witch on Grindledown Hill."

"Oh, I see. It's one of those classic Dorset folklore tales." Churchill gave a cynical laugh.

"Oh, I'd dismiss it as folklore right enough," replied Grieves, "if I hadn't seen it with my own eyes."

"That would make it seem all the more real, I suppose," replied Churchill, gulping down a sip of hot tea. "Is that everything, Mr Grieves?"

He sat back in his chair and continued to regard her with a fixed gaze. "That's everything."

"And you'd like me and my trusted assistant, Miss Pemberley here, to carry out some investigations into these strange happenings?"

"I would indeed, Mrs Churchill."

"Do you have any theories of your own?"

"None. If only one of these things had happened I'd probably have been able to explain it away somehow, but there's some sort of tinkering going on in the churchyard that I just can't understand. That's why I'm here."

"I must say now that this seems to be rather a tricky case, Mr Grieves, but we'll do our best. Nothing has ever managed to stump us so far, has it, Miss Pemberley?"

. . .

Once Mr Grieves had left, Pemberley made some more tea and Churchill placed her foot back up on her desk.

"Is it just me, Pembers, or is there a lingering odour of the tomb in here? We could do with a little potpourri to freshen the air."

"How on earth are we going to investigate this one, Mrs Churchill?" said Pemberley, placing the tea tray on her employer's desk.

"We'll have to sneak around the graveyard at night to find out who's been causing all this mischief."

"You can count me out."

"You can't be *counted out*, Pembers. It's your job!"

"Not if it involves wandering about graveyards at night it's not! I'd rather resign."

"Resign? Don't be so ridiculous! You're one of the fixtures and fittings of this place."

"I'm not going into St Swithun's graveyard at night, and that's the end of it. It's enough of a struggle going there in the daytime."

"I can't say it tops the list of places I'd like to spend a night, but we have a case to solve. Anyway, we could bring Oswald with us. He's quite fearless."

"He's not fearless at night; he hates the dark. The only place Oswald wants to be at night is under the eiderdown next to me."

"Oh dear. I'd hoped that by inviting Oswald to join us you could also be persuaded, Pembers. Please come with me… I really don't want to spend a night in the church-yard on my own."

"You could ask Mr Grieves to join you."

Churchill gasped. "That man? He gives me the chills sitting across the desk from me in my own office. Can you imagine spending a night with him in the graveyard? It's quite unthinkable."

"Maybe he could just do it on his own, in that case. Surely he doesn't need us to help him."

"He clearly does or he wouldn't have asked for our help."

"We could refuse to investigate the case."

"And turn down good money?"

"Neither of us wants to investigate it."

"Can you imagine what it would do to the reputation of this detective agency if we were to turn the case down? People would assume we were inept. At least our reputation is intact at the present time. People know we get our cases solved."

"But the downside is we've been given a creepy one this time."

"I'm sure there's a simple explanation Mr Grieves has overlooked."

"Grass growing on Saul Mollikin's grave? No one can explain that away."

"Perhaps we're dealing with someone who merely wished to carry out a little maintenance in the churchyard. Perhaps they decided that removing lichen from headstones and scattering a rose and some grass seed about is what was needed. They probably thought Mr Grieves wasn't doing a good enough job of maintaining the graves but felt too frightened to say it to his face. I know I would be, and I'm not often frightened of people, as you well know."

"But what about the exploratory hole in Benjamin Grunchen's grave?"

"That was probably a family member. Mr Grieves said himself that he hadn't spoken to the family about it yet. I know the case sounds rather sinister, but perhaps it can all be easily cleared up."

"Without spending a night in the churchyard?"

"Let's hope so. I feel the need for a change of air, Pembers. That tomb smell is still lingering in here. Would you like to accompany me?"

"What about your ankle?"

"Resting it on my desk has made no difference at all, so I may as well keep it moving."

Chapter 5

A SMALL CHILD with a stick was chasing a flock of pigeons as Churchill and Pemberley walked along the cobbled high street. Mrs Thonnings waved at them from the window of her haberdashery shop and Mr Perret the greengrocer gave them a nod as he arranged a display of cabbages.

"How's the ankle faring?" Pemberley asked.

"It's holding up, thank you. I don't like to grumble, as you know."

The two ladies passed the bank and came across a shopfront that had been freshly painted in a pleasing pistachio green.

"I say," said Churchill, pausing beside the shopfront. "Does the bank have a new neighbour?"

"Yes. This used to be Mr Borridge's barber shop."

"What happened to Mr Borridge?"

"No one wanted to visit him after that incident with Mr Sparrow and the cut-throat razor."

"Ah yes, I remember now. It was always rather a down-at-heel sort of place anyway, but look at it now!" Churchill admired the paintings of pleasant rural scenes that had been neatly positioned in the shop window. "It's a picture gallery of some sort, wouldn't you say?"

"It certainly appears to be."

"Pickwick's Gallery," Churchill read from the newly installed sign. "How delightful, and what an extremely welcome addition to Compton Poppleford high street. A shop of this ilk lends a certain class to an area, wouldn't you say? We were practically falling over picture galleries when I lived in Richmond-upon-Thames, but to discover one here in this rural backwater is quite something."

"Even the people you term 'rustics' like to hang pictures on their walls, Mrs Churchill."

"I shall have to poke my little nose in here to see what they have inside. We'd better leave Oswald outside, though. Don't you have a lead to attach him to something?"

"I don't, but I'm sure he'll wait here nicely for us."

"I fear your abounding trust in him might be misplaced, Pembers. Churchill pushed the shop door open. "Pickwick..." she mused. "Isn't that the name of the awfully pleasant chap who had his sandwiches eaten by Oswald at the summer fete? Oh look, here he is!"

The smartly dressed Mr Pickwick with his neat grey moustache gave the two ladies a smile as they stepped through the door.

"Well, fancy not mentioning your wonderful new gallery to us, Mr Pickwick!" enthused Churchill.

"Oh, I've only just got it off the ground. There's not a great deal to speak of at the moment. Only a few pieces so far."

Churchill glanced around, noticing the walls were fairly bare. "But what you do have looks quite delightful, doesn't it, Miss Pemberley?"

"Indeed it does."

"Actually, I think the fact you don't have many pictures

31

yet makes the ones you do have look all the better. Don't you think so, Miss Pemberley?"

"Possibly."

"Personally, I can't abide shops that are filled with clutter. I find it quite off-putting and distracting."

"You liked Mr Harding's cookshop, Mrs Churchill," said Pemberley.

"Mr Harding? I can't say I recall him."

"I recall you being quite taken with him."

"Is that so?" commented Mr Pickwick with a wry smile.

"No, I can't remember him at all," snapped Churchill. "Now, Mr Pickwick, where did you find these delightful artworks? Do you source them from auctions? Or from local artists?"

"Oh, I do a bit of everything; I'm just starting out with it all really. And I must confess that yours truly may have had a hand in one or two of them."

Churchill gasped. "Your good self, Mr Pickwick? An artist?"

"I wouldn't call myself that, exactly. I just started dabbling a little when I retired."

"Can you show us some of your works?"

"If you insist." He gave an embarrassed cough. "I've hidden them right at the back here." He led them toward the rear of the shop, then paused beside a maritime scene painted in oils. "HMS Devastation," he mumbled.

"Crikey! That's rather a hair-raising name for a ship."

"She was scrapped in 1908."

"And you painted this all by yourself?"

"I'm afraid so."

"What a talent you are with a brush! HMS Devastation... A naval man, are you, Mr Pickwick?"

"Goodness, no. I wish I could say that I'd done something that exciting. Alas, no. I was a mere insurance salesman for forty years."

"There's nothing *mere* about being an insurance salesman. It's a most important job!"

"Very kind of you to say so, Mrs Churchill. I fear you flatter me a little."

"No more than you deserve, Mr Pickwick."

Churchill felt a little warmth in her face as he fixed her with his intelligent blue eyes. She turned toward a painting depicting a bowl of fruit to prevent him noticing her blushes.

"I like the colours in this one."

"Do you really? They're not quite as vibrant as I would have liked. There's a little too much of a bluish hue to it."

"Then why do you have it in your gallery?"

"Because Mr Pickwick painted it himself," responded Pemberley. "Look at the signature."

Churchill peered at the bottom right-hand corner of the painting and saw the word 'Pickwick' scrawled there.

"Good gracious, Mr Pickwick!" she exclaimed. "This is your own work, too? It's quite astonishing. And to think you wasted all those years as an insurance salesman when you could have been a professional artist!"

"Oh, I don't know about that." He glanced down at the floor and shuffled from one foot to another. "I've always enjoyed fooling around with oils, but my talents don't stretch much further than that."

"I must respectfully disagree! I'll tell you who would enjoy this new gallery, Mr Pickwick. Lady Darby, that's who. Miss Pemberley and I were chatting to her just yesterday at the fete, weren't we, Miss Pemberley?"

Her trusty assistant nodded.

"A simply delightful lady," continued Churchill. "I'm sure she would like this picture." She paused beside the portrait of a distinguished-looking man in a long curly wig and a red velvet tunic.

"The Duke of Marlborough," said Mr Pickwick. "I didn't paint this one."

"What else have you painted in here?" asked Churchill. She glanced around keenly and Mr Pickwick pointed to a portrait of a mature, dignified-looking lady seated in a chair beside a large window.

"Viscountess Bathshire," he announced.

Churchill gave an impressed nod. "A personal friend of yours, is she??"

"Of sorts." He scratched his temple. "Her father-in-law was at school with my father."

"I see," said Churchill, who was warming more to Mr Pickwick with every passing moment. She found herself feeling slightly envious of Viscountess Bathshire, who appeared to be so blessed that she had little to do other than repose in a chair and enjoy being painted by a well-mannered gentleman of a convivial nature.

~

"Oh look, here we are in the *Compton Poppleford Gazette* with Mr Butterfork and Mrs Thonnings," said Pemberley as the two ladies enjoyed a plate of jam tarts back at the office.

Churchill walked over to Pemberley's desk, tea and jam tart in hand, and peered down at the photograph. "Oh yes. Taken when that brusque photographer accosted us. He's not a very good photographer, is he?"

"Why not?"

"He's taken the picture from rather a strange angle. It makes my bosom appear far bigger than it is in real life, wouldn't you say?"

"Hmm." Pemberley filled her mouth with jam tart in a bid to excuse herself from replying.

"Oh, and there's Mr Pickwick," said Churchill, spotting him in another photograph taken at the fete. "Standing shoulder to shoulder with Inspector Mappin, nonetheless. I can't imagine the pair of them having much in common. He's such a delightful fellow."

"Inspector Mappin?"

"You knew I was talking about Mr Pickwick, Pembers. There's no need for your funny little wordplay games."

"I can't understand why he became an insurance salesman when his father was at school with Viscount someone-or-other."

"He's clearly a man who doesn't fall for all the trappings," replied Churchill loftily, "which demonstrates great strength of character. It's all too easy to subsist on the charity of one's rich friends, but it takes a real gentleman to stand on his own two feet, launch himself out into the big wide world and earn an honest wage."

"You appear to have formed rather a high opinion of Mr Pickwick, Mrs Churchill."

"Who wouldn't? He's an erudite, respectful and humble gentleman; well-connected while refusing to boast about it."

"Aside from painting his rich friends and displaying their pictures on the walls of his gallery."

"Only one wall, Pembers. And besides, one of his pictures featured a bowl of fruit."

"Perhaps he holds Viscountess Bathshire in no higher regard than a bunch of grapes, in that case."

"Exactly. He's the modern sort who fails to be impressed by wealth and status. Whether you're an earl or a chimney sweep, he treats everybody just the same."

"How do you know that?"

"Oh, one can just tell these things." Churchill bit into another jam tart. "I must say you seem rather sceptical of our new friend, Pembers."

"Not sceptical, Mrs Churchill, just wary."

"Why on earth would you be wary of Mr Pickwick?"

"I noticed the way he looked at you."

"At *me*?" Churchill felt a surge of heat rise up in her face. She guzzled down the jam tart and tried to recover herself. "What do you mean, Pembers? He looked at me? Of course he looked at me... we were having a conversation!"

"It was the *way* he looked at you."

"Which way?" She took a large gulp of tea.

"Rather bashful and... dare I say it... a little flirtatious."

It took all the willpower Churchill could muster to keep the swig of tea inside her mouth rather than spraying it all over the *Compton Poppleford Gazette* in surprise. She had to concentrate for a few seconds before she felt able to swallow it down.

"Miss Pemberley!" she exclaimed. "*Flirtatious* is a word best confined to the nation's youth! It's for bashful maidens and awkward young bachelors in their first bloom of adulthood."

"And old retired insurance salesmen."

"Nonsense. Absolute nonsense!" Churchill marched over to the hatstand. "Come along, Oswald, let's take you out for your walk."

"Why are you going out for another walk?" asked Pemberley.

"I need a relaxing stroll by the river. I drank my tea while it was still rather hot."

Chapter 6

CHURCHILL RETURNED to the office approximately two minutes later once her embarrassment had subsided. "Forget the relaxing stroll by the river, I've realised we should be doing something more useful with our time. I'm afraid there are no two ways about it, Pembers. We're going to have to visit St Swithun's churchyard."

"Oh no. Must we?"

"We have a case to work on."

"I really don't like this case."

"If we go to the churchyard in the daytime, we can get ourselves accustomed to it. Then we'll feel ready to go in the night-time."

"I don't want to go in the night-time, Mrs Churchill."

"Well, if we manage to solve the puzzle in the daytime we won't need to."

"I hope we can solve it nice and quickly then, without any trouble. This is my least favourite case ever!"

"Surely Atkins had some macabre cases."

"He once had to spend a night in a haunted house."

"There you go."

"But he didn't make me go with him. Therefore, I don't think you should make me go with you."

"I hope you don't mind me saying so, Pembers, but you tend to make rather a lot of fuss about these things. We're only going to a churchyard, for heaven's sake."

"Where lots of *dead* people are buried."

"But they can't harm us now, can they? It's the living who cause the problems. And besides, we'll have God close by in the church to protect us."

"God isn't actually *in* the church."

"Well, perhaps not directly inside it, but the presence of a church is usually enough to ward away evil spirits. Have you ever known anything bad happen in a church?"

"Yes."

"Really? What?"

"Sister Prudence hit me over the head with a hymn book when I bit my nails during Mass."

"I highly doubt we'll find Sister Prudence and her hymn book prowling around the churchyard today. And besides, St Swithun's is Church of England."

"That wouldn't stop Sister Prudence."

The two ladies and Oswald walked down the lane that led up to the pretty little church, which was so old it appeared to have slumped a little into the ground.

They entered the churchyard beneath the kissing gate, and from there a paved path led up to the church door. Oswald scampered here and there, sniffing around in the long grass.

Churchill glanced at the crooked headstones standing either side of her and shivered. "These graves the sexton mentioned... do you know where any of them are?"

"I know which one is Saul Mollikin's, because the fact no grass has ever grown on his grave has passed into village lore."

"Which one is it, then?"

"It's over there, by that yew."

"In the dingiest part of the churchyard, I see."

Churchill shivered again as the two ladies walked toward the giant yew tree.

"There he is," said Pemberley, pointing to a headstone that bore Saul Mollikin's name. "And the sexton isn't wrong; I spy some new blades of grass."

Churchill peered down at the bare patch of earth in front of the headstone and, with an involuntary shudder, noticed a few small fronds of fresh green. "Well I never," she declared. "Bald with slight signs of new growth. Mr Mollikin's grave bears a remarkable resemblance to Mr Grieves's head, doesn't it? Didn't Greives say he was cursed by a witch?"

"Yes, the witch on Grindledown Hill."

"Do we know why?"

Pemberley shrugged. "I think the original reason has been lost in the mists of time."

"I see. Then perhaps there's a possibility he wasn't cursed at all."

"Yes, there is, but it helps to explain why the grass refuses to grow on his grave."

"Until now... Four years later."

"A hundred and four."

"Oh yes, silly me. He died in 1828, not 1928. Which makes the whole thing even spookier, for some reason." Churchill squirmed uncomfortably and glanced around. "I don't like this little dank corner very much, Pembers. Shall we look at the other graves?"

"I'd rather just leave the place altogether."

"So would I, but we have duties to attend to. Now, we should be able to find Arthur Brimble's grave quite easily because it has a rose on it, according to Grieves."

After a few minutes of searching, Churchill and Pemberley found Arthur Brimble's final resting place with a withered rose lying at the foot of the headstone.

Churchill gave yet another shudder. "Who placed this thorny bloom here, Pembers?"

"Why are you asking me? That's what Grieves wants us to find out, isn't it?"

"Yes, I realise that. It was a… one of those questions people ask when they're not expecting an answer."

"Rhetorical."

"I don't think it's that; I must have meant something else. Anyway, I think the presence of this rose can easily be explained. I know Grieves said Brimble has no direct descendants, but a distant family member must have visited to pay their respects. The descendant of a sibling, or a cousin even. A Brimble who lives in another country, like America, and sailed across the great Atlantic to lay a rose on Mr Brimble's grave as he or she passed through."

"Passed through to where?"

"I don't know. London, probably. That's the nearest point of interest for Americans, isn't it?"

"There are many interesting places for Americans in these parts, Mrs Churchill. There's the old castle at Bridgington Stanley. Americans like castles and they don't have many over there."

"But they're hardly likely to have heard of Bridgington Stanley, are they? And even if they had, it would still support my theory that a distant Brimble family member was passing through and placed a rose on old Arthur Brimble's grave. Now then, who else did Grieves mention? Sally

Fletcher, wasn't it? I suppose we'll have to wander around the place trying to find her now."

Fifteen minutes later the two ladies found themselves standing in front of Sally Fletcher's headstone.

"Grieves has a point," said Pemberley. "Mrs Fletcher's headstone does look very well maintained."

"Not a spot of lichen on it," added Churchill. "I can understand Grieves's concern. Who would spend time clearing the headstone of a lady who died... how many years ago was it, Pembers? I can't be bothered to work it out again."

"Fifty years."

"Fifty long years."

"Perhaps it was someone who planned to clean all the headstones and they just so happened to make a start on Sally Fletcher's."

"A fairly sound theory, except for the fact they surely would have shared such a plan with the sexton."

"Perhaps they wanted to do it in secret."

"Why would they want to do it in secret?"

"Perhaps they commented to Grieves that some of the headstones looked a bit licheny and suggested he clean them, to which he took exception. So they decided to clean the headstones themselves, but in the dead of night so as not to be spotted by him."

"In which case Grieves would have a suspect, wouldn't he? It must have been the person who told him the headstones looked licheny. Is that an actual word?"

"Yes, I believe it is. In that case, we need to find out from Grieves if anyone suggested the headstones should be cleaned."

"I assume the old chap would have considered it himself if they had. He may resemble a dragged-through-a-hedge-backwards version of Count Dracula, but I'm sure the man's not a complete fool. Shall we find the final one? Benjamin Grunchen, I believe."

"The grave with the exploratory hole."

"It's all very odd indeed. I shall need a nice cup of tea once we're finished here. In fact, I may even require something a little stronger."

The two ladies were making their way through the churchyard when Pemberley gave a sudden yelp and dashed off across the grass.

"Pembers?" Churchill called out. As she looked in the direction of her departing secretary, she saw the unmistakable form of a small dog digging enthusiastically. "Oh no," she puffed, taking off after her.

A moment later she caught up with her secretary, who was holding the grubby-pawed dog under one arm and admonishing him.

Churchill glanced down at the damage he had done. "Well, what was once an exploratory hole in the grave of Benjamin Grunchen is now a small crater. We need to get this filled up, Pembers, and quickly!"

"I know that. I'm just busy telling him off for the moment."

"Don't waste your time doing that," replied Churchill, scooting down onto her hands and knees. "Let's just fill this hole." She began sweeping the dirt into little mounds with her hands. "Goodness, Oswald has managed to dig quite deep, hasn't he? He's almost exhumed the poor chap!"

Pemberley put Oswald down, knelt down next to Churchill and did her best to return the soil to the hole. "It would have been helpful if he hadn't dispersed it so far and wide," she muttered.

"It would have been helpful if he hadn't dug it out at all," added Churchill. "We need him to be an asset to our team; a detective dog, if you will. At the moment he's simply creating extra work for us."

"Oswald is quite capable of becoming a detective dog!"

"How?"

"He'll prove himself to you, Mrs Churchill, just you wait and see."

"I shall await that moment with bated breath," she replied. "I've always wondered what that phrase means, come to think of it. What is *bated breath*, exactly?"

"Do you often use words you don't know the meaning of?"

"Yes. Doesn't everyone?"

"No, never. I don't like to be caught out." Pemberley got to her feet and surveyed their handiwork. "Oh, why do holes never refill themselves properly?" she lamented. "Even when you replace all the earth the hole is still there."

"Don't forget about the exploratory hole that was there before Oswald got to it."

"Grieves told us it was small. This one certainly isn't small."

"Help me up, Pembers. My legs don't appear to have any oomph left in them."

Pemberley helped Churchill stagger to her feet as she inspected the ground around them.

"The only solution I can see is to take some earth from another hole," said Churchill.

"We don't need more than one hole, Mrs Churchill. Grieves wouldn't be at all happy about it."

"Then we'll just have to leave it as it is."

"Leave this big hole in Benjamin Grunchen's grave, you mean?"

"What else can we do? Fill a bucket with soil from your garden and bring it back here?"

"What an excellent idea. I shall do just that."

"What nonsense, Pembers! Come on, there's nothing more we can do here. I need an urgent spot of tea and cake before I collapse."

Chapter 7

"WE ACHIEVED nothing at all in the churchyard yesterday," said Churchill the following morning. "Let's hope today is a little more fruitful."

"I don't see how it can be; the case is completely baffling," replied Pemberley. "I think we should tell the sexton we have no idea what to do about the whole thing and leave it at that."

"Absolutely not! There can be no question of us giving up on a case. It's simply not what we do at Churchill's Detective Agency."

"That's a shame."

"I refuse to be defeated, though I acknowledge it's a tricky one. I'm beginning to think each strange occurrence could be an isolated event. Perhaps one person decided to place a rose on Mr Brimble's grave, another decided to clean Mrs Fletcher's headstone and a third chose to dig a hole in Mr Grunchen's grave."

"And then a dog chose to dig an even bigger hole in it."

"Indeed. That was most unfortunate."

"And the grass on Mr Mollikin's grave?"

"An anomaly of some sort."

"That's your explanation?"

"Some things are mere anomalies, Pembers. They defy explanation."

A slam of the office door downstairs caused both ladies to jump. They grew even more alarmed as heavy footsteps thundered up the stairs.

"Good grief," said Churchill, rising to her feet. "Something's afoot!"

A red-haired woman in a tea dress burst into the room and flung herself into the chair opposite Churchill.

"Oh dear, I'm all of a quiver!"

"Whatever has happened, Mrs Thonnings?"

The flame-haired lady clutched her chest. "Oh dear! My heartbeat is all over the place. I fear I may die!"

"You look perfectly healthy to me," replied Churchill, trying to remain patient. "Now, please tell us what has sent you into this paroxysm."

"Oh, it's too awful!"

"If you're not going to tell us what it is, I'm afraid there's nothing we can do about it."

"There's nothing anyone can do about it. He's dead!"

"What the jiggins? Who's dead, Mrs Thonnings?"

"Mr Butterfork! He's been murdered, and all his money has been taken!"

"How awful!" Churchill's mouth hung open. "When did this happen?"

"Inspector Mappin was called after a gunshot rang out in the night. Someone has shot Mr Butterfork dead! He should never have bragged about all that money. It was only a matter of time before someone came for it!"

"Maybe so, but he still didn't deserve to be murdered."

"No, he didn't. It's completely awful! I'm sure whoever

it was could have just taken the money without killing him."

"Putting an end to the poor chap's life certainly sounds like an extreme measure," said Churchill. "Quite unnecessary, if you ask me."

"Perhaps the culprit murdered Mr Butterfork to avoid being recognised," said Pemberley.

"Good point, Miss Pemberley," said Churchill.

"Maybe Mr Butterfork knew his killer?" continued Pemberley. "The poor man may have been murdered to guarantee his silence."

"An even better theory, my aide-de-camp. You're becoming quite the sleuth these days."

"I'm merely posturing theories. I may be wrong, of course."

"I suspect you're on the right track. Why else would a man make the leap from burglar to murderer? To protect his identity, no doubt. Mr Butterfork must have known him!"

"He could have put on a mask," said Mrs Thonnings.

"Mr Butterfork?"

"No, the murderer. If he'd worn a mask there would have been no need to commit the murder because Mr Butterfork wouldn't have known who he was."

"That's a good point," said Churchill.

"The murderer must be kicking himself for not wearing a mask now," said Pemberley. "He's probably realised there was no need to go around shooting the poor man dead, and now he'll find himself in infinitely more trouble when he's caught."

"He certainly will," said Churchill. "Poor Mr Butterfork. I must say it was quite uncalled for. I suppose that hapless Mappin is investigating the case, is he?"

"Oh yes," replied Mrs Thonnings. "He'll soon catch the culprit, I'm sure."

"I can't say I share your certainty."

"Mr Butterfork was such a lovely man." Mrs Thonnings's voice cracked. "And he was so generous with his money. Only last week he gave me five pounds."

"Five pounds? Why on earth would he give you such a vast sum of money?"

"Because he was a generous man. You saw how he was at the summer fete. He was handing out money to anyone and everyone. If ever I asked him for money, he'd give it to me just like that! He didn't ask any questions, nor did he want it repaid. I did offer, of course, but he just gave me more money instead. He was a true gentleman, and we'll never see the likes of him again."

"I believe you're right, Mrs Thonnings. It will be a struggle to find someone else who'll give you a regular income with no questions asked. What a generous man indeed. Unusually generous, if you ask me."

"He was the kindest gentleman I've ever met. He didn't have a single bad bone in his body," continued Mrs Thonnings. "I never heard him exchange an angry word with any other living soul; neither man nor beast. His heart remained as pure and white from the moment he drew his first breath to the time he drew his last. The Lord God has had one of his angels returned to him on this, the darkest of all days."

"Goodness, Mrs Thonnings. You're really going to miss your regular stipend, aren't you?"

"I am, Mrs Churchill. I'm a widow, you see."

"The lack of a husband isn't sufficient reason to feel hard done by, Mrs Thonnings. Miss Pemberley here has managed quite well her entire life without ever having one at all."

"I know, but then that's Miss Pemberley for you."

"What do you mean by that?"

"Yes, what *do* you mean by that?" asked Pemberley.

"You're just different from everyone else, aren't you, Miss Pemberley?"

"I certainly am," she replied proudly.

"You seem to have taken that as a compliment, Miss Pemberley," said Churchill. "Anyway, let's return to the matter in hand, and that is the tragic demise of Mr Butterfork. Do you know anything more, Mrs Thonnings?"

"Only that he was shot and his money was taken. That's all I know."

"Where did Mr Butterfork live?" asked Churchill.

"Crunkle Lane."

"Do you know where that is, Pembers?"

Her secretary nodded.

"Then take me there at once!" Churchill responded, rising to her feet.

"Are you planning to solve the case, Mrs Churchill?" asked Mrs Thonnings.

"It's a little too early to promise anything like that, but I'd be interested to find out a little more."

"Won't that annoy Inspector Mappin?" asked Pemberley.

"Of course it will, but since when did we start worrying about that? Fetch your hat and coat, Miss Pemberley. There isn't a moment to lose!"

Chapter 8

"ANY IDEA which number Crunkle Lane belonged to Mr Butterfork?" asked Churchill as she, Pemberley and Oswald made their way along the high street.

"I don't, but I imagine it'll be the house with a lot of hullabaloo outside it."

Situated close to St Swithun's church, Crunkle Lane was only a short walk from the office. It was a tree-lined lane boasting an assortment of little houses built at varying points in Compton Poppleford's history.

"There's the hullabaloo," said Churchill, pointing to a crowd of people gathered outside a red-brick house with a green door. A young, spotty-faced police constable standing just outside it was making a studious attempt to ignore the noisy onlookers.

"It looks like quite an ordinary house for a man with a lot of money," commented Churchill as they drew nearer.

"Yes, it's exceedingly ordinary."

"Wasn't it said that he didn't trust the banks and kept all his worldly wealth in a tea chest in his bedroom?"

"Yes, that's right."

"Do you know how long he's lived in the village, Pembers?"

"Not terribly long. About a year, I think."

"Any idea where he lived before that?"

"No idea at all."

"I wonder where his fortune came from."

"I heard it was inherited from an elderly aunt."

"Just the money? No property?" Churchill asked.

"Apparently so."

"How interesting. When one inherits wealth there's usually a bit of property thrown in."

"Maybe there was but it went to someone else."

"Quite possibly."

"Let's go and see if we can find out more."

The two ladies made their way through the crowd toward the constable.

"May I enquire as to what has happened here, Constable?" Churchill asked.

The spotty-faced police officer opened his mouth as if to reply, then seemed to think better of it. He reached into his pocket and pulled out a piece of paper.

"I need to consult my list," he replied.

"I'm sure there's no need for that, Constable. I merely enquired as to what had happened to Mr Butterfork."

The constable frowned at the slip of paper in his hand, then observed Churchill closely. "It's Mrs Churchill, isn't it?"

"That's correct."

He frowned at the paper again. "Your name's on the list, I'm afraid."

"What does that mean?"

"It means I'm not allowed to answer any of your questions."

"What nonsense! Why on earth not?"

"I don't know."

"Let me see that."

"I don't think it's allowed."

"Of course it's allowed. If my name's on a list I have a right to read it!"

"You're not meant to. It was given to me for my eyes only."

"Who else is on the list?"

"Erm…"

"You can tell me, you know."

"Erm…"

"All right then, just tell me who wrote the list."

"It's a police matter."

"I think I already know. Just show me the infernal list and then I'll leave you alone."

"Do you promise?"

"Of course. Now, show me that list, my good man."

The constable handed Churchill his piece of paper and she quickly examined it.

"This isn't a list," she said scornfully, "it's only got one name on it! Look at this, Pembers. That lunk-headed Inspector Mappin calls this a list!"

Pemberley glanced at the paper and shook her head.

"How do you know Inspector Mappin wrote it?" asked the constable.

"Call it a hunch." She returned the piece of paper. "You can answer the questions posed by my aide-de-camp here instead."

"Me?" said Pemberley.

"Yes. As your name doesn't feature on Mappin's list, Miss Pemberley, you can go ahead and obtain the details we require. Oswald and I will go and mingle with the crowd to see what else we can glean."

. . .

"Mr Butterfork died from a single shot to the side of the head," Pemberley told Churchill a short while later as the two ladies lingered on Crunkle Lane.

"Goodness me. A veritable execution! Has Mappin found the murder weapon yet?"

"No."

"How interesting. And where was the body found?"

"On the floor."

"Of which room?"

"His bedroom. He was dressed in his nightgown and dressing gown, and the tea chest he stored all his money in was empty."

"Goodness me. Poor old Mr Butterfork. The fact he was dressed in nightwear suggests to me that the robbery occurred sometime between his usual hours of retiring and rising."

"They believe the robbery took place late yesterday evening."

"Did any of the neighbours hear anything?"

"Mrs Strawbanks in the house opposite heard the shot at about ten o'clock."

"Did she raise the alarm?"

"Yes, she telephoned Inspector Mappin and he came round immediately. He summoned some constables to help and telephoned for the police doctor. Mr Butterfork died almost immediately."

"Did he live alone?"

"Yes, but his housekeeper, Mrs Hatweed, lives close by. Her house is a little further along this lane."

"She must be terribly sad about his death."

"She will be."

"What do we know of any visitors to Mr Butterfork's house yesterday?"

"That's an interesting question. A dark figure was seen, apparently."

"Is that so? And where exactly was this dark figure seen?"

"Here in this lane, directly outside Mr Butterfork's house. It was a little after nightfall, at about half-past nine. The figure was wearing a long, dark coat with a dark hat, and was seen standing there looking up at an upstairs window. And then the figure was seen to walk away."

"Interesting indeed. Who saw this dark figure?"

"Mrs Strawbanks."

"It sounds as though she'd be an interesting lady to talk to. Did she see anything else suspicious?"

"She saw the same dark figure running away from Mr Butterfork's home shortly after the gunshot sounded."

"The culprit making his escape, then."

"That's what Inspector Mappin believes."

"And does he know where the culprit ran off to?"

"Along this lane and down into the churchyard. You can just make out the churchyard wall from here."

Churchill peered in the direction of Pemberley's pointed finger. "So you can."

"He vaulted the churchyard wall, apparently."

"Gosh. And do they know where he went from there?"

"No, the trail goes cold after that."

"Is there any other description of this dark figure aside from the long coat and hat?"

"None. It was dark, you see."

"Yes, I realise that. I just thought someone might have seen a few facial features when the culprit ran beneath a street lamp or something like that."

"I'm afraid not."

"Well, this is all very interesting. Is there any indication that the dark figure forced his way into Mr Butterfork's home?"

"None at all. No windows or doors were forced, and neither were any accidentally left open."

"Another interesting finding. Then he could have called at the door and Mr Butterfork may have admitted him."

"Yes, it seems likely that Mr Butterfork let him in. It's possible the murderer pushed his way in once the door was opened, but it's also possible that Mr Butterfork allowed him to enter freely."

"Very interesting indeed. Pembers, may we pause for a moment while I congratulate you on the sheer volume of information you managed to glean from that spotty-faced constable outside Mr Butterfork's house? He refused to speak to me, but he certainly spilled the beans to you!"

"That's because your name was on the list."

"Yes, there's no need to remind me of that. Let's take a little saunter down to the churchyard and see what's happening over there. Where's Oswald?"

Pemberley gave a sharp, shrill whistle, which startled Churchill to such a degree that she was sure her feet momentarily left the ground. The little dog emerged from between the legs of those in the crowd seconds later.

"Must you make that wretched noise, Pemberley?"

"It worked, didn't it? Oswald came back to me."

"That's something to be pleased about, I'm sure. It was almost worth the ruptured ear drums."

The two ladies and their mischievous dog began walking toward the churchyard.

"Mr Butterfork must have known the culprit quite well if he admitted him to his home in his nightwear," commented Churchill.

"That offers a good explanation as to how the murderer got inside his home."

"A few crimes in and I think we're getting rather good at analysing these cases, aren't we? I'm beginning to feel quite well practised at this now."

"There's just one problem."

"What might that be?"

"We're not supposed to be investigating this case. No one's tasked us with looking into it; that's Inspector Mappin's job."

"Ah yes. There is that, I suppose."

"The only case we have at present is Mr Grieves's churchyard mystery."

"And that can be our way in!" enthused Churchill. "The sexton asked us to investigate strange goings-on in the churchyard, and that's just what we're going to do. If it just so happens that Mr Butterfork's murderer made his escape via the churchyard, then so be it."

"I don't think Inspector Mappin will be satisfied with that explanation."

"Of course he won't. He's never satisfied with any of our explanations."

"He'll accuse us of meddling again."

"And what's new there? All we need do is carry out some quiet investigations. He needn't know anything about it."

"We're not particularly good at doing things quietly, are we?"

"We're getting better at it all the time, Pembers! Even I would admit that I wasn't the most subtle of individuals when I first arrived here from Richmond-upon-Thames, but I like to think I've learned some of Compton Popple-ford's ways now and have mastered the craft of sneaking around with the shadowy imperceptibility of a black cat at dusk."

Chapter 9

Two constables were bent over the ground beside the churchyard wall with the gangly, dark-suited photographer from the *Compton Poppleford Gazette* standing close by.

"I wonder what they've found," said Churchill. "Shall we go and ask them? We can pretend we're complete ignoramuses, which might encourage them to explain what they're doing. Men tend to enjoy explaining things to ladies, don't they?"

Oswald ran up to the two police officers and sniffed them enthusiastically.

"Good morning, Constables," said Churchill cheerily. "What are you up to there?"

One of the officers, a man with a thick brown moustache, stood up and eyed them suspiciously. "Will you please keep your dog away? We don't want him interfering with the evidence."

Pemberley gave another shrill whistle and Oswald returned to her side. She quickly attached a lead to his collar.

"Evidence, Constable?" Churchill queried. "Whatever do you mean?"

"Footprints, ma'am."

"There must be quite a few footprints in this old churchyard. May I ask why you're particularly interested in these ones?"

"We believe they may be connected to a crime, ma'am."

"Good grief! Really? Which crime might that be?"

"Have you not heard?" replied the moustachioed constable, giving Churchill an incredulous look. "We're investigating the murder on Crunkle Lane."

"Oh, that crime! Yes, I've heard about that crime all right. Goodness! You think those footprints have something to do with it, do you?"

"Yes. The culprit ran down Crunkle Lane, just over there," he said, pointing over the wall. "And then he vaulted over the wall here and left these footprints, right next to the final resting place of Barnabus Byers."

"Well I never!" Churchill stepped closer. "We're looking at the footprints of a murderer, are we?"

"Indeed we are, ma'am."

"Gosh." Churchill peered closer at the spot where the grass had been crushed beneath the feet of the culprit, leaving large indents in the soft earth beneath. A tape measure had been laid alongside it.

"Have you worked out the size of his feet?"

"We believe he takes a size nine," said the other constable, a young man with spectacles.

"Does he indeed? How interesting. And where did he go after jumping over the wall?"

"We're yet to ascertain that."

"Over here!" said Pemberley from a short distance away. "It looks as though he jumped over Betsy Wolfwell."

"Really?" replied Churchill. She walked over to where Pemberley was standing and saw that the grass had been crushed in a similar manner, as if someone had leapt over the grave. "Goodness!" she continued. "That's certainly a compression made by someone moving at speed, isn't it? One couldn't make such a dent in the grass by simply stepping over it at walking pace."

"Let's have a look," the moustachioed constable said with a scowl. He marched over and surveyed the dent in the grass before giving a reluctant nod. "We've got another one over here, Dawkins. Bring the tape measure."

"Righty-ho, Russell."

"It seems odd that the culprit was happy to take the life of a human being yet couldn't bring himself to step on the grave of a deceased person," mused Churchill.

"There's a piece of snagged material on this hawthorn bush," said Pemberley, who was busy examining a small branch extending out from an area of shrubbery.

"Is that so?" exclaimed Constable Russell, his frown deepening.

Churchill strode over to where Pemberley was standing. "Allow me to examine it more closely," she said, pulling a magnifying glass from her handbag and peering at the piece of fabric through it. "Dark in colour, perhaps even black. Snagged from an item of clothing as someone moved past at speed, I'd say."

"Let's have a look," said Constable Russell, marching over and reaching for the magnifying glass.

"Don't you have your own magnifying glass, Constable?"

"We left it at the station."

"I see." She handed him the glass and he looked through it.

"Very interesting indeed," he commented. "We believe

the culprit was wearing a long, dark coat, and this piece of material certainly could have come from such an item. Photograph, please!"

The gangly photographer lumbered over and took some images of the fabric fragment from a variety of angles.

"And we'll need some photographs of the footprints next to Betsy Wolfwell's grave. Dawkins is just laying out the tape measure." He pulled the piece of fabric off the thorn and rolled it between his fingers. "Yes, it feels as though it could have come from an overcoat of some sort."

"Worsted or double-worsted?" asked Churchill.

"I've no idea."

"Even when you look through the magnifying glass?"

The baffled constable peered through the glass at it again. "I don't know. I've no idea about threads of wool."

"I know just the woman who will," said Churchill. "Mrs Thonnings from the haberdashery shop knows her worsteds from her double-worsteds, doesn't she, Miss Pemberley?"

"She certainly does."

"Why don't you ask Mrs Thonnings?" suggested Churchill.

"All right, then," said Constable Russell.

"There's something over here, too," said Pemberley, observing the rear end of Oswald as he sniffed at a shrub, his tail wagging.

"What is it now?" asked Constable Russell gruffly, walking over to her with the magnifying glass and piece of material in his hand.

"The murder weapon itself!" announced Pemberley proudly.

Churchill hurried over and joined the constable as he peered beneath the bush to see daylight glinting on metal.

"Good grief, it is as well!" she crowed. "A pistol. Good grief!"

"Over here, Dawkins!" the constable called out. "And bring that photographer chap with you!"

The two men strode over.

"Photographer chap?" said the photographer. "I've already told you my name is Smith."

"Sorry, I couldn't remember it. I got rather excited all of a sudden with all the evidence we've been finding."

"The evidence *Miss Pemberley* has been finding," corrected Churchill.

"Oswald found the gun," added Pemberley.

"He's such a wonderful detective dog. Whatever would you have done without us, Constables?" asked Churchill.

"We'd have found it all eventually."

"Are you sure about that?"

"Oh, yes. We'd only just made a start on the first footprint when you arrived."

"What's going on?" murmured a low voice behind Churchill.

The sound alone was enough to chill her bones.

"Mr Grieves," she said, turning to greet the dark figure of the sexton topped with his usual wide-brimmed hat. "There's been quite a palaver in your churchyard today."

"I can see that."

"It seems Mr Butterfork's murderer made his way through it at a speedy pace. He's left footprints, torn off pieces of overcoat and even deposited the murder weapon here!"

"Has he indeed? All in my nice, quiet churchyard?"

"Rather inconsiderate of him, wasn't it?"

"It was even less considerate of him to commit the murder in the first place," added Pemberley.

"Well yes, that is true."

"I'd been meaning to pay you another visit, Mrs Churchill," muttered Grieves.

"Oh?"

"Before all this murdering business occurred, I noticed there had been more strange happenings in this here churchyard."

"Oh dear, such as?"

"Significant trampling all over the graveyard, resulting in an overall flattening of the grass. I don't object to grass being flattened, as a rule, but it happens to be home to some rather nice wildflowers at the moment."

"And someone's flattened them?"

"Squashed them into the ground. And as for the hole in Benjamin Grunchen's grave, it's grown exponentially."

"Is that so?"

"I think it was even bigger at one stage, but someone, or some*thing*, has attempted to refill it."

"How extraordinary. Any more headstones cleaned of lichen?"

"None that I've noticed."

"Any more fresh roses on the graves of people long since deceased?"

He shook his head. "Just the trampling and the hole."

"Well, thank you for informing us, Mr Grieves. We'll get on to it right away."

"Will you? You don't appear to have got on to it at all since we last spoke."

"That was only a day or two ago, and we've been carrying out some surveillance, haven't we, Miss Pemberley?"

"Yes, we have. In fact, it may have been us who—"

"So there you have it, Mr Grieves," interrupted Churchill. "We'll let you know as soon as we've discovered the truth behind these mysterious occurrences."

Chapter 10

"ON BEHALF of Churchill's Detective Agency, I am awarding you, Oswald Pemberley, the medal of merit." Churchill attached the medal to Oswald's collar while Pemberley held him still.

"Oh, look at his little face," cooed Pemberley once the medal was secured. "He's so proud of himself!"

"And so he should be. He found the gun used to shoot Mr Butterfork, after all."

"Well, that's yet to be confirmed by the ballistics experts at Bovington."

"A mere formality, I suspect. It's quite clear to me that the murderer vaulted over the churchyard wall and landed next to Barnabus Byers. Then he jumped over Betsy Wolfwell, caught his coat on the hawthorn and threw the murder weapon into a shrub."

"It certainly seems that way."

"And if it wasn't for Oswald's hard work the murder weapon would still be lying there undiscovered!"

"They probably would have found it eventually."

"Constables Russell and Dawkins? I consider it highly

unlikely. Anyway, the important thing is that Oswald carried out a good deed and has a medal to prove it."

"I'll put his award from the fete on his collar as well." Pemberley attached the red rosette. "There! He's a decorated hero now."

"He certainly is."

The two ladies were still admiring him proudly when they heard footsteps on the stairs. A familiar red-haired lady stepped into the room moments later.

"Good afternoon, Mrs Thonnings!" said Churchill. "You seem a good deal calmer now than when you last visited. In fact, I'm tempted to say you look rather pleased with yourself."

"Do I?" She made herself comfortable in the chair beside Churchill's desk. "I suppose I am, really. I didn't realise the fact was written all over my face, however."

"Indeed it is; clear for all to see. You need to perfect your poker face, Mrs Thonnings."

"I'm no good at it."

"All it takes is a little practice."

"I practise often, but I never manage it. I suppose that explains why I always lose at strip poker."

Churchill stared at the haberdasher, her mouth agape. "Well, there's always bridge," she suggested. "Anyway, I feel as though we've strayed from the point somewhat. May I ask what you're so pleased about, Mrs Thonnings?"

The red-haired lady smiled. "You're going to be so proud of me."

"Gosh, am I?"

"Yes, it appears that I have excellent investigative abilities after all."

"Have you indeed?"

"Yes. The police came and consulted me to get my expert opinion."

"Ah, would that have been in relation to the piece of fabric we found in the churchyard, by any chance?"

Mrs Thonnings's smile faded a little. "How do you know about that?"

"I sent the police to you myself. Miss Pemberley found the piece of material snagged on a twig of hawthorn, so I suggested to the constables, who were fumbling about in the churchyard haplessly, that they might like to speak to you in the hope of identifying its source."

"Did you indeed?" The smile returned to Mrs Thonnings's face. "It was very kind of you to consider me, Mrs Churchill. Thank you. Oh, look at Oswald!"

The little dog had paraded himself into the centre of the room, as if to show off his medal and rosette.

"Has he won another dog competition?" asked Mrs Thonnings.

"No, he's been carrying out the police force's work for them," replied Churchill. "He's been suitably rewarded for his efforts and is now officially a detective dog."

"Oh, how wonderful! He's still scratching himself an awful lot, though. I noticed that at the fete the other day. Does he have fleas?"

"Absolutely not! Oswald would never have fleas!"

"I didn't mean it as a slur on his character, Mrs Churchill. All dogs get fleas, no matter how clever they are. Even detective dogs can get them."

"I see. Does he have fleas, Miss Pemberley?"

"I don't know."

"What do we do about it if he does?"

"I think it's customary to dip them in kerosene," replied Pemberley.

"Gosh, I can't imagine him liking that." Churchill started scratching at her shoulder. "I feel rather itchy myself now. Why did you have to go and mention fleas, Mrs Thonnings?"

"I just wondered."

"Sometimes it's best not to wonder these things aloud. Why not just do it quietly instead? That way we won't have our important conversations interrupted. Now, what did you discover about the piece of fabric from the murderer's coat?"

"I believe it's a woollen twill."

"Worsted or double-worsted?"

"Neither. I think it's from a woollen twill of dark grey; not black, as the constable had first assumed."

"So had we. Very interesting indeed. Dark grey, you say?" Churchill scratched the back of her neck.

"Yes. And twill rather than plain weave."

"So the murderer was wearing a dark grey woollen overcoat with a twill weave?"

"That's what the snagged fabric suggests. If it actually came from the murderer's overcoat, that is."

"I see. So the police need to question anyone who possesses a dark grey twill overcoat."

"Yes. And I've explained to them the difference between twill and plain weave."

"Which is?"

"In plain, the warp and weft weaves cross one another at right angles. In twill, a diagonal pattern is formed by crossing multiple counts of weft and warp threads. For example, a common twill is two warp threads crossing two weft threads, and the pattern is slightly offset on each row to create a diagonal pattern. Another type is—"

"That all sounds fascinating, Mrs Thonnings," interrupted Mrs Churchill, scratching her knee. "A very detailed explanation indeed. How about our coats hanging over there?" She pointed to the cloak stand. "Can you tell us which type of weave they are?"

"I expect so."

Mrs Thonnings got up from her seat and examined them closely.

"Mine is the taupe one," said Churchill. "It cost a pretty penny from a boutique in Sloane Square, but that was fifteen years ago, so it's worn well. The sort of bluish-greyish-greenish coat is Miss Pemberley's."

"Plain weave," announced Mrs Thonnings.

"Miss Pemberley's, you mean?"

"No, I was referring to yours, Mrs Churchill. Miss Pemberley's is a little more interesting. It appears to be a type of basket weave."

"I see. And mine's just plain?" Churchill tried to reach an itch between her shoulder blades.

"Yes."

"I see. Well in that case I've a good mind to return it. You wouldn't believe the price they charged me for it back then!"

"Plain weave doesn't denote poor quality, Mrs Churchill," said Pemberley. "It's the quality of the wool that matters."

"Ah yes, there is that, I suppose. I expect that's of a rather superior quality. Can you examine the quality of the wool for us, Mrs Thonnings?"

"Is that really necessary?" asked Pemberley. "Isn't there a risk that we're becoming rather pernickety about our overcoats?"

"I want to make sure they charged me a fair price, Miss Pemberley."

"You've been wearing it for fifteen years, Mrs Churchill. I'd say you've had your money's worth!"

"Right you are, then." Churchill shuffled the papers on

her desk. "Well, Mrs Thonnings, I think it's fair to say that your knowledge of threads and weaves and the suchlike has proved quite indispensable."

"I'm so pleased you think so, Mrs Churchill! Does that mean you'd be interested in recruiting me?"

"I think you're best placed to continue working in the field in which you're already an expert, Mrs Thonnings. Namely, haberdashery."

"Oh, do you think so?"

"Very much so. But you never know when your expert knowledge may be called upon again. Thanks to your work the list of murder suspects can be narrowed down to those who own dark grey twill coats; a very significant development indeed. I hope that fool Inspector Mappin uses the intelligence wisely, although I think we already know he won't."

"I think you sometimes underestimate him, Mrs Churchill," said Mrs Thonnings. "He couldn't have been a police inspector all these years if he was completely hopeless at his job."

Chapter 11

FOOTSTEPS on the stairs announced the impending arrival of another visitor. The three ladies paused and waited to see who would appear. Moments later, a man with bushy brown mutton-chop whiskers and wearing an inspector's uniform stepped into the room.

"Good afternoon, ladies," he said, removing his hat. "It seems you're having quite the gathering here."

"It's only us and Mrs Thonnings, Inspector. And we still have enough iced fancies to go round, don't we, Miss Pemberley?"

"We have three."

"Three? What happened to the others?"

"They've been eaten."

"Eaten? I can't think how. Anyway, Inspector, what brings you here? You must be rather busy at the moment with all this murder business going on."

"I'm very busy indeed." He hung his hat on the hatstand.

"And I must say you're looking rather stern. Aren't you at least going to thank Oswald for his unrivalled sleuthing skills? He was the one who found the murder weapon, you know."

"I shall come to that."

"He's our decorated detective dog, Inspector! Look at all the awards on his collar."

"Very good. He's also the scrappy little thing that caused me to swerve dangerously on my bicycle last week."

"That was almost certainly another dog, Inspector. Our dog is an exceptionally well-trained hound, which is no doubt why he was able to find the gun used to shoot Mr Butterfork. Your men would have missed it altogether if it hadn't been for Oswald."

"I highly doubt that, Mrs Churchill. Russell and Dawkins are perfectly competent."

"Miss Pemberley found a torn piece of fabric from the assailant's coat and, from that Mrs Thonnings was able to identify the type of coat the culprit was wearing."

"I was," added Mrs Thonnings proudly.

"Off the top of my head, Inspector," continued Churchill, "I can't quite picture what your men actually achieved in the churchyard."

"An awful lot of police business is conducted away from the eyes of the general public, Mrs Churchill. And I must, ahem…" He paused to clear his throat. "I must…" He scratched beneath his collar, clearly feeling uncomfortable. "I must…"

"Must what, Inspector?"

"I must express my, ahem, *thanks*."

"Your thanks?"

"Yes, that's correct."

"Did you hear that, Miss Pemberley and Mrs Thonnings? Inspector Mappin has thanked us!"

"He still hasn't thanked Oswald, though," said Pemberley.

"He's a dog," replied the inspector. "He can't understand what I'm saying."

Pemberley let out an indignant gasp.

"But," stressed the inspector with a raised finger, "I do have a little something for him here." He reached into the pocket of his jacket and removed a paper bag. He took a bone out of the bag, crouched down in the middle of the room and waved the treat in Oswald's direction.

"Here, little doggy woggy!"

Churchill's toes curled at the unusually high tone of his voice.

"The police inspector man has a little reward for you!" he added.

Oswald regarded Inspector Mappin suspiciously for a moment, then swiftly reconsidered and happily bounded over to fetch his reward.

"Oh, thank you, Inspector!" gushed Churchill. "How lovely to see you do something nice for a change."

He returned to full height and frowned. "I often do nice things."

"Do you?"

"Yes. You probably just don't see me do them."

"I can vouch for the fact that Inspector Mappin does nice things," added Mrs Thonnings, "behind closed doors."

"When have you and the inspector been behind closed doors together, Mrs Thonnings?"

"That's quite enough of that," responded Mappin. "Now, returning to the matter of the Butterfork case, I'm extremely grateful for all the work you've done—"

"But…"

"But there will be no need for any more assistance from you, Mrs Churchill. I have the matter firmly in hand."

"Who are your chief suspects, Inspector?"

"I'm afraid I can't discuss the matter with anyone from outside the police force, Mrs Churchill."

"I see. Did you put my name on your list, Inspector?"

"Which one?"

"There's more than one list?"

"For what?"

"I don't know, you tell me! All I know is that when we approached the spotty constable at the door of Mr Butterfork's home he said he wasn't allowed to speak to me because my name was on the list."

"Why did you feel the need to approach the constable in the first place?"

"We were just passing, weren't we, Miss Pemberley? And we were interested to find out what all the kerfuffle on Crunkle Lane was about. I consider it most rude of you to go putting my name on lists."

"It was merely a precaution, Mrs Churchill. I know how adept you are at pumping people for information, and Constable Wiggins is just a young lad. He's only been with the force three months, and the poor chap's too green to withstand the likes of you."

"Then perhaps you should have someone more experienced attending your murder scenes, Inspector!"

"A rural community must do what it can, Mrs Churchill, and if the villagers would allow us to get on with our jobs unhampered the likes of Constable Wiggins would be able to acquit themselves perfectly well."

"You could call for assistance from Scotland Yard, Inspector."

"And have one of those big heads take over my investigation? No thank you."

Churchill felt a snap of anger. "My dear departed husband was detective chief inspector at the Yard for a good number of years, Inspector Mappin. I do hope you aren't including him in your description of *big heads*!"

"Certainly not, Mrs Churchill, especially as Detective Chief Inspector Churchill is no longer with us."

"Good," responded Churchill, her feathers feeling decidedly ruffled. "Now, I should like to request that my name be removed from any lists you may have written it down upon. I have no interest in involving myself in your investigation, Inspector Mappin."

"That's reassuring to hear."

"The case Miss Pemberley and I have in hand merely concerns the churchyard, so I must forewarn you that there may be a slight overlap as we go about our business."

"What sort of case could possibly involve the churchyard?"

"A little investigation into the things that go bump in the night. Isn't that right, Miss Pemberley?"

Her secretary shuddered.

"It's not for Grieves, is it?" asked Inspector Mappin.

"It is indeed. He told me he'd contacted you about the mischief taking place down there but you'd shown no interest in investigating it."

"I told him I can't investigate everything that happens in the village. I'm a busy man with a lot on my plate. I don't have time to find out who moved a flower from one grave to another or whatever it was."

"It's a little more complicated than that, but don't worry your important police inspector head about it. Miss Pemberley and I have it *in hand*, to borrow your own expression."

"Good. Then the next time you see my men investigating in the churchyard you'll leave them well alone, won't you?" He retrieved his hat from the hatstand.

"Even if we discover another piece of crucial evidence, such as the murder weapon?"

"Seeing as you've already done that, it's unlikely you'll find anything else of significance."

"I see. We'll make that same assumption then, and if we do happen to find any further evidence we'll just leave it be, shall we?"

"Well, you could mention it to the constables."

"Oh, we could, could we? This is all terribly confusing."

He put his hat on, clearly exasperated. "There's no need to split hairs, Mrs Churchill. You just get on with whatever you're doing in the churchyard and leave me to apprehend Mr Butterfork's killer."

"Of course, Inspector. Understood. Good luck with that."

Chapter 12

"The sole purpose of our visit to Mrs Hatweed this morning is to pretend to be returning the shillings her lately departed employer gave us at the summer fete," said Churchill to Pemberley as they walked along Compton Poppleford high street with Oswald at their heels.

"But we gave the rest of our money to Mrs Roseball on the jam stall."

"Yes we did, but Mrs Hatweed doesn't know that. We can use the shillings as an excuse to speak to her."

"To ask her some probing questions about the circumstances of Mr Butterfork's death, you mean?"

"Oh no, because that would constitute meddling in the eyes of Inspector Mappin."

"But we are really, aren't we?"

"Are what?"

"Going to ask some probing questions."

"I don't think that's quite the right way to go about it, Pembers. We need to fully accept that the one and only reason we're visiting Mrs Hatweed is to return Mr Butterfork's money. If we suspect, even for a moment, that there's a dual purpose to our visit we shall be knowingly meddling."

"I can't really see a difference."

"There's a *huge* difference, believe me. But if it so happens that Mrs Hatweed also decides to impart a few facts about Mr Butterfork's demise, we shan't stop her."

"So we're returning the shillings while secretly hoping she'll spill the beans."

"Yes."

They continued on their way, waving at Mrs Thonnings through the window of her haberdashery shop, scowling at Mrs Higginbath through the library window and acknowledging Mr Pickwick with a morning greeting as he stood outside his picture gallery.

"I'm sure he's been waiting there all morning just for you, Mrs Churchill," whispered Pemberley once they had passed him.

"Nonsense."

"He has, you know. He's still looking at you."

"Stop turning around and gawping at him, Pembers!"

"It's *you* he's interested in, not *me*."

"You can stop all this teasing right now," scolded Churchill. "Any more of that and I shall start looking for a new assistant!"

"Oh, you wouldn't, would you?" said Pemberley, sounding quite forlorn.

"I'd be forced to."

"It was only meant as a little joke."

"It's worn rather thin, I'm afraid. Too thin, in fact. Where's Oswald?" Churchill looked down but saw no sign of the little dog. Then she glanced behind her just in time to see him trying to clamber up Mr Pickwick's legs.

"Oh dear. Please go and fetch him, Pembers."

"But wouldn't you like to? Seeing as it's Mr—"

"No!" interrupted Churchill. "*You* go. I have no interest whatsoever in that man!"

Pemberley went back to fetch Oswald and returned with him in her arms.

"Was he annoyed?" asked Churchill.

"Not at all. He was rather excitable and hoping for a little treat."

"What sort of treat?"

"A pig's ear, I expect."

"I meant Mr Pickwick, not the dog."

"Mr Pickwick might like pig ears, too."

"Perhaps he does; I have no interest either way. Come along now, Pembers. We've wasted enough time already this morning."

Mrs Hatweed had a head of brown curls and red cheeks. She wore a voluminous pink housecoat and filled the doorway of her small cottage.

"Miss Pemberley!" Her curls bounced as she greeted the wiry secretary with a smile. "I haven't seen you since Inspector Mappin's birthday party. Do come in. And this must be Mrs Churchill you have with you. Do come in, Mrs Churchill, it's a pleasure to finally meet, I've heard all about you."

"Do you mind if Oswald comes in as well?" asked Pemberley.

"Not at all. I love dogs." Mrs Hatweed beamed at him. "Especially ones wearing medals. Come on in, all of you."

"Inspector Mappin's birthday party?" whispered Churchill to Pemberley as they followed Mrs Hatweed into her front room. "That must have been a barrel of laughs."

"It was, actually," replied Pemberley. "He's quite different when he's not on police duty, you know."

Churchill gave a derisory snort.

"Is everything all right?" asked Mrs Hatweed.

"Oh yes, I'm fine. Something just caught in my throat," replied Churchill.

"I'm sure a lovely cup of tea will sort that out."

"Thank you, I'm sure it would."

"As would a slice of walnut cake, I imagine."

"You're a woman after my own heart, Mrs Hatweed."

Churchill, Pemberley and Oswald settled themselves on a velour settee in the small, cosy front room.

"Goodness, what a lot of shepherdesses," commented Churchill, surveying the china ornaments arranged along the mantelpiece, windowsill and every other available surface.

"They're very precious to me," said Mrs Hatweed.

"That's nice."

"They're all I really have now, given that I see so little of Ernie these days. I'd better go and make the tea." She left the room.

"What a lot of shepherdess dusting she must have to do," said Pemberley. "I couldn't keep up with it myself."

"Who's Ernie?"

"Mrs Hatweed's son. Look, there's a photograph of him there. There are rumours going around that he's inside."

"Inside where?"

"Prison!" whispered Pemberley.

"Good lord! Really? Well, that explains why she sees so little of him, I suppose."

"Now, what can I do for you, ladies?" asked Mrs Hatweed when she returned to the room with a tea tray. She rested it on the floor, pushed Oswald away from the plate of biscuits, moved several shepherdesses from a little table and placed the tea tray on it.

"We have something of Mr Butterfork's to return to you," said Churchill.

"Oh," replied Mrs Hatweed sadly as she poured the tea. "It's not money, is it?"

"Yes. Two shillings, to be precise." Churchill retrieved her purse from her handbag and began to count out the money.

"Oh, don't worry about that," replied the housekeeper, "it's only two shillings. And besides, what can Mr Butterfork do with them now? He's…" She let out a loud sob as she sank back into the armchair with a cup of tea in her hand.

"I'm so sorry, Mrs Hatweed," said Churchill. "It must have been a terrible shock for you."

"It was awful. Awful, I tell you! He was always ready for his two boiled eggs every morning, you see. He'd be sitting there at the breakfast table with his napkin tucked into his collar just waiting for me. Every single day until that fateful morning when his chair sat empty as he lay on the floor of his bedroom, stone cold dead!"

"It's truly dreadful."

"Eight long months, and then he was just gone in the blink of an eye."

"Eight months? Is that how long he lived in the village?"

"I believe he lived here for about a year. I moved to the village eight months ago and became his housekeeper after the previous one died."

"That was Mrs Fingle, wasn't it?" asked Pemberley.

"That's right," replied the housekeeper sadly.

"She drowned in the river during a midnight swim," Pemberley explained to Churchill.

"Golly, how tragic!"

"It was very sad indeed," said Mrs Hatweed. "Mr

Butterfork was terribly upset about it. That's when I stepped in and became his housekeeper."

"During the time you were Mr Butterfork's housekeeper, did you encounter anyone who might have harboured a wish to murder him?" asked Churchill.

"No! No one at all. But then it was a robbery, you see. Someone knew he kept all that money in his tea chest."

"And with all due respect to the deceased gentleman, he didn't exactly keep his money a secret, did he?"

"He was very generous. He couldn't help himself."

"And at no time did he express any wish to bank his wealth with Mr Burbage?"

"He didn't trust the banks."

"I see. That's a great shame, because if he had done so he would no doubt still be with us now."

"He never imagined anyone would steal his money, Mrs Churchill. He was too trusting, you see."

"With the exception of bank managers."

"Apart from them, yes."

"And would you say that it was rather common knowledge among the villagers that Mr Butterfork kept his fortune in the tea chest in his bedroom?"

"Yes, I'd say that it was."

"That doesn't exactly narrow down our list of suspects, does it?"

"No, it doesn't. Oh, it really is awful!"

"Do you know anyone who owns a long, dark grey overcoat, Mrs Hatweed?"

"I might do. I can't immediately recall anyone who does, but then they might own one without me realising it."

"Did you see anyone in a dark grey overcoat loitering near Mr Butterfork's home at around the time of the murder?"

"Well, there was the dark figure, wasn't there? Is that who you mean?"

"Yes. Do you remember Mr Butterfork receiving a visit from someone wearing said coat?"

"Male or female?"

"I suppose we can't be entirely sure, though I suspect it was a male as the culprit appears to have left man-sized footprints in the churchyard."

"I didn't see anyone wearing a dark grey coat, male or female."

"Did he receive any visitors shortly before his death?"

"Oh, yes."

"Can you recall who they were?"

"The police have already asked me this, so I can remember quite clearly. There was Mrs Strawbanks."

"The lady who lives opposite Mr Butterfork?"

"Yes."

"Who else?"

"Mrs Thonnings."

"I see."

"Mrs Roseball."

"The lady who makes jam?"

"Yes. And Mr Pickwick."

"Oh. Any others?"

"No, just those four."

"Three ladies and one man," said Pemberley. "Mr Pickwick is the only man."

"He certainly appears to be," replied Churchill.

"Interesting, don't you think, Mrs Churchill?" Pemberley added.

"Sort of. Although recent visitors to Mr Butterfork's home are unlikely to be culprits, aren't they? They wouldn't have wished to make it so obvious by visiting Mr Butterfork during the day and then returning during the

EMILY ORGAN

hours of darkness to shoot him. I should think the murderer would have stayed well away until the appointed time so no one would make a connection between the culprit and his victim."

"Then why did you ask about Mr Butterfork's visitors?" asked Mrs Hatweed.

"It's helpful to be able to rule them out."

Pemberley frowned. "You're ruling them out because you don't believe the murderer would have visited Mr Butterfork on the day he was murdered?"

"The murderer may have done, but not in such an obvious way that Mrs Hatweed here or others might have spotted him. If Mr Pickwick were the murderer, for example, I sincerely doubt he would have been happy to be seen paying him a visit. Don't you agree, Mrs Hatweed?"

"It could have been a bluff," replied the housekeeper. "Perhaps he thought nobody would suspect him because he was a friend of Mr Butterfork's."

"Was he a friend?"

"Yes. Apparently they used to work for the same insurance company."

"Gosh. Mr Pickwick never mentioned that to me."

"I don't believe they were *friends* as such; just acquaintances."

"Well, that is a coincidence. Does that mean Mr Butterfork once lived in London like our good friend Mr Pickwick?"

"Yes, he did."

"And is that where he came into his money?"

"He inherited it from an elderly aunt. He was her favourite great-nephew, you see. She lived in Benton Thurstock."

"Which is where?"

82

"A great long way away. Over on the other side of Dorset, in fact."

"And was this coming into money the reason why Mr Butterfork moved from London to Dorset?"

"Apparently so. When he heard she was unwell he left his job in insurance and moved to Benton Thurstock to nurse her."

"Would he have done so if she'd been as poor as a church mouse, do you think?"

"Of course he would! He loved his great-aunt very dearly."

"What brought him to Compton Poppleford?"

"He lived in his great-aunt's house for a while after her death but didn't feel very settled in that part of Dorset. He didn't care for their ways over there."

"What sort of ways?"

"Just their manner of doing things."

"Such as?"

"I don't know, to be exact, but I've heard they have a certain way of doing things over on that side of the county. Anyway, he happened to be passing through our village on the way to Melching Mummerton one day, and here he stayed."

"He never made it to Melching Mummerton?"

"No, and it's probably just as well, really."

"How so?"

"If you think Benton Thurstock's bad you really don't want to go visiting Melching Mummerton."

"I can't say I have a fixed opinion on Benton Thurstock, to be quite honest with you, Mrs Hatweed."

"Oh, you will if you ever go there… which is strongly inadvisable, of course."

"I must say I'm quite intrigued now."

"It's on the border with Hampshire, and you know

what border towns are like. Melching Mummerton, on the other hand, is dangerously close to Devon."

"Why *dangerously*?"

"Have you ever been to Devon, Mrs Churchill?"

"No, but I'm considering it for a little holiday."

There was a sharp intake of breath from Mrs Hatweed. "Don't do it, Mrs Churchill."

"Why ever not?"

"My sister's son-in-law went to Honiton once and was never the same again."

"Goodness, why not?"

"They won't speak of it, Mrs Churchill. The whole family refuses to speak of it. Whatever happened was very bad, that's for sure." Mrs Hatweed shuddered and drained her teacup.

"Well, I can understand why Mr Butterfork chose Compton Poppleford. It's a very nice place indeed," said Churchill. "All we need to do now is find out who murdered him."

"Well, we already have the four suspects who visited him the day he died," said Pemberley.

"They're not *suspects*, Miss Pemberley."

"But they could be. And Mr Pickwick is one of them."

Chapter 13

"PERHAPS THE FOUR visitors could be considered suspects if one of them happened to own a dark grey overcoat," said Churchill, "but I doubt Mr Pickwick owns one. He doesn't seem the type. Have you ever seen Mrs Strawbanks wearing a dark grey overcoat, Mrs Hatweed?"

"No, I can't say I have."

"What was her business with Mr Butterfork?"

"I couldn't tell you the entirety of their conversation, as I'm not one for listening in, but I did overhear her telling him about a fence of hers that had fallen down."

"What did she expect him to do about that? Ah, wait, I think I see it now. She was hoping he would contribute toward a replacement, was she?"

"Now you put it in those terms, Mrs Churchill, I suppose that may well have been the reason she visited him. She spent quite some time complaining about how it had crushed her dahlias and explaining that replanting her flowerbed wouldn't come cheap. As for the cost of the new fence, that was something else altogether. And if Mr Strawbanks had still been alive he would have happily erected the new fence because that was something he'd always enjoyed doing, but as she's a widow now she would have to go to the expense of finding a man to do that sort of work, and men who do that sort of work have been in the habit of putting their prices up lately. She remembered that in her mother's day there were lads aplenty willing to put in a day's work and expect nothing more for their trouble than a tankard of scrumpy, but those days are gone now, more's the pity."

"It sounds as though you overheard the entire conversation, Mrs Hatweed."

"No, barely any of it. That was just what she was saying as I passed by the door."

"Do you know whether Mr Butterfork stumped up the money?"

"I don't know, but I suspect he did. He was ever so generous, wasn't he?"

"And what about Mrs Roseball? What was the purpose of her visit?"

"I happened to pass by the door again briefly while she was there. I heard her discussing the weather and then telling him about her cat, Theophilus."

"That's a fancy name for a cat."

"It's Oswald's middle name as well," added Pemberley.

"Is it really?" asked Churchill. "What a funny coincidence. I hadn't realised Oswald was in possession of a middle name."

"He wasn't until a moment ago."

"So, on hearing the name of Mrs Roseball's cat just now, Miss Pemberley, you made the impromptu decision that it would be a nice middle name for Oswald, did you?"

"Yes."

"I see. And what of Theophilus, Mrs Hatweed? Were cats of great interest to Mr Butterfork?"

"Not at all; he preferred dogs. He would have loved your little Oswald."

"Mr Butterfork had no interest in cats, but Mrs Roseball told him all about her own kitty just the same. Why so?"

"Poor little Theophilus hadn't been well recently. Mrs Roseball had done her best at looking after him but his health was making no improvement, so she needed to take him to the village veterinarian. At least, she would have done so if she could have afforded to, but being what they are, veterinarians don't come cheap, and she really couldn't put it off any longer. She'd been so terribly worried about the whole affair it had been keeping her up all night."

"And Mr Butterfork gave her the money for the vet's bill, did he?"

"I would imagine so. He was a—"

"Generous man, yes. Now then, let's discuss Mrs Thonnings. What did she want him to pay for? Actually, don't give me any clues… I want to guess this one myself. She probably visited him to talk about buttons and bows, and how a good number of customers are asking for items that aren't in stock, and instead of ordering them in they've been swanning off to the big haberdasher's in Dorchester instead, and if it continues like this for much longer she'll go out of business. The only solution, and a rather urgent one at that, would be to replace the ageing display stands with something a little more modern, making it possible to display a wider range of stock within the same amount of space. But with these modern display stands costing an arm and a leg… Well, it's all well and good when you're the large haberdasher's in Dorchester, but when you're a little haberdasher's in a village, and run by a widow… Am I on the right track here, Mrs Hatweed?"

"I've no idea."

"You didn't happen to hear any of their conversation while you were passing by the doorway?"

"No, none at all." Her expression was one of great disappointment. "I'm not one for listening in, but I did notice they kept their voices quite low. And I also heard a bit of chuckling."

"Perhaps she was whispering sweet nothings into his ear," commented Pemberley.

Churchill felt her stomach turn. "Gosh, what a thought."

"And Mr Pickwick?" asked Pemberley. "Do you know why he visited Mr Butterfork?"

"It all sounded very dull to me... what I heard of it while I was passing by, anyway. It was all gentlemen's topics. Business, mainly."

"Discussing business, were they? Two retired men?"

"They worked together in insurance many years ago, you see, and I suppose old habits die hard."

"What exactly were they discussing?"

"I can't say that I know. My mind is entirely uneducated on the matter, and I didn't understand half the words they were using, no matter how hard I tried. It took me back to the days when Mr Hatweed used to talk about profits and percentages and predicaments. None of it made any sense to me. Ladies' brains simply don't work that way, do they?"

"Speak for yourself," said Pemberley.

"Now, now, Miss Pemberley," said Churchill. "Let's make allowances for the fact that housekeepers don't always need to know about profits and percentages."

"They should know a few things about predicaments," replied Pemberley.

"Only if they find themselves in one." Churchill turned

to Mrs Hatweed. "I suppose it suffices to say that the long and short of it is you don't know what Mr Pickwick discussed with Mr Butterfork, but it sounded rather boring."

"*Very* boring. Would you like another slice of walnut cake?"

"It would almost be rude not to. Thank you, Mrs Hatweed. Now then, Mr Butterfork appears to have freely allowed the assailant into his house, as there was no sign of a break-in. Was he in the habit of leaving his doors and windows open?"

"No. He liked to keep the doors locked, front and back, on account of all the money he had stashed in the house."

"Which door did you leave by on the day of his murder, Mrs Hatweed?"

"The back door."

"Do you have a key for it?"

"Yes. I was in the habit of locking it every evening after I left. It was still locked the following morning, but the front door had been left unlocked."

"Was that unusual?"

"Yes. It was usually still locked and bolted from the night before when I arrived each morning. Mr Butterfork didn't often go out before I arrived, you see. He would get himself up and dress, then wait at the breakfast table for his eggs."

"Then Mr Butterfork must have unlocked the front door at some point during the night?"

"He must have done."

"Could it have been left unlocked accidentally?"

"It could have been, but I've never known Mr Butter-fork do such a thing."

"But he could have forgotten to lock it on this occasion,

and someone might have happened to stroll in off the street on the very day he left it unlocked."

"It seems too coincidental to me," said Pemberley.

"I agree, my trusted assistant. The alternative is that someone called on him that evening and he opened the door to greet them. Did he often receive visitors of an evening?"

"Only occasionally," replied the housekeeper, "and if he'd arranged for someone to visit, he was in the habit of asking me to stay on a while longer to prepare a bit of supper for them."

"So this could have been an unexpected visitor?"

"Undoubtedly."

"What were Mr Butterfork's usual movements?"

"Quite like anyone else's, really. He had a slight limp; an injury from the war, he told me. But other than that he moved fairly normally."

"I meant his routine, Mrs Hatweed."

"Oh, why didn't you say so?"

"What were his usual comings and goings? Was he the sociable type?"

"Not enormously. He went out two evenings a week: every Tuesday to the Masonic Lodge and every Thursday to play cards with Mr Pickwick."

"I see. Nothing to raise any great suspicions there. And how much money do you imagine the murderer made away with?"

"I have no idea. Enough to fill a tea chest, I suppose."

"Initially, perhaps. But he was in the habit of giving it away, wasn't he?"

"Yes, that's true."

"When did you last look inside the tea chest?"

"Oh, I never looked inside it! The contents of that tea chest were Mr Butterfork's concern and no one else's. The first time I saw inside it was the morning after his murder, when it had been left open." The housekeeper gave another loud sob and pulled a handkerchief from the pocket of her apron to dab at her eyes.

"There, there, Mrs Hatweed," said Churchill. "The culprit won't get away with this, you can be sure of that."

"It can't have been easy for him to run off with all that money about his person," said Pemberley.

"No, it wouldn't have been," agreed Churchill. "And although Mr Butterfork may have given a good deal of it away, there must have been enough left on that fateful night for someone to resort to murder in order to get their hands on it."

The two ladies and Oswald left Mrs Hatweed's home and walked down Crunkle Lane toward the churchyard. Churchill felt a shiver as they passed Mr Butterfork's house, the windows of which had been shuttered up.

"Poor Mr Butterfork," she lamented, recalling the ruddy-cheeked man in the boater hat with scrumpy slopping from his tankard as the Morris dancers performed. "I can't deny that I found him rather irritating while I was having a go at that coconut shy at the summer fete, but he was only enjoying himself, wasn't he?"

"And he helped you win a coconut," added Pemberley.

"He did, and it was most kind of him. That reminds me, it's still sitting on my mantelpiece. I really don't know what to do with it."

"You drink the milk and then eat the inside bit."

"I suppose one does. I don't find the whole idea particularly appetising, if truth be told."

"You could make coconut cake with it."

"That sounds rather more appealing. I must say,

Pembers, I'm slightly disappointed not to have received an invitation to Inspector Mappin's birthday party."

"He probably didn't know you well enough by then. You'd only just arrived in the village."

"It was fairly recent then, was it?"

"Yes, it was shortly after you arrived in Compton Poppleford. I think we were investigating the death of Mrs Furzgate at the Piddleton Hotel back then."

"That wasn't long ago at all! You'd have thought he'd have invited a newcomer to the village along to make her feel welcome."

"That's not really the sort of thing Inspector Mappin does, is it? And besides, you had recently trampled on his wife's geraniums."

"People really do bear grudges about the smallest of things around here."

"Oh look, there's something shiny in the gutter," said Pemberley, reaching down to the ground. "It looks like somebody's lost a ring." She pulled a handkerchief out of her pocket and picked it up. Then she stood to show Churchill the thick band of gold.

"It looks like a gentleman's ring," commented Churchill. She retrieved her reading glasses from her handbag and peered closely at it. "With some sort of insignia on it, too. Is that a bookend? No, I think it might be some sort of bridge."

"It's the square and compasses," replied Pemberley. "The sign of the Freemasons."

"Of course," said Churchill. "I knew that really, I was just looking at it upside down. Detective Chief Inspector Churchill was a mason."

"As is the owner of this ring."

"How interesting. I wonder whom it belongs to."

"It could be a clue," said Pemberley.

Churchill glanced toward the churchyard wall at the end of the lane. "By Jove, Pembers, it could indeed! This is the route the murderer must have taken from Mr Butterfork's house to the churchyard. It may belong to the murderer himself!"

"It could!" replied Pemberley. "We can't be certain, though. I wonder why the police didn't find it."

Churchill made a scoffing sound. "You've seen how they search for things, Pembers, they're hopeless. Let's hang on to this for now; it could be a clue."

"Shouldn't we give it to Inspector Mappin?"

"Why would we do that?"

"For two reasons. Firstly, because someone may be looking for it, and secondly because it could be an important piece of evidence in the murder investigation."

"It might be an important piece of evidence, or it might not. I say we hang on to it for now and see where our investigations lead us." Noticing the dubious look on Pemberley's face, she continued. "I'm not suggesting we keep this ring indefinitely. I just think we should hold on to it for a few days. We'll make sure it becomes reunited with its rightful owner one way or another."

Chapter 14

PEMBERLEY MADE a pot of tea once they had reached the office, then fetched a small wooden box from a cupboard and brought it over to Churchill's desk. "This is Atkins's old fingerprint dusting kit," she announced. "I've been itching to use it for ages. Let's try dusting the ring for prints." Pemberley set about inspecting the various little pots inside the box.

"Isn't the ring rather small for identifying fingerprints?"

"Yes, but it's worth a go, don't you think?" She took out one of the pots. "I think this powder would work best." She selected a small brush with long, soft bristles. "And this brush will be just the ticket."

Pemberley set the ring on a piece of blotting paper at the centre of Churchill's desk, and her employer watched as she opened the tin of dark powder and dipped the brush into it. Pemberley held the brush over the ring for a moment before beginning to dust over it with light, flitting movements.

"There's a certain method to this," she explained. "You

can't just splodge the brush on, like daubing paint onto a canvas."

These light, floaty movements continued for a while, the bristles only lightly touching the ring.

"Can I have a go?" asked Churchill.

"Just let me reveal the fingerprints first."

"Why can't I reveal the fingerprints?"

"Because it requires a certain amount of training."

"How can I learn if you won't let me have a go?"

"I shall be happy to teach you, Mrs Churchill, but on another object to begin with, such as your teacup or the plate that had the butterfly cakes on it."

"From what I can glean, there isn't much to it other than wafting the brush around rather aimlessly."

"There's *much* more to it than that, Mrs Churchill. So much more!"

"Can you see any fingerprints yet?"

"I can see markings of some sort."

"Well, I suppose that's not altogether surprising. All that powder you're wafting about is making my nose itch."

Pemberley fetched a magnifying glass from her drawer and peered closely at the ring. "Hmm. There are fingerprint smudges all over it, but I can't find a clear enough print for it to be of any use. I shall take a photograph all the same."

"When can I have my go?" Churchill asked again as Pemberley fetched the Brownie camera and wound it on.

"Once I've taken the photograph," Pemberley replied.

"Actually I'm beginning to wonder if it's such a good idea after all. I can't tell you how tickly that powder has made my nose."

Just as Pemberley depressed the shutter button on the camera, Churchill let out an enormous sneeze, which set

Oswald barking and caused Pemberley to stagger backwards in surprise.

"Now I've gone and taken a photograph of the ceiling," fumed Pemberley. "That's a whole frame completely wasted!"

"I think we've wasted too much of our time dusting for fingerprints anyway, Pembers. Even if we managed to identify a print on that little ring, how would we know whom it belonged to? Can you think of a way to go about fingerprinting all the Freemasons in Compton Poppleford?"

Pemberley scowled. "I wanted to try it out, all the same. Mr Atkins and I spent many a fun hour dusting pieces of evidence for fingerprints."

"Well, that is lovely to hear, but it doesn't really help us at the present moment. What we need to do is identify the owner of this ring somehow. I think he'll be missing the thing, so what better way than to advertise the fact that we're in possession of it?"

"By placing a notice in the newspaper, you mean?"

"That's exactly what I mean. Now, tidy away your little fingerprinting set and I'll start drafting something." Churchill picked up a pen and paper and began to write.

Once she had finished, she read it aloud to Pemberley: "'A gentleman's gold ring bearing the insignia of the Freemasons has been found on Crunkle Lane. If this ring is yours, or you know whom it may belong to, please visit Churchill's Detective Agency at your earliest convenience.'"

"No, no, that's all wrong."

"What do you mean it's *all wrong*?"

"For one thing, it needs to be as short as possible. The *Compton Poppleford Gazette* charges sixpence for twenty words and a halfpenny per word after that. The message you've written would cost us almost a shilling."

"Daylight robbery! Is that awful Trollope gentleman still the editor?"

"Yes."

"Well, no wonder. The man's a disgrace!"

"He is. To prevent any chancers coming forward we'd best avoid describing the ring in too much detail. The gentleman who comes to collect it from us will need to describe the ring so we know he's the rightful owner."

"Of course. That goes without saying."

"So you can't say that it has the Freemasons' insignia on it."

"But how will he know to get in touch if we don't?"

"The owner of the ring will be missing it and is therefore likely to be on the lookout for notices about lost rings."

"Ah, very good."

"Shall I rewrite the notice?"

"Be my guest, Pembers. I'm beginning to lose interest in it now."

"Oh, don't be like that, Mrs Churchill. It'll be more than worth it if it helps us catch the murderer."

"Now you put it like that, it certainly will be. If it even belongs to the murderer, that is."

Once Pemberley had rewritten the notice, she read it aloud to Churchill: "'Found. Gentleman's gold band ring, near Crunkle Lane. Enquire at Churchill's Detective Agency.'"

"That's it?"

"It's all that's needed."

"How many words is that?"

"Thirteen."

"Excellent. That'll bring the price down a little. Let me

work it out. If it's sixpence for twenty words, what will it be for thirteen? How do you divide sixpence into thirteen?" Churchill scribbled some cursory numbers onto a piece of paper. "My old governess, Miss Spitly, would tell you mathematics was never my strongest subject. That said, she must be long dead now, as she looked incredibly ancient back when I was a girl."

"It'll still be sixpence."

"What?"

"It's a flat fee; the minimum amount payable."

"Then we should increase the number of words! We need to get our money's worth, Pembers."

"I'm not sure that's necessary."

"I won't rest until we've added seven more words."

Churchill rewrote the notice and read it aloud, "'Found. Handsome gentleman's gold band ring was retrieved from Crunkle Lane and is in safe hands. Enquire Churchill's Detective Agency.'"

"I don't think the word '*handsome*' is needed."

"Of course it isn't, but I'm making sure we get value for money."

"Is it the ring that's handsome or the gentleman?"

Churchill considered this for a moment. "It would be rather nice if the ring belonged to a handsome gentleman, wouldn't it?"

"As handsome as Mr Pickwick?"

Despite her best attempts to control her face, Churchill felt her cheeks reddening and her mouth lifting at the corners. "No, I mean yes... I mean, I don't know."

"He is rather handsome, don't you think?" continued Pemberley.

"Any notion of whether he's handsome or not has never crossed my mind, Pembers. Mr Pickwick is just a man like all the rest of them. Now, I'm going to stow the ring safely inside my desk drawer here and run along to the *Gazette* office to get this notice placed."

Chapter 15

CHURCHILL'S ROUTE back from the *Compton Poppleford Gazette* offices took her, not entirely unintentionally, past the bank and Pickwick's Gallery. She was quite thrilled to spy Mr Pickwick standing outside in the sunshine.

"Isn't it a delightful afternoon?" he said. "I'm just taking a little fresh air. It seems such a shame to be stuck indoors."

"But you have a charming indoors, nonetheless."

"Thank you."

"Please accept my deepest commiserations, Mr Pickwick, on the sad passing of your dear friend Mr Butterfork."

"Ah, yes." He blinked, then made a face as though he were swallowing something painful. "Thank you, Mrs Churchill," he said solemnly. "You're very kind."

"I heard from his housekeeper that you used to play cards together once a week."

"We did indeed. I visited him on the day of his death, actually. It was only a fleeting visit, but I'm glad now that I was able to see him. To think that would be the last time…" His eyes grew moist as he focused on a distant point along the high street.

"I'm certain the culprit will be found," said Churchill.

"I absolutely hope so. The poor chap didn't deserve it at all. It's so dreadful." He cleared his throat. "On a lighter note, I've taken delivery of some new pictures this morning. Would you like to see them? They're not up on the wall yet, as I'm still deciding where to put them."

"I do have ten minutes to spare, so why not?"

He moved aside to allow Churchill space to step inside the gallery. She glanced around and noticed several pictures resting against the counter.

"Are these the ones?" she asked, walking over to them.

"They are indeed. I bought them at an auction in Dorchester last week, and the chap's just brought them over. They're all landscapes."

He picked up the first one, which depicted a large weeping willow with its branches trailing into a winding river. Two small boys with fishing nets crouched on the riverbank to the right of the picture, watched by a little scruffy dog.

"Oh, that looks just like Oswald!" chimed Churchill. "How lovely to see him in a painting."

"Percival!" a woman's voice called out from the rear of the shop. A trim lady in a fashionable rose-coloured jacket and matching skirt stepped through a door behind the counter. Her fair hair was neatly waved and her lips were painted crimson. "Oh, I'm so sorry!" she added as soon as she saw Churchill. "I didn't realise you were with a customer."

"Not just any old customer," said Mr Pickwick. "This is Mrs Churchill!"

The lady smiled, and Churchill did her best to return it, but a sour taste lingered in her mouth. She felt foolish for assuming Mr Pickwick was a bachelor or widow, when right here in the shop was his attractive lady wife. She realised it would have been extremely unlikely for a man as pleasant as Mr Pickwick to have remained unattached.

"Mrs Churchill, this is my sister, Miss Agnes Pickwick," he announced.

A grin spread across Churchill's face. "Mr Pickwick's *sister*!" she enthused. "How lovely to meet you!"

"I'm helping Percival with his latest venture," explained Miss Pickwick. "What do you think of the gallery so far, Mrs Churchill?"

"I think it's a simply wonderful addition to the high street."

"It is rather, isn't it?"

"It brings a little class and culture to the village. I lived latterly in London, you see, so I'm quite accustomed to the arts."

"That really is delightful to hear, Mrs Churchill. I do hope you'll visit us regularly from now on."

"Oh, I shall."

"Do please excuse me for a moment, I have something to attend to."

"Of course."

Miss Pickwick disappeared back through the door behind the counter.

"May I ask whereabouts in London you lived, Mrs Churchill?" asked Mr Pickwick.

"On the south-western periphery. Richmond-upon-Thames, to be precise."

"A very nice place indeed. I'm well acquainted with London."

"Are you, Mr Pickwick? How interesting. Do you hail from the Big Smoke yourself?"

"From just outside it, like you. Kent, actually, but I

worked in London town for many years in my insurance job, so I know it like the back of my hand."

"How wonderful. Who'd have thought it? And here you are bringing your cultured ways to the great unwashed in Dorset!" Churchill laughed sheepishly, quickly realising her comment might have sounded rather snobbish. "I'm only joking, of course. There are some perfectly nice and well-educated people here – my secretary, Miss Pemberley, being one of them, of course."

An unexpected rumbling noise came from beneath Churchill's feet. "Good grief! What was that?" she exclaimed.

"Workmen, I'm afraid," replied Mr Pickwick. "We've had a spot of bother in the basement – a bit of a leak – so we've had to get some men in to look at it. They're under strict instruction not to make too much noise while the gallery is open, as it can be rather off-putting for our customers."

"Oh, I don't mind, Mr Pickwick. You obviously need to have your leak fixed."

"Indeed. Agnes is supervising them."

Mr Pickwick showed Churchill the pictures that had arrived that morning. "There was another painting at the auction which quite took my fancy, but unfortunately a rival buyer snapped it up. It was a charming depiction of the Royal Academy of Arts at sundown. Are you familiar with the building?"

"On Piccadilly? I most assuredly am, Mr Pickwick. I used to attend many of the exhibitions there, in fact."

"Why, so did I. Perhaps we were both there at the same time and didn't know it!"

"I feel sure that we must have been at some point."

Churchill felt enchanted by his eyes, which matched the azure blue of the sea in a recent advertisement she had seen for the French Riviera. She imagined being there with him at that very moment. "In fact, you seem so familiar that I feel sure our paths must have crossed in London town at some point," she added.

"Yes." He nodded. "I'm sure they did, Mrs Churchill. There's certainly something very memorable about you."

"Oh, do you think so?" She felt heat rise into her face once again. "I've been told that a few times before, but not always for the most flattering of reasons!"

"I meant it purely as a compliment, Mrs Churchill."

"Did you? Well, there's no need to be so terribly nice to me. I must say that it's quite uncalled for."

He chuckled. "Oh, I beg to differ."

"Then I suppose we shall have to disagree on that front, Mr Pickwick." Churchill heard a tinkling girly laugh, realising moments later that the noise had come from her. She also registered the fact she hadn't been able to draw herself away from his eyes for several minutes.

Mr Pickwick cleared his throat. "I wonder..." he began. Then he paused and glanced up at the portrait of Viscountess Bathshire. "I hope you don't mind me asking you this, Mrs Churchill..."

"Asking me what, Percy? Sorry, I mean Percival. I mean Mr Pickwick."

He smiled. "My dearest friends call me Percy."

"Do they? It's a lovely name."

"Anyway, I was wondering whether you would allow me to paint you."

"Paint *me*, Mr Pickwick?" Churchill's heart skipped several beats. "Like Viscountess Bathshire?"

"Yes. You rather remind me of her, in fact."

"Do I? Goodness, well that is quite the compliment." She smoothed her lacquered hair, half-bashful and half-flattered. "I really don't know what to say!"

"How about yes?"

"Well yes, of course! How wonderful. I'd be delighted to let you paint me. Oh gosh, I don't believe I have anything suitable to wear!"

"I'm sure you do, Mrs Churchill. Just settle on something you feel comfortable in. I often tell my sitters to wear their normal clothes, as I believe that's what best reflects their personalities."

"Pearls, a twinset and a tweed skirt, then?"

"That sounds perfect. There's only one rather trifling matter I should mention."

"Which is?"

"Unfortunately, my studio is quite unusable at the present time. It's an adapted summerhouse, and the roof was taken clean off during the spring gales."

"Oh dear."

"Indeed. It's currently under repair, so I was wondering whether you'd feel comfortable being painted in your own home, Mrs Churchill."

"In *my* home?"

"Yes."

"*You* in *my* home, Mr Pickwick?"

"Yes, I realise it's not the ideal situation. By all means ask a friend to be present if you wish. I really wouldn't mind."

"Oh, I'm sure that won't be necessary. I can trust you to behave yourself, can't I?"

It was Mr Pickwick's turn to blush. "Absolutely, Mrs Churchill. I shall be on my very best behaviour."

Chapter 16

"THAT'S a nice little ditty you're humming, Mrs Churchill," commented Pemberley as Churchill returned to the office. "What is it?"

"Oh, I don't know," replied Churchill whimsically as she placed her handbag on her desk. "A little aria I must have picked up somewhere."

"I don't believe I've ever heard you sing before."

"No? I'd have said that I sing quite a bit."

"It's the first time I've heard it. Something rather pleasing must have happened at the offices of the *Compton Poppleford Gazette* while you were placing our notice about the ring."

"Nothing pleasing ever happens at the offices of that local rag."

"Then why are you in such good spirits?"

"Well, I happened to bump into Mr Pickwick on my way back."

"Ah, now I understand quite well."

"No you don't, Pembers, as I haven't explained it yet."

"It's Mr Pickwick. What further explanation could be required?"

"It's not just Mr Pickwick. In fact, the gentleman himself is neither here nor there as far as I'm concerned."

"You don't mean that."

"Pembers, bumping into Mr Pickwick was little more than a formality. What really put a spring in my step is the fact that I'm to be painted."

"By Mr Pickwick?"

"Yes indeed."

Pemberley paused for a moment as she considered this. "But why?"

"Why not? He clearly enjoys dabbling in a bit of portraiture."

"But why you?"

"It's funny you should say that, Pembers, because that was my immediate reaction when he first asked me. But he happened to mention that he felt there was something quite memorable about me."

Pemberley gave a bemused snort.

"What is that noise supposed to mean?"

"It seems he has a healthy stock of lines with which to woo a lady."

"There was absolutely no wooing involved, Pembers! He's painting me in much the same way as he painted Viscountess Bathshire. And he certainly didn't woo her!"

"How do you know that?"

"Because she's married to Viscount Bathshire."

"That doesn't seem to stop people these days."

"Oh Pemberley, that's enough! I won't entertain this crude conversation a moment longer. Now, let's get on with our work. We have a murder case to solve, remember?"

"Inspector Mappin has a murder case to solve, you mean."

"It'll never be solved with that man in charge. Earlier today I was speaking to a close friend of Mr Butterfork's, and when I saw the sadness in his face at the loss of his dear friend I just knew I had to do something about it."

"Was this close friend Mr Pickwick, by any chance?"

"It doesn't matter who it was. Now, fetch your coat and hat, Pembers, and let's pay Mrs Strawbanks a visit. She's the one who reported hearing the gunshot, so I'd like to hear what she has to say."

"Oh, hello Mrs Churchill, Miss Pemberley," said Mrs Strawbanks as she opened the front door of her ancient-looking cottage. She wore half-moon spectacles and her hair was tied up in a colourful headscarf. Another scarf was draped around her shoulders, and various beaded necklaces and bracelets rattled as she moved. "Hello there, little Oswald. Do come in, all of you. I imagine you're keen to speak to me about poor old Mr Butterfork across the road."

"We are a little intrigued, Mrs Strawbanks, it has to be said," replied Churchill as they stepped inside the cottage.

"More than a little intrigued, no doubt."

She led them through to the front room, which had brightly patterned walls and an equally vibrant carpet. A tortoiseshell cat on the windowsill hissed at Oswald, who hid behind Pemberley's skirts.

"You're private detectives, aren't you? I bet you can't resist trying to solve this case. After all, the local police force isn't up to much, is it? Being married to an inspector of the yard for as long as you were, Mrs Churchill, must surely have equipped you with a degree of sensibility when it comes to investigations like this."

"Thank you, Mrs Strawbanks," replied Churchill, feeling slightly alarmed that this lady she had never met before seemed to know so much about her.

Churchill and Pemberley seated themselves among the beaded cushions on a little velvet settee until Mrs Strawbanks trundled in with a tea trolley.

"Here are a few cakes for you, Mrs Churchill. I know how much you like cake."

"Do you indeed?"

"Yes, I've seen you standing in that bakery below your office quite a number of times."

"Right." Churchill couldn't recall ever having seen Mrs Strawbanks in the bakery.

"You're probably wondering what I saw the evening Mr Butterfork was murdered," continued Mrs Strawbanks.

"Yes, we are."

"I've written it all down." She poured out the tea, sat down in an armchair then picked up a notepad from an occasional table beside her. "Six o'clock," she announced, peering over her half-moon spectacles at Churchill, who was preoccupied with a custard slice. "You'll probably want to write this down."

"Oh right, yes of course." Churchill put her plate down and started wiping her fingers on her serviette.

"I can write it down," volunteered Pemberley.

"Oh, thank you, Miss Pemberley," said Churchill. "You write and I'll listen intently."

"Six o'clock," announced Mrs Strawbanks again. "Mrs Hatweed the housekeeper left for the evening. I saw her come through the side gate, which confirms that she left via the back door."

"Jolly good," replied Churchill.

"Seven o'clock."

Churchill took another bite of custard slice before realising Mrs Strawbanks was expecting her to respond. "Yes?"

"Mr Butterfork was seen to open his front window and water the Busy Lizzies in his window box."

"Lovely."

"He was observed to close the window again, and – now this is an important detail – *and* push the latch across."

"He locked the window?"

"Yes. As he always did, of course."

"Good."

"Eight o'clock."

"What happened then?"

"Nothing."

"Oh."

"I just included it to show I surveyed the lane at that time and nothing was happening. Just for the record."

"I see. And nine o'clock?" asked Churchill.

"Wait!"

"Oh?"

"There's another entry at a quarter to nine."

"Right. What happened then?"

"Mr Butterfork was seen to peer out from an upstairs window before drawing the curtain across."

"How interesting."

"It really is quite interesting, because he seemed to have become more watchful of late. I noticed him looking out of that window in the evenings, as if to check whether anyone was loitering outside his home."

"And was there?"

"Not at the time he looked out, no. Now, there are two upstairs windows in his home that face out onto the lane. I saw him looking out of the window to the right as you view his house from here. I have reason to believe that was the window of his bedroom."

"I see. And the other room?"

"A box room, I believe. The guest bedroom is at the rear of the property."

"Right. Was there an entry for nine o'clock?"

"By then Mr Butterfork had drawn the curtains at the downstairs window and at the box room window. Dusk was upon us at that hour. I imagine he drew the curtains at the rest of the windows too, but as those aren't visible from my home I couldn't be certain about that. I expect you'd like to know when the dark figure first appeared, wouldn't you?"

"You seem to have an uncanny ability to read my mind, Mrs Strawbanks."

"Thirty-five minutes after nine o'clock."

"That's when the dark figure appeared?"

"Yes. Duchess did one of her strange little meows, and I observed the figure standing directly in front of Mr Butterfork's home. It appeared to be looking up at his bedroom window."

Churchill shivered. "You describe the dark figure as '*it*', Mrs Strawbanks, as though it were something not quite human."

"Well it wasn't human, was it? Shooting poor Mr Butterfork like that."

"It gives me the willies," added Pemberley.

"How was this dark figure dressed?" asked Churchill.

"In a long dark overcoat and a dark hat."

"Could the overcoat have been dark grey, do you think?"

"It may have been. It was difficult to tell at twilight. I decided to go outside and investigate further," continued Mrs Strawbanks, "but by the time I'd changed out of my house shoes and put my shawl on it was gone."

"Well I never. It sounds quite spooky."

"I walked up and down the lane a little way. There was some cloud that night, but when the moon was out it was quite bright. I took my electric torch with me and caught neither sight nor sound of the dark figure."

"That was rather brave of you, Mrs Strawbanks."

"Nothing fazes me, Mrs Churchill. I suppose you'll want to know when I heard the gunshot."

"Yes please."

"It was shortly after ten o'clock. I'd just done my hourly check of the lane, which didn't amount to much because it was nautical twilight and the moon was behind a cloud."

"Nautical?" queried Churchill. "We're about ten miles from the sea here."

"It's a scientific term used to describe the period of time when the sun is between six and twelve degrees below the horizon," explained Pemberley.

"Goodness! Despite all the years I've been on this earth there continue to be certain facts to which I am completely oblivious. So you checked the lane, Mrs Strawbanks, and then?"

"I began to retire for the night. I was just changing into my nightgown when the shot rang out as clear as day."

"I suppose a gunshot would be rather distinct whether it was day or night."

"Duchess wouldn't stop meowing. I had to change back into my day clothes, then I rushed downstairs, put my shoes on and dashed out into the lane. That's when I saw it."

"*It?*"

"The dark figure again, Mrs Churchill, fleeing down the lane. The moon happened to emerge from behind a cloud at that moment, so I had a good view."

"What did you see of the dark figure?"

"Much as before: a dark overcoat and a dark hat."

"Was the figure carrying anything?"

"Yes, it appeared to be. It was running away from me, but I couldn't see its arms. It was as though they were held out in front of it, clutching the bundle of Mr Butterfork's money. Then it reached the churchyard wall, jumped over and disappeared into the darkness."

"What did you do then?"

"I telephoned Inspector Mappin. I didn't know for certain that the gunshot had occurred inside Mr Butterfork's home, although I had my suspicions, having seen the dark figure standing there. I called on Mrs Hatweed while I was waiting for Inspector Mappin to arrive. It took a moment to rouse her, and by the time I'd managed it the inspector had arrived."

"Thank you, Mrs Strawbanks, that was all very interesting. Mrs Hatweed told us you visited Mr Butterfork on the day of his death. Is that right?"

"Yes. He kindly offered to pay for my replacement fence. He was an extremely generous man."

"Did he mention he was expecting a visitor that evening?"

"No, he mentioned nothing of the sort. I wasn't expecting it either. It was a Sunday, and I'd never known him receive visitors on a Sunday evening. There's no doubt about it, Mrs Churchill; a burglar sprung himself upon that poor man before taking his money and ending his life!"

Chapter 17

"I BELIEVE the time has come for us to create another dependable incident board, Pembers," said Churchill when she arrived at the office the following day.

"For the case of Mr Butterfork?"

"Yes."

"But we're not even officially working on it."

"We're working on the churchyard case for Mr Grieves, and given that the murderer made his getaway through the churchyard we need to consider the broader picture, as it were. We need to understand the events leading up to the moment the culprit found himself dashing through the churchyard."

"I'm not entirely convinced by that."

"Oh, come on, Pembers. You'd like to solve another murder, wouldn't you? We can't leave it all up to that hapless Mappin."

"Then we have two cases to work on at present."

"I prefer to consider it as one main case split into two subcases. The first subcase relates to the mysterious goings-on in the churchyard, while the second relates to the murder of Mr Butterfork. I realise no one has officially tasked us with investigating the murder, but two seasoned private detectives like ourselves couldn't possibly stand by and watch the local constabulary make a complete hash of it. You saw those constables in the churchyard, didn't you? I'm surprised they manage to tie their own shoelaces of a morning."

The two ladies set about sticking pins in at significant points on the map and connecting them with pieces of string.

"Do we have a photograph of the late Mr Butterfork, Pembers?"

"Yes, there's the picture of us standing with him and Mrs Thonnings beside the coconut shy at the summer fete from the *Compton Poppleford Gazette*."

"Isn't there another picture of him we could use?"

"That's the only one I can think of. Mr Butterfork hadn't been in the village long, so there aren't many photographs of him knocking about."

"Oh, I suppose it'll have to do."

Pemberley went to fetch the newspaper.

"I don't like the idea of us appearing on our own incident board, Pembers. Can we cut him out of the picture?"

"Let me see." Pemberley found the photograph in the newspaper. "Not very easily, no. Look, he has one arm around you and the other around Mrs Thonnings."

"Goodness, so he has."

"I'll cut myself out, as I'm just standing on the periphery. I often do that when a photograph's being taken in the hope I'll be left out of it." Pemberley proceeded to prune one end of the picture. "Now we just have Mr Butterfork flanked by his two lady friends."

"Mrs Thonnings might qualify as such, but I only met the fellow once. Are you sure you can't trim me out?"

"It would take his left arm off."

"That wouldn't really matter. We'd still have most of him."

"But isn't that rather disrespectful given that he's just been murdered?"

"It's a slip of paper from a cheap newspaper, Pembers, it matters not a jot. You can apologise to the spirit of Mr Butterfork as you remove his left arm if needs be, but please take me out of the picture. Now, let's get on with moving the pictures and pins and string about. It might give us some fresh ideas about the case."

"While I remember, I also have a photograph of Mr Grieves we can put up there."

"Why on earth do you have a photograph of the sexton?"

"It's from a case Mr Atkins was working on about eight years ago."

"Mr Grieves was a suspect?"

"No. We worked out he might have been about to become a victim. There was a murderer around at the time who was killing people in alphabetical order. Mr Grieves had a lucky escape because Atkins caught the murderer just after Frederick Fulboat was slain."

"Crikey, and you think Mr Grieves might have been next?"

"Yes. His name was Gregory Grieves, and he lived in Garland Grove at the time."

"Factors that would have been most appealing to someone intent on murdering people in alphabetical order."

"Exactly. It was a very worrying time. Henrietta Higginbath was so concerned she went to stay with her sister in Weston-Super-Mare."

"I'd have gone a great deal further than that if I'd been in danger of death on the basis of my name."

"Me too. It wasn't as if the murderer was averse to travelling, either. He even went as far as Charmouth on one occasion."

"Whom did he murder there?"

"Charlie Chamberlain."

"How terribly sad. But well done to Atkins for apprehending the man. Now, let's dig out that picture of Gregory Grieves and stick him up on the board."

Churchill felt a chill down her spine as Pemberley did so. She regarded the photograph of the sexton with his gaunt face, long beard and steely eyes.

"He hasn't changed his appearance over the years, then?"

"No, he's always looked like that."

"I think the alphabet murderer would have had a change of heart if he'd come face to face with the man. Don't you find him vaguely terrifying?"

"Yes I do, now you come to mention it."

"Do we really need his photograph up on the incident board?"

"Probably not." Pemberley took the picture down and laid it, face up, on Churchill's desk.

"Not there, Pembers. Hide him somewhere. Preferably at the back of a deep drawer in one of those filing cabinets."

They heard footsteps on the stairs as Pemberley did so.

"Helloee!" A red-haired lady popped her head around the door.

"Oh, hello there, Mrs Thonnings. You're just in time to admire our incident board," said Churchill.

Mrs Thonnings joined her at the board and surveyed

it. "It looks very impressive indeed. But hold on a minute. Why is my picture up there?"

"You visited Mr Butterfork on the day of his death."

"You don't consider me a suspect, do you?"

"No, not at all. Far from it. He had four visitors that day, and we're quite certain none of them could possibly be the murderer."

"That still doesn't explain why my picture's up there."

"It was the only one we could find of Mr Butterfork."

"Oh. Can't you just cut me out of the picture?"

"If we do that Mr Butterfork will lose his right arm," said Pemberley. "He's already lost his left. He would look ever so strange standing there with no arms."

"What happened to his left arm?"

"Let's not stray too far from the topic," said Churchill. "Any of the four who visited him on the day of his death could prove to be a valuable witness, Mrs Thonnings. Perhaps you saw the dark figure loitering outside his home when you visited."

"I didn't, I'm afraid. I don't think I've ever seen a dark figure during the daytime."

"Come to think of it, neither have I. Do you mind me asking the purpose of your visit to Mr Butterfork?"

"He was an old friend. Actually, he wasn't really, come to think of it, because I'd only known him for about six months, but it felt like I'd known him forever." Her voice cracked.

"Jam tart, Mrs Thonnings?"

"Thank you."

"Was Mr Butterfork your lover, Mrs Thonnings?" she asked.

This was a question Churchill immediately regretted asking when she was forced to cover her head to protect herself from the spray of jam tart crumbs that erupted from Mrs Thonnings's mouth in response. Mrs Thonnings then began to choke.

"Oh dear," lamented Churchill. "Can you please fetch Mrs Thonnings a glass of water, Miss Pemberley?"

A few moments later the redness in Mrs Thonnings's cheeks had subsided and the choking noises had become intermittent.

"It went down the wrong way," she explained. "I hate it when that happens."

"There's no need for it, is there?" sympathised Churchill. "Now, perhaps you can confirm for me whether or not you and Mr Butterfork were—"

"Absolutely not!" retorted Mrs Thonnings. "What sort of a woman do you think I am?"

"I wasn't casting aspersions on your character, Mrs Thonnings. I was merely wondering what the nature of your relationship was."

"We were good friends," she replied. "I was visiting him that day to discuss his haberdashery needs."

"And what were they?"

"He'd lost a button from his trousers."

"I see. Isn't that something his housekeeper would have seen to?"

"He told me Hatters was the best housekeeper he'd ever had, but that she could turn her hand to absolutely anything except sewing. Apparently, she had once sewn a button onto his dinner suit trousers and they had fallen down while he was giving a speech at the annual Compton Poppleford Cricket Club dinner."

"Oh dear, how embarrassing."

"He hadn't worn a belt that evening because he'd lost it, so you can imagine the sight of him when the button gave way."

"I'd rather not."

"He always consulted me with regard to any patching, mending and general sewing from that moment on. I sewed on countless buttons, replaced a number of zips and patched up numerous snags and tears for Mr Butterfork."

"In just six months? It sounds as though the chap was rather hard on his trousers. It makes you wonder what he must have been doing in them."

"He lived life to the full, Mrs Churchill."

"It seems his trousers did the same."

"I still have a pair I was halfway through mending." Mrs Thonnings swallowed back a sob. "I don't suppose there's any use in me finishing them now."

"Oh, I think you should finish them," said Pemberley. "What if Mr Butterfork happens to be looking down on us? I think he'd be rather upset to find that his trousers were never mended."

"If Mr Butterfork were looking down on us now, Miss Pemberley, I think he would make allowances for Mrs Thonnings's grief and not expect her to finish mending his trousers. It's not as if he'll be able to pay her for them, is it?"

"But he's already paid me," replied Mrs Thonnings. "Ten times over, in fact. He was such a generous man."

"Mrs Hatweed seemed quite upset by his death," said Churchill.

"Oh, Hatters would be. She adored him."

"And with a son in prison, of all places."

"Yes, that's her great shame. He fell in with the wrong crowd, but she maintains his innocence."

"A policeman friend of my dear departed husband, Detective Sergeant Dickie Harlow, used to say that the prisons were full of innocent men."

"How awful," exclaimed Pemberley. "They should be released!"

"It's a policeman's joke, Pembers. It refers to the fact that every inmate claims to be innocent, but generally speaking they're not."

"Police officers have an odd sense of humour."

"They do, and particularly DS Harlow. Now then, back to Mr Butterfork. It's quite clear that the motive in this case was robbery," said Churchill. "That makes it rather difficult to identify a suspect, because just about everybody knew that Mr Butterfork kept his money in a tea chest in the bedroom."

"But why murder him?" asked Mrs Thonnings. "Why not wait until the house was empty before going in to steal the money?"

"A very sensible question," said Churchill, "and one that isn't easy to answer. It seems a fair bit of planning went into this attack because the murderer clearly knew about the chest of money and armed himself with a gun. The presence of a weapon suggests he was expecting to be confronted by someone."

"And also that he intended to murder Mr Butterfork."

"But was it the intruder's intention to kill him? Or did it happen because matters got out of hand? Maybe there was a struggle between the two of them and Mr Butterfork was shot by mistake."

"It sounded like an execution to me from the description of the scene," said Pemberley.

Churchill winced and took a sip of tea. "In which case, we must assume the murder was deliberate."

"But he didn't have to be killed," said Mrs Thonnings. "The murderer could have just waved the gun around and Mr Butterfork would have let him take the money. Mr Butterfork would never have risked his life for it."

"In that case, Mr Butterfork must have been killed because he knew who the robber was," said Churchill.

"After all, he let the man into his home. Only, the robber didn't want to be identified after the money was taken."

Mrs Thonnings shook her head sadly. "It's awful. There was no need for it at all. If the burglar had entered that house unarmed and asked nicely for the money, I'm sure Mr Butterfork would simply have handed it over."

"And then reported him to the police," added Churchill. "Which is exactly what our thief didn't want."

Chapter 18

"I've done my best to fill the hole and level it off," said Mr Grieves, "but it'll be a while before the grass grows over it again. It's a shame really, as this is one of the nicest plots in the graveyard."

Churchill pondered over the word 'nice' being used to describe a grave as she stood next to the final resting place of Benjamin Grunchen with Pemberley and Oswald.

"What have you discovered during your investigations to date?" asked Grieves.

Churchill felt a chill as his icy eyes turned upon her.

"I'll be honest with you, Mr Grieves, not a great deal. Our theory at the moment is that a relative from America placed the rose on Arthur Brimble's grave as he or she happened to be passing through, and that someone decided to clean the headstones and began with Sally Fletcher. Has anyone recently suggested to you that the headstones should be cleaned?"

"No."

"Not even the vicar?"

"No."

"I see."

"That's all you've got?"

"Well, there has been the minor distraction of a terrible murder taking place this week, and our investigations have been hampered by the work of the police."

"Those two constables?"

"And the photographer. It's been quite difficult for us to get any work done at all. But here we are this morning, ready to get cracking with it."

"Then you'll be interested to hear that another rose has been placed on Arthur Brimble's grave," said the sexton.

"What a lovely gesture."

"It was placed there last night," replied Grieves, "so it's unlikely to have come from another American relative who just happened to be passing through, as you put it. This was no lovely gesture; somebody's playing games."

"It's rather an odd game to play."

"Exactly. Which is why I asked you to investigate it, Mrs Churchill." He gave a sigh. "But if you're not up to the task—"

"Oh, we're up to it all right!"

"Are you?"

"Yes!"

"Right, then I shall await your findings."

"We shall report back to you with our findings very soon, Mr Grieves."

He touched the wide brim of his hat as an acknowledgement and strode away.

"Why didn't you just tell him we're not up to it?" asked Pemberley once the sexton was out of earshot.

"I could never countenance telling anyone we're not up to something. It simply isn't done!"

"But we don't even want this case. We have no idea

how to solve it, and we're busy trying to work out who murdered Mr Butterfork instead."

"I'm sure there's a simple explanation for all this, Pembers. We'll have it worked out in no time."

"I really don't see how. And why didn't you ask him about Mr Butterfork?"

"Why would I ask him about Mr Butterfork?"

"You heard the description Mrs Strawbanks gave us. The dark figure was wearing a long, dark overcoat and a hat. That description could be a match for Mr Grieves!"

"Except the coat he wears is black, while the piece of fabric torn from the culprit's coat was dark grey."

Pemberley mulled this over. "Perhaps he also has a dark grey coat. Maybe he was only wearing his black coat today because the dark grey one had a piece ripped from it when he was making his getaway."

"I suppose it's possible, but Mr Grieves strikes me as the sort of man who only ever wears one coat. You've seen how shabby it is. He has the appearance... and odour... of a man who always wears the same clothes. And besides, if you felt we should have questioned him about Mr Butterfork, why didn't you pipe up yourself?"

"He frightens me."

"What, old, tall, thin, gaunt-faced Mr Grieves dressed all in black with an icy stare? Actually, he frightens me too, but we mustn't let that put us off. Not everyone we work with will be friendly and cuddly."

"Who *is* friendly and cuddly?"

"I can't think of anyone off the top of my head. Oswald?"

"Of course!"

"Jolly good. Right then, let's be on our way."

The two ladies and their dog walked down the path that led to the church gate.

"Oh, goodness!" Churchill stopped in her tracks and gripped Pemberley's arm.

"What is it?"

"Look!" Churchill pointed at a dark-haired man walking past the churchyard wall. He was wearing a dark grey overcoat.

"Who is it?" asked Pemberley.

"I've no idea, but did you see what he was wearing? Come on, we need to follow him."

"Why?"

"To see if we can find out who he is."

"Just because he's wearing a dark coat?"

"Yes!"

The two ladies hurried out of the churchyard and followed the man along a cobbled lane.

"What if he notices us?" asked Pemberley.

"He may well notice us, but he won't know we're following him, will he?"

"What if he realises we are?"

"He won't because we'll be very subtle. If he turns around, we'll pretend we haven't noticed him at all. You could point at something in a tree and I could nod appreciatively."

"That seems an odd thing to do."

"It does, but it's the sort of thing two old ladies might do during an afternoon stroll while paying no heed to the person walking in front of them. Quick, point at a tree!"

"Why?"

"I'll do it then," hissed Churchill, pointing at a nearby shrub. "He turned around!"

"That's not a tree, it's a shrub."

"I panicked! Just nod appreciatively, as if we're discussing the shape of its leaves."

Pemberley nodded.

"You look perplexed, Pembers."

"I am."

"Try to look appreciative instead."

"Of a shrub?"

"Surely you have basic acting abilities?"

"Not really."

"Acting is an essential skill for a detective. How else can we work undercover?"

"We normally get found out whenever we try to do that."

"That's because we haven't yet perfected our acting skills. Right, he's turning the corner at the end of the lane. Let's hurry along. We don't want to lose him."

Churchill and Pemberley scampered after the man, with Oswald trotting behind. The lane led into a little park as they turned the corner.

"Cowslip Park," announced Pemberley.

The dark-coated man entered the park through a little iron gate. He gave them a brief glance as he closed it behind him.

Pemberley swiftly pointed at a nearby ash tree.

Churchill nodded appreciatively. "Well done, Pembers. That was quick thinking."

The two ladies and their dog entered the park a few moments later and observed the man strolling along a path which ran through an avenue of sycamore trees. Close by was a pond, where several nannies tended to small children as they splashed about in the water.

"What a pretty little park," commented Churchill.

Oswald ran off to greet another dog, and the two canines began weaving their way in and out of the sycamore trees.

"Let's keep up with our man," said Churchill as two nannies walked past them pushing large perambulators.

127

"Are we the only grown-ups in this park who aren't employed as nannies?" she whispered.

"It's a popular place for them to bring their charges, probably because the high gates and fences stop the children running away."

"Looking at some of these nannies, I can't say I'd blame the children for wanting to run away. There's a rather interesting-looking building at the edge of the park over there. Is it a chapel?"

"It's the Masonic lodge."

"Masonic? As in the Freemasons?"

"Yes."

"How very interesting. And it looks as though our man is heading straight for it."

As they drew closer, Churchill saw that the lodge was an elegant, single-storey building of golden stone. It had arched windows surrounded by sculpted stonework and an arched wooden doorway that wouldn't have looked out of place on a medieval church.

The two ladies watched as the man in the dark coat unlocked the elaborate wooden door before stepping inside and closing it again.

"Well I never, Pembers. A man in a dark grey overcoat entering the Masonic lodge, and a Freemason's ring found on Crunkle Lane. This is all beginning to appear rather intriguing, isn't it? If only we could knock at the door and ask him a few questions about Mr Butterfork. Ladies aren't permitted inside such places, more's the pity."

"And quite right, too."

"What on earth makes you say that?"

"What lady, in her right mind, would wish to enter a Masonic lodge? I can't think of anything more tedious."

"Right. Well, anyway, it's no secret that the Freemasons are a secretive bunch."

"They are. And that's not terribly helpful when it comes to investigating crimes."

"You're right, Pembers. Secrecy tends to play havoc with these things. There can be no doubt that the ring belongs to a member of this lodge; it could even belong to the man in the dark grey coat himself. But who is he?"

"Why don't we just wait and see who comes to claim the ring?"

"Because I'm growing impatient. We could try to work out which men in the village are Freemasons. That would help narrow down the list of potential owners."

"Freemasons don't often admit to non-Freemasons that they're Freemasons."

"True, but I don't think we need to ask anyone the question directly. Which day of the week did Hatters say the weekly meetings took place?"

"On a Tuesday. Oh, I see! We could just be taking a little wander through this park at the time of the meeting and we'd be able to see which men were masons!"

"Exactly."

"But won't they spot us gawping at them? There aren't many obvious hiding places around here, are there? It'll be rather difficult to watch all the comings and goings without being noticed." Pemberley glanced around them. "There are plenty of trees to hide behind, I suppose."

"Plenty for *you* to hide behind, perhaps, but I don't see many with a trunk wide enough to accommodate me. What I need is a nice large oak or a horse chestnut, but I can't see anything suitable close by. A bit of dense shrubbery would also have been perfect to hide within, but I don't see any of that close to the lodge either. What sort of park is this with no suitable hiding places?" Churchill pondered this a little further. "I think we may need to alter our appearance a little. We'll have to pay a visit to Dorchester and purchase a few suitable accessories."

A large lady approached them on the path, a small pink hat pulled over her head of brown curls.

"Mrs Hatweed!" said Churchill cheerily. "How nice to see you."

"I'm just out for my evening walk," she replied, stopping to look over at the Masonic lodge. "Oh, how they must miss him there."

"Mr Butterfork?"

"Yes. He always looked forward to his weekly meetings."

"We've just seen an interesting gentleman wearing a dark grey coat walk in there."

"What's so interesting about him?"

"Because we believe the murderer was wearing a dark grey coat."

"Like the man who just walked in there? Oh, I see!" Her eyes widened. "You mean to say the murderer walked into that building just now?"

"We don't know for sure that it's him, but the man we saw was certainly wearing a dark coat."

"Oh." Her shoulders slumped. "I suppose a lot of people wear dark coats, don't they? My own is quite dark." She glanced down at her woollen coat, which no longer had any hope of being buttoned across her midriff, if it ever had.

"Yours is dark brown, though, Mrs Hatweed. We're looking for a dark grey one."

"I see. Well, good luck with that. I'll keep an eye out for one myself and let you know. There was something I forgot to tell you when you visited the other day."

"Oh yes? What was that?"

"Mr Butterfork only ate one boiled egg on that last morning."

"Is that so?"

"He normally had two, you see. I boiled him two, but he only managed one. I'd never known that happen before. He was very apologetic and told me he was feeling a bit egged out."

"How very interesting. Thank you, Mrs Hatweed."

Chapter 19

CHURCHILL WAS WALKING to her office the following morning when a shiny motor car pulled up outside the town hall and an elegant lady dressed in yellow stepped out.

"Lady Darby! What a delight to meet you again."

"Oh, good morning. It's Mrs Churchill, isn't it?"

"Indeed it is. You have a good memory for faces, Lady Darby."

"Thank you, Mrs Churchill, I like to think so. You're a private detective, isn't that right?"

"Yes."

"I really find that rather fascinating because – and I hope you don't mind me saying so – you're a lady of more mature years, and I think it most unusual that a lady of your…"

"Vintage?"

"Ah yes, vintage. What a wonderful choice of word. That puts it so well, don't you think?"

"Yes, I do."

"I'm of a certain vintage myself!" added Lady Darby, and the two ladies shrilled with polite laughter.

"Oh, Lady Darby, how amusing!" enthused Churchill.

They chatted a while longer. Churchill spoke of her years in Richmond-upon-Thames, her friendship with Lady Worthington, and the long and distinguished career of Detective Chief Inspector Churchill in the Metropolitan Police. Then she asked a good number of questions about Lady Darby's hobbies, social activities and good works.

"Golly, look at the time," said Lady Darby. "I'm almost twenty minutes late for my meeting with the mayor!"

"Oh, I'm so terribly sorry, Lady Darby. I really didn't mean to detain you."

"It's quite all right, Mrs Churchill. To be quite honest, I'd much rather stop outside here for a chat with you than sit in the draughty town hall listening to that old tortoise. I'm going about my husband's business, you see, as he's still rather incapacitated on account of his foot."

"Ah, yes. I do hope he's up and about soon; more for your sake than his, by the sound of things."

"Yes. A gentleman's business is very dull, I can vouch for that. Anyway, Mrs Churchill, it really has been lovely talking to you, and I do hope to see you again soon. In fact…"

She paused to consider something, and Churchill desperately hoped the words that followed would include an invitation to some sort of highbrow event. She held her breath until Lady Darby spoke again.

"…Bertrand and I are having a little garden party in a few weeks' time."

"Oh, are you?" Churchill gushed with a heavy exhale. "How lovely!"

"Yes, and we're really looking forward to it. It'll only be a small affair, you understand."

"Naturally."

"Indeed, and it's likely to be even smaller than usual as a couple of people can no longer make it. Actually, truth be told, it's the gamekeeper and his wife. My husband dismissed him after he was shot in the foot."

"The gamekeeper shot your husband in the foot?"

"No, he did it himself. But he likes to have someone to blame when bad things happen, so he sacked the gamekeeper."

"Oh."

"Anyway, the long and the short of it is, I can extend an invitation to you and a guest if you'd like to join us."

"I'd be more than delighted to, Lady Darby. What a wonderful invitation!" Churchill felt herself grinning so widely that the sides of her mouth ached. "How very lovely indeed."

"Good, then that settles it. I shall have an invitation sent out to you. Now, I mustn't keep the mayor waiting a moment longer. Goodbye, Mrs Churchill!"

"Goodbye, Lady Darby!"

"Another aria, Mrs Churchill?" asked Pemberley as she sauntered into the office.

"A whatty?"

"You're humming to yourself again. More good news, is it?"

"Oh, not really. Although it appears that I shall soon receive an invitation to a little soiree at Gollendale Hall."

"How nice."

"It is rather, isn't it? I just bumped into Lady Darby and had quite a long chat with her. It turns out we get along like a house on fire. It's remarkable how many things we have in common."

"Oh yes? Such as?"

"All sorts of things. It made me realise there are several refined people in these parts after all. In fact, that reminds me," Churchill checked her watch. "I have my first sitting with Mr Pickwick at eleven."

"Where?"

"In my little cottage, of all places."

"Really?"

"His studio doesn't have a roof at the moment."

"How convenient."

"I'd say it was most *in*convenient! We'll have to make do in an inferior setting."

"Which just happens to be within the privacy of your own home, Mrs Churchill."

"He can hardly paint me in the office, can he, what with all the interruptions we have here? I've always dreamed of being painted, but I never imagined it would one day come to fruition. The practice is most commonly associated with the aristocracy, of course, so I never believed a mere commoner such as myself would prove interesting enough to become the subject of a painting."

"Striking up a friendship with an artist seems to be quite useful in that respect," replied Pemberley. "Perhaps you'll become Mr Pickwick's muse."

Churchill laughed. "Oh, I shouldn't think so."

"You could be another Elizabeth Siddall."

"I suppose I could be if I had any idea who she was."

"She was the muse for a number of pre-Raphaelite painters."

"Oh, them."

"She married Dante Gabriel Rossetti."

"A sensible move when your surname is as dull as Siddall."

"How long will Mr Pickwick be painting you for?" asked Pemberley. "We have work to be getting on with."

"Ah yes, but today our work will be taking place tonight."

"What do you mean by that?" Pemberley groaned as the realisation dawned on her. "Don't tell me we're going back to that churchyard!"

"All right then, I won't. But it's the only way to progress our investigation, and there really is nothing to fear. The night is just the same as the day, only there's a little less light about."

"A lot less light."

"We'll take torches."

"But we'll have to extinguish them once we're in the graveyard or we'll be seen by whoever it is we're supposed to be investigating."

"Only for a short while."

"That's the bit I'm least looking forward to."

"I'll be there with you, Pembers, and so will our trusty detective dog. You'll have to keep him on a leash, though. We can't have him ruining our surveillance."

"I'm sure you don't really need me there."

"Go on my own, you mean?" Churchill shuddered. "Never!"

"You could ask perfect Mr Pickwick to go with you."

"Perfect? Why perfect?"

"Isn't he?"

"How should I know? Anyway, he's not a detective. He's a retired insurance salesman and amateur artist."

"But I'm sure he'd look after you well, Mrs Churchill."

"Don't waggle your eyebrows at me in that suggestive manner, Pemberley."

"Why don't you ask him?"

"Stop it! There's no need for that."

"I saw one of the Flatboots leaving Pickwick's Gallery with a wheelbarrow the other day."

"Well, that's the Flatboots for you."

"I'm surprised Mr Pickwick allowed him inside with his wheelbarrow."

"Mr Pickwick is an extremely accommodating man. Now, it's time for an early elevenses, and then I shall be on my way."

Chapter 20

DESPITE HAVING SPENT several hours tidying and rearranging her cottage the previous evening, Churchill was concerned that it still looked untidy. She checked her appearance in the looking glass countless times, wondering whether she should change her powder-blue twinset for the dusky-pink one. A knock at the door confirmed that she had no time to change her mind, and she felt her heart flutter as she answered the door to find Mr Pickwick standing on the doorstep with his easel and box of paints.

"What a smart jacket, Mr Pickwick. Is it Harris Tweed?"

"It is indeed. You clearly have an eye for these things, Mrs Churchill."

"Oh, well I'm rather partial to Harris Tweed myself. What's good enough for those Outer Hebrideans is good enough for me, I say!" She gave a shrill, nervous laugh that made her eardrums ache. "Ahem. Do come in, Mr Pickwick. My abode is rather humble, I'm afraid. I'm renting it from Farmer Drumhead while I search for a desirable residence. In fact, it's not much of a setting for the portrait at all. Perhaps I should have hired some theatrical props."

"No need, Mrs Churchill." Mr Pickwick rested his easel and paints on the floor and surveyed the small room with his hands on his hips. "Simple is best. The only thing we need is a good amount of daylight, so I think we should seat you beside the window. Do you mind if I move the dining table a little?"

"Do please move whatever needs moving, Mr Pickwick."

He made a space beside the window in the dining area and placed a chair next to it.

"Now, if you could sit right there, Mrs Churchill, I'll decide on the best place to set up my easel."

"Of course. I'd be delighted." She took a seat and watched as he arranged his equipment.

"I wonder if you could move your knees a little to the left, Mrs Churchill."

"Certainly."

"Then perhaps you could move your right shoulder back a little and try a winsome gaze out of the window."

"Winsome, Mr Pickwick? Golly, I don't think I've ever been winsome in my entire life."

"There's a first time for everything, Mrs Churchill. The light is falling beautifully on you now."

"Is it really? Well, there's a wonder. Oh, I've been terribly remiss and forgotten to offer you a cup of tea."

"That would be lovely. Thank you, Mrs Churchill."

"But is it all right if I move?"

"Quite all right."

"It won't put you off?"

"Not at all; it's important that you feel relaxed. If I need you to hold a pose for any length of time I shall ask."

Still feeling flustered, Churchill made a quick pot of tea

in the kitchen, then carried the tray in to her guest and placed it on the dining table. "I'm in blue. Do you think blue is the right look?"

"It's perfect, Mrs Churchill."

A swell of relief caused some of the milk to slop onto the tea tray in response. "Oh, thank you. I'm pleased to hear that. Whoops, I appear to be all fingers and thumbs this morning. Let's hope you're not the same or it'll be rather a disastrous portrait!" She laughed nervously again.

"Do take a seat, Mrs Churchill, and try to relax."

"Oh, I will, yes." She sat down in the chair, slid her knees to the left, moved her right shoulder back and gazed winsomely out of the window.

"Simply delightful," said Mr Pickwick.

"Do you think so?"

"Absolutely."

"Oh, I am pleased to hear that. Are we allowed to talk?"

"Yes, of course."

"I'm not very good with silences, you see. But just let me know when you're painting my mouth and I'll keep it still."

"By all means move your mouth and the rest of your body, Mrs Churchill. You can't be expected to hold the same pose all day or you'll stiffen up, and we wouldn't want that, would we?"

"Indeed we wouldn't."

The pair discussed the weather at great length, soon discovering they had both holidayed in the Lake District. Once the merits of various lakes and fells had been exhausted, Churchill decided it would be a wasted opportunity if she failed to ask Mr Pickwick about his friend Mr Butterfork.

"You worked with Mr Butterfork in the insurance world, I hear."

His paintbrush paused. "Ah, yes." He rested his brush down on the little table next to him and rubbed his brow with the cloth he normally used to wipe his brushes. "He was a fine chap."

Churchill wasn't sure whether to tell the artist he had smeared blue paint across his forehead during this emotional moment. She thought it best to save it for later. "His housekeeper, Mrs Hatweed, told me that."

"A good lady. Hatters looked after him well. 'My Hatters boils the perfect egg...' That's what he always used to say. He adored her." Mr Pickwick dabbed at his eyes with the rag, leaving patches of blue on both cheeks.

Churchill felt she really ought to say something, but he had cocked his head a little and fixed his eye on the furthest corner of the room, as if to recall further fond memories of his friend.

"He was an underwriter, you know," Mr Pickwick continued. "A very clever man with an innate skill for risk contingency. I don't believe the company had to pay out a bean on any of the contracts he'd underwritten."

Having found herself privately scoffing at Mrs Hatweed's admission that she couldn't follow conversations about business, Churchill realised how dull the discussions between Mr Pickwick and Mr Butterfork must have been.

"The commission was good, too," continued Mr Pickwick, "and he earned very penny of it."

"His vast riches came from a great-aunt, though, am I right?"

"That's correct."

"And although he was a very clever undertaker—"

"Under*writer*."

"Oh yes, silly me. Despite all this clever underwriting business, he chose not to put his money in the bank?"

"I know. Foolish, isn't it? But that was old Jammy for you."

"Jammy?"

"That was his nickname. Butterfork, butter, butter and cream, cream bun and jam, jammy."

"Oh, I see. Like one of those public school nicknames you hear."

"Except it was an insurance company nickname."

"Did you have an insurance company nickname yourself? Actually, let me guess it. Erm, Pickwick papers, paper, linen draper, er... linen?"

"No, it was just plain old Mr Pickwick for me."

"Why's that then?"

"Jammy was popular, you see. Only the popular chaps had nicknames."

"I struggle to believe you weren't popular, Mr Pickwick!"

"I was just a salesman; not even a broker. The brokers were quite revered, but it was the underwriters who were the top dogs. They always got the first sitting in the canteen."

Churchill began to feel a bit sorry for Mr Pickwick, who had blue paint on his chin as well as his cheeks and forehead by this point.

"Did Jammy make any enemies within the grand world of insurance?" she asked.

"Yes."

"Really?"

"All those he refused to underwrite!" he said with a laugh. "And the ones who had to pay higher premiums after his recalculation of risk!"

He laughed again, and Churchill joined in to give the impression she knew all about insurance jokes.

Once the laughter had subsided, she broached the subject of enemies again. "Is there anyone you can think of who might have wanted to harm Mr Butterfork?"

"Apart from the many enemies he made during his underwriting days, no."

"I think we can safely assume that someone who felt aggrieved by his underwriting work would have been unlikely to murder him for it."

"You're right, Mrs Churchill, it would be rather unlikely. Not completely impossible, but unlikely. The attack on Jammy was robbery, plain and simple. Someone went in there, took the money and shot the poor..." The rag was held up to Mr Pickwick's face again.

"Oh dear, I am sorry." Churchill felt the urge to comfort Mr Pickwick. She got up from her seat and walked over to him.

"You mustn't see the painting!" He grabbed the easel and turned it away from her. "No one must see my work until it's complete!"

"I understand," replied Churchill, standing rather awkwardly beside him and wondering whether she should continue to comfort him or return to her seat. She realised he was probably wondering why she had stood up in the first place. "I didn't come over here to look at it. I came to... Oh, it doesn't matter, I'll sit back down again. By the way, Mr Pickwick, you have blue paint all over your face."

Chapter 21

INSPECTOR MAPPIN STRODE into Churchill and Pemberley's office that afternoon. "Right then, let's see it." He removed his hat, tucked it under his arm and stood in the centre of the room officiously.

"And a good afternoon to you, too, Inspector," replied Churchill. "What brings you here, then?"

"The ring. Let's see it."

"The handsome ring?"

"The gentleman's gold ring you placed a 'found' notice for in the classifieds."

"Oh, then the newspaper has finally published it. Jolly good. Does it belong to you?"

"No."

"Ah, well we're waiting for the rightful owner to turn up, you see."

"Any such finds should be handed in at the police station."

"We didn't think you'd want to be bothered with it, Inspector. You have such a lot on your plate, as you so often remind us."

"Finds must be handed in to me so that the relevant persons can enquire at the police station and be reunited with them. This is especially important when it comes to items of value. We have a safe down at the station. Do you have a safe, Mrs Churchill?"

"The drawer in my desk is quite adequate, Inspector."

He snorted in reply.

"And it's filled almost to the brim with women's bits and pieces, so any man would be quite put off if he started rummaging about in there."

"That's your security system, is it, Mrs Churchill? Women's bits and pieces?"

"Absolutely, and judging by the flushed appearance of your face I'm guessing you'd be put off rummaging in there yourself, Inspector."

"But a thief wouldn't. They have totally different standards, you see." The inspector hitched up his trousers and sat down at Churchill's desk. "I'm rather interested in the location where this ring was found," he continued. "Crunkle Lane, wasn't it?"

"Yes, the scene of the murder. Do you think the ring could have been involved somehow?"

"I'm quite sure you had already made the connection, Mrs Churchill. And your discovery of the ring suggests you've been sniffing around the area. I need you to hand over the ring, not only because I can keep it in the safe until it's claimed, but also because it could be an important piece of evidence."

"But we put in the notice that it needs to be collected from this detective agency. I shouldn't think the owner will be happy when I tell him he has to head down to see you instead. And besides, he might be afraid to ask you for the ring."

"Why so?"

"Because he could be the murderer, and the last thing he'll want to do is start fraternising with the law. Besides, Miss Pemberley and I have hatched a little plan."

The inspector groaned.

"Shall we tell him about our plan, Miss Pemberley?"

"I suppose we'll have to."

"Indeed. Our plan, Inspector, is to wait and see who arrives to collect the ring, and then we'll have ourselves a murder suspect!"

"Just because someone lost his ring on that lane doesn't mean he committed the murder, Mrs Churchill."

"No of course not, which is why he'd only be a suspect. And this particular ring suggests the suspect could be a Freemason!"

He raised an eyebrow. "A Freemason? How?"

"Ah, perhaps I should explain. We believe the ring belongs to a member of the Freemasons, as it bears the square and compasses insignia. Now, Inspector, perhaps we can reach a little agreement."

"Oh dear. What sort of agreement?"

"We hold on to the ring for a further three days unless it happens to be claimed by its owner. I think that's only fair, as our notice asked the owner to visit this detective agency. If no one has claimed it after three days, we shall happily pass it on to you."

Inspector Mappin grunted. "And if someone does claim the ring, you'll tell me who it was?"

"Of course. I think that all sounds very fair, don't you?"

The inspector got up from his chair. "The ring was probably dropped in Crunkle Lane some time after the murder, otherwise my men would have spotted it much sooner."

"I wouldn't be so sure about that, Inspector. Need I remind you who discovered the murder weapon?"

"There's no need to remind me, Mrs Churchill, I've already dished out my thank yous." He surveyed the wall. "Interesting incident board," he commented.

"Ah, yes. That's for our churchyard case," said Churchill.

"It looks as though it relates to the Butterfork case to me."

"Only because some of the evidence from that case was found in our churchyard, Inspector. It's caused the two cases to overlap a little."

"You're not trying to solve the Butterfork case, are you?"

"Absolutely not!"

"It seems the ring is a waste of time," said Pemberley once Inspector Mappin had left. "If it doesn't belong to the murderer there's really no need for us to be bothered with it."

"Pfft, you're taking Mappin's word for it, Pembers. How else would it have found its way onto the ground in Crunkle Lane if it hadn't fallen from the finger of the fleeing culprit?"

"Perhaps one of the Freemasons walked along there at some point."

"I suppose he could have done, but which one?" Churchill opened the drawer in her desk and began to look for the ring, which she had carefully wrapped in a hand-kerchief.

"Where's it got to?" she said, rummaging around in the drawer. "Have you ever noticed that with drawers, Pembers?

Often the last thing you put in them ends up being right at the bottom, at the back. How does it even do that? It must somehow wiggle and worm its way into the most inaccessible part of the drawer possible, as if it knows you're after it. Where *has* it got to? I only put it in here two days ago, and I can't find the handkerchief it was wrapped in either… Oh dear."

A sense of panic began to grip Churchill as she pulled the drawer out and emptied it onto her desk. Two hat pins, seven buttons, a pot of rouge, six hair pins, three penny coins, a small bottle of perfume, five unpaired earrings, a bottle of smelling salts, four hair rollers, a pot of cold cream, three papers of headache powder, two half-crown coins, numerous beads from a broken necklace, a tube of lipstick and a stale gingerbread biscuit scattered themselves across the desktop.

"There's no ring here, Pembers. Where's it gone? Have you taken it?"

"No! Why would I take it?"

"I don't know. Someone must have. It wasn't me, so I figured it could only have been you. Oh, where is it?"

"Are you sure you put it in that drawer?"

"Yes, I think so."

Churchill flung open the other drawers in her desk and Pemberley grabbed her arm to stop her hurling out their contents.

"There's no need to make such a mess, Mrs Churchill. I'm sure we'll find the ring after a careful search."

"But it's gone, Pembers, don't you see? Somebody's taken it!"

After twenty minutes of careful searching, Churchill and Pemberley had to resign themselves to the fact that the ring had indeed been taken.

"We've been leaving the door unlocked recently," commented Pemberley. "Perhaps that's how the thief got in."

"I'd say it was! What do you mean we've been leaving the door unlocked?"

"Just that. It's been unlocked."

"I lock the door whenever I come and go, Pembers. You clearly don't, and that's how we've come to be robbed."

"Actually, I'm not sure you do, Mrs Churchill. I've found the door unlocked a number of times first thing in the morning after you've been the last to leave the previous evening. It's a common habit in Compton Poppleford to leave doors unlocked, so it's quite normal and not really a problem unless you have something worth stealing."

"I might have forgotten to lock the door one day last week, but apart from that I've locked it every day without fail."

"With the exception of last night."

"I definitely locked it last night."

"Are you sure?"

"Yes."

"How sure?"

"Very!"

"Do you specifically remember locking the door yesterday evening, or is it possible that you merely have a general memory of locking it?"

"General memory? What are you on about, Pembers? I locked it!"

Pemberley sighed. "I suppose we should report the theft to Inspector Mappin."

"Absolutely not! We reassured him the ring would be safe in my drawer with all the women's bits and pieces, didn't we? It would be a great embarrassment to admit that the ring hadn't been stowed safely after all. The thief clearly knew what he was looking for, didn't he? Nothing else appears to have been taken."

"It's because we advertised the fact we had the ring in the *Compton Poppleford Gazette*."

"Of course! That's what did it. That snivelling editor Mr Trollope has a lot to answer for. Now, what do we say to the rightful owner when he arrives?"

"We'll have to explain that it's been stolen."

"And look completely foolish? Not likely. There's only one thing we can do, Pembers. We'll have to buy an identical ring and give it to the rightful owner."

"That would cost a fortune!"

"It's still preferable to admitting we've lost the ring."

"Perhaps the rightful owner was also the thief."

"I like that idea! Maybe he came to collect the ring from us yesterday evening and noticed the door was unlocked."

"I thought you said you'd locked it."

"I can't exactly remember now whether I did or not."

"It was unlocked this morning."

"Then I must not have. So he tried the door handle and came up to this office. Finding it vacant, he decided to look for the ring himself. He clearly isn't someone who feels too bothered by a drawer full of women's bits and pieces. He must have been very keen to get his ring back."

"We'll never know who the ring belonged to if he was the one who took it."

"Oh, darn it!"

"Unless he didn't take it, and then we'll be faced with someone asking us for a ring we no longer have. But at least we would know his identity if that were the case."

"The situation is less than ideal whichever way you look at it, isn't it?" Churchill began to put her belongings back in the drawer. "Where did the gingerbread biscuit go?"

"I gave it to Oswald."

"But he's not allowed biscuits! You've told me that time and time again."

"He was frightened when you emptied the women's bits and pieces all over your desk. I gave it to him to calm his nerves."

"I'm in even greater need of calmed nerves, Pembers. This is a sorry mess indeed."

Chapter 22

LATE THAT EVENING, Churchill, Pemberley and Oswald set off down the dark high street, which was lit at distant intervals with dim lamps. Churchill had hoped to see some moonlight, but a brisk wind was blowing the heavy clouds across the sky.

She switched on her torch as they left the high street and ventured down the lane toward St Swithun's church. Churchill hardly dared admit to herself that there was an almost unnerving silence in the air. The sound of their footsteps echoed on the cobbles.

"What do you suppose the relevance of the two boiled eggs could be, Pembers?" asked Churchill, desperately trying to distract herself from the dark.

"Which eggs might they be?"

"Don't you remember Hatters telling us Mr Butterfork only consumed one boiled egg on that last morning instead of his usual two?"

"Ah, yes. Apparently he felt a bit egged out."

"Could that be a clue?"

"It doesn't sound like one to me."

A sudden flash from a pair of bright eyes startled Churchill and she gasped.

"What is it?" asked Pemberley. "I was just beginning to calm down. What did you see? Oh, I really want to go home!"

"Just a cat," replied Churchill, shining the beam of her torch on the animal as it slunk away. The very last place she wanted to be visiting at this hour was the dark, cold, silent churchyard. "Don't worry, Pembers," she said tremulously. "We'll be fine. There's nothing to fear at all."

"What if the murderer's nearby?"

"Even if he is, he's hardly likely to murder us, is he?"

"He might well do. Perhaps he likes lurking around in the churchyard. After all, that's where he was last seen, isn't it?"

"But he wouldn't murder us."

"How do you know that?"

"He murdered Mr Butterfork while committing a robbery, Pembers. You and I have nothing worth stealing."

"He might take Oswald."

"Not a chance. I feel quite sure Oswald would bite his hand off."

"Good evening!" said a cheery voice.

Churchill and Pemberley gave a simultaneous yelp.

"It's only me."

"Who is *me*?" Churchill flashed her torch around until the beam rested on a lady wrapped in scarves and beads. "Oh, it's you, Mrs Strawbanks. Why are you walking around in the dark without a torch?"

"I don't need one, Mrs Churchill. I know my way around here in the dark."

"I see."

"On your way to the churchyard, are you?"

"Yes. How did you know?"

"I heard Mr Grieves had asked you to investigate the strange happenings. Rather you than me, Mrs Churchill. I may walk around without a torch, but you certainly wouldn't catch me venturing inside that churchyard in the dead of night!" She gave a nervous laugh and disappeared into the darkness.

"Now I really, really don't want to go in there!" quivered Pemberley.

"We'll be fine," replied Churchill unconvincingly. "What's the worst that could happen?"

"We'll be frightened witless, never recover our senses and have to live out the remainder of our days in an institution."

"What a sobering thought." Churchill took a deep breath and tried to muster all the courage she could find. "Come along, Pembers. It wouldn't do to turn back now."

Churchill paused once they had passed through the gate. "Goodness, it really is especially dark inside the churchyard, isn't it?"

"It's a particular type of darkness," observed Pemberley. "One that I find extremely dark and sinister."

"I wouldn't say *sinister*," replied Churchill as bravely as possible.

"Oh, but it is. We're the only living people in here."

"Now you're just dwelling on minor details to make it seem more frightening than it really is. And besides, you've quite forgotten about Oswald."

"And he's the only living dog here."

"That may be so, but there's still no reason to worry. Where's he got to, anyway?"

"I don't know."

The two ladies shone their torches around, hoping to find their wayward companion. The torchlight bounced off the walls of the church, a yew tree, the grass and a number of headstones, but there was no sign of the dog.

"Oh no, something must have got him!" wailed Pemberley.

"What sort of *something*?"

"I don't know. Whatever sort of something lives in churchyards. The thing that put a rose on Arthur Brimble's grave, removed the lichen from Sally Fletcher's headstone, made a hole in Benjamin Grunchen's plot and caused grass to grow on the grave of Saul Mollikin!"

Churchill felt a shudder. "It's not a *thing*, Pembers. There must be a logical explanation for all that."

"Such as?"

"We don't know yet. That's why we're here, isn't it?"

"And now the wretched thing has Oswald!"

"No it hasn't. I can see him over there." The light from Churchill's torch revealed a small, scruffy dog sniffing at the base of a tomb. "If, for want of a better word, there happened to be a *thing* in this churchyard, don't you think Oswald would be growling at it? Instead, he's bimbling about, happy as Larry and without a care in the world."

This observation appeared to help Pemberley relax a little. "Actually, you're right, Mrs Churchill. Oswald has a very strong sense of evil."

"There's no doubt that dogs, and many other species of animal, for that matter, have a good sense for these things. A *sixth* sense, I suppose it is."

"That sixth sense came in extremely useful when we all lived in caves, apparently."

"People in Compton Poppleford used to live in caves?"

"They did everywhere, the world over."

155

"Ah, you're referring to prehistoric times. From the way you spoke I assumed people living in caves was recent history around here. Mind you, it probably is for some of the more rustic types. And before you accuse me of being derogatory about the rural provinces, Pembers, we had the same problem in Richmond-upon-Thames. It wasn't unusual to see someone of a practically Neanderthal nature strolling around. Not local, of course; they'd taken the train up from somewhere like Staines or Feltham, I imagine, and were usually a little too hairy. It's quite disconcerting to encounter someone with that much hair, isn't it? It's not natural these days, especially when you consider—"

"Are you talking a lot because you're nervous, Mrs Churchill?"

"Me, nervous? Of course not. I don't think I've ever—"

"It's the dark churchyard, isn't it? I'm beginning to think you're as nervous as I am."

"I simply don't have the disposition to be nervous, Pembers. It's not in my bones, nor in my blood. I'm the sanguine type, you see. Good grief!" A sudden noise sent a freezing shiver down her spine. "What was that?" She took several steps back toward the relative safety of the church gate.

"I think Oswald growled," replied Pemberley, "but I don't know what it was aimed at. Perhaps he's come across the evil *thing* after all."

"Oh, don't say that, Pembers. It's much too dark and creepy here to start speculating and making matters worse than they already are."

Pemberley gave a shrill whistle to call Oswald over, but he didn't reappear. Churchill shone her torch in the direction of the last sighting but there was no sign of him.

"Where is he?" she whimpered.

"He can't be far away or we wouldn't have heard him."

"Which can only mean that the evil thing must also be close by!"

There was another low growl, and the beams of the ladies' torches frantically crossed and re-crossed the graveyard.

"Come here, Oswald!" Pemberley called out, her voice cracking. "Oh dear," she added when he still didn't return. "We'll have to go and look for him."

"Really?" All Churchill's bravado had left her now. "Can't we just wait by the gate until he comes back?"

"He might be in trouble!"

"That dog is always in trouble, Pembers, but he has a knack for getting himself out of it. There's no need for us to get involved in his capers this evening."

"We can't just abandon him."

"We're not abandoning him. We're merely waiting beside the gate until he's finished whatever it is he's up to."

"But what if he's found the *thing* we were looking for?"

"We came here to carry out surveillance, Pembers, not to look for a *thing*."

"He's found something, that's for sure. Don't you think we should find out what it is?"

"By all means go and have a look, Pembers. I'll just wait here by the gate."

"You're not frightened, are you, Mrs Churchill?"

"Frightened? Surely you know me better than that by now."

"Then why won't you come with me to find Oswald? He may have been carrying out some of his clever dog detective work again for all we know. He may even have solved Mr Grieves's case."

"I doubt Oswald has done so single-handedly while we've been standing around the churchyard."

"Fine, then I'll go and fetch him myself."

"I thought you were afraid of the dark?"

"I don't have time for all that when my dog needs me. Will you be all right if I leave you here quaking in your boots, Mrs Churchill?"

"I'm not quaking!"

"You're obviously too scared to search the churchyard for poor Oswald."

Pemberley strode off into the darkness with her torch, and Churchill felt so affronted by the suggestion of her being scared that she quickly followed. Besides, remaining with Pemberley seemed preferable to standing on her own in the dark. She felt the hairs on the back of her neck prickle as she followed her assistant. She wished she were in the cosy kitchen of her cottage, sitting in her easy chair by the stove enjoying a hot toddy. She also wished she had never agreed to take on the churchyard case. She made a mental note to be a little choosier in future.

"Oswald!" Pemberley called out. "Where are you? Oh dear, I do hope he's safe."

The wind moaned eerily through the bell tower and Churchill felt her knees begin to quake. "We must have almost crossed the whole churchyard by now," she said. "Isn't Saul Mollikin's grave near here?"

"Yes, it is."

Churchill thought of the strange grave with its fresh blades of grass and felt an extra-strong shiver. She found herself fighting the strong urge to turn tail and run out of the churchyard as quickly as her legs would carry her.

"It'll be a miracle if we ever get out of this churchyard in one piece, Pembers."

"Why on earth would you say that, Mrs Churchill? You

surely don't believe something's about to attack us, do you?"

"I just don't know, Pembers. Perhaps we'll be cursed."

"In a churchyard?"

"Yes. Whatever it is, I have a feeling something terribly bad is about to happen to us."

"Why didn't you say so when we were walking here this evening? It would have saved us having to wander around the churchyard in the dark trying to find Oswald."

"I didn't realise it would be this bad."

"I did try to warn you."

"I know."

"You should listen next time."

"I should, but I probably won't. Once I'm back at home with a nice brandy and lovage in my hand I shall probably forget about all the horrors of the churchyard. If we ever get out of here, that is."

"We will—"

Pemberley's reply came to an abrupt end as Churchill emitted a scream louder than she'd considered herself capable of making. She dropped her torch and flapped her hands in terror, her whole body consumed by a paroxysm of fear.

"Mrs Churchill! Mrs Churchill!" pleaded Pemberley. "What is it? What's happened? Did you see something?"

"Over there! On that grave! It's coming out!"

"Coming *out*?" shrieked Pemberley. "*Coming out of the grave?*"

"Yes! It's coming for us!"

Churchill felt Pemberley's hand grip tightly around her arm.

"What is?" she squeaked. "What's coming for us?"

Pemberley swept her torchlight across the graveyard until it came to rest upon the glaring white of bone.

Then it was Pemberley's turn to scream.

Resting at the foot of a headstone close by was a grinning skull with the deepest, darkest eye sockets Churchill had ever seen.

"We have to get out of here!" Churchill wailed. "It's cursed! We're doomed!" She turned to run, but quickly realised she could see nothing in the blackness behind her with her torch still lying on the ground somewhere.

"I, I... I d-don't think it's m-moving," ventured Pemberley, as the quivering beam of her torch rested on the skull once again. "In fact, it's not attached to anything. The rest of the body isn't there. It's just the head."

"I can't decide whether that's better or worse!" wailed Churchill.

"At least it can't chase us."

"How do you know that?"

"Because it's just a head."

"Oh, get me out of here, Pemberley. I can't take a moment more of this! Which way did we come in? Oh, it's so dark. Oh, help!"

A short, sharp bark brought Churchill back to her senses.

"He's back!" rejoiced Pemberley as the scruffy little dog scampered over to them in the torchlight.

"Oh, thank goodness!" said Churchill with relief. "Now we really must go." Her heart was pounding in her chest, fit to burst.

"Here's your torch," said Pemberley, stooping to pick it up from the ground. "I just stepped on it."

"Does it still work?"

Pemberley gave it a shake and the beam came on. "Yes." She handed it back to Churchill. "Now, let's get out of here."

The two ladies had only taken a few steps when Oswald began to growl again.

"Oh dear," said Pemberley.

Churchill was struck dumb. Looming ahead of her in the torchlight was an ominous dark figure. Her knees gave way and she knew nothing more.

Chapter 23

"Mrs Churchill?"

Pemberley's voice sounded distant, but when the buzzing noise in Churchill's ears subsided she was able to hear it more clearly.

"Mrs Churchill?"

"Yes, Miss Pemberley. I'm here." She wasn't sure exactly where *here* was, but Churchill did know she was lying down and that her head ached. "What are you wiping my face with, Pembers?"

"I'm not."

"What is that, then?"

Torchlight shone into her eyes.

"Ouch!" she said.

"Oswald was licking you better, Mrs Churchill."

"How very thoughtful of him. Where am I? Please don't tell me I'm still in that accursed churchyard."

A deep chuckle made her jump.

"Was that you, Pembers? What's happened to your voice?"

"Nothing," came the reply. "This voice belongs to Grieves."

"Mr Grieves the sexton? What are you doing here?"

"Frightening old ladies in the churchyard, that's what. Allow me to help you up, Mrs Churchill. Are you able to stand?"

She whooped with surprise as two large hands slid beneath her arms and lifted her up.

"Goodness, I think so. What just happened?"

"You fainted after catching sight of the church sexton," replied Pemberley.

"That large, scary thing?"

'That's me," responded Grieves, hoisting Churchill onto her feet. "Hold on to my arm if you still need some support, Mrs Churchill."

"I do feel a little woozy still, if truth be told." She gripped his arm. "Strewth, what a terrible palaver? Can you please get us out of here, Mr Grieves? My assistant and I have had more than enough for one day. One night, I mean. One *week*, even."

"Of course."

"Would you like to borrow my torch?"

"No, that's all right," he said. "I can see very clearly in the dark."

Oswald gave another low growl.

"He doesn't like me, that dog," said the sexton as he led them along the path.

"Was it you he was growling at earlier?"

"Yes. There I was keeping watch and the little fellow wouldn't leave me alone."

A terrible memory descended upon Churchill. "Oh, and the skull. Good grief! Did you know that someone's skull has come out of their grave, Mr Grieves?"

He gave another chuckle. "Oh, you've met Jake."

"Jake?"

"The skull. I've been leaving him out in the churchyard at night in the hope of scaring off whoever's been causing mischief."

"You could have warned us, Mr Grieves. He frightened two elderly ladies half to death!"

"I should have done, in hindsight. Although it seems that I frightened you even more than Jake did."

"Indeed you did. Creeping up on us in the dark like that; it shouldn't be allowed!"

"I was coming to let you know your dog was on the loose."

"I see. What were you doing in the churchyard, anyway?"

"I'm the sexton. It's my job to look after it."

"You often hide out here at night, do you? Lurking about in the shadows?"

"I've had to keep a check on things, Mrs Churchill, as you well know. Did you see anything suspicious, by the way?"

"Erm, no. We came to the churchyard this evening to find out what was happening, but instead we've been scared witless by a macabre prop placed on a grave as some sort of practical joke."

"I put it there to scare people away."

"Well, it worked. I certainly shan't be setting foot in this churchyard ever again."

"How do you intend to solve the case if you're not willing to come back again, Mrs Churchill?" asked Pemberley.

"I'll think of something."

"You seem rather fidgety today, Mrs Churchill. Is something bothering you?" asked Mr Pickwick, paintbrush in hand.

"Oh I do apologise, Mr Pickwick. Is it ruining your painting?"

"Not at all." He sat back and smiled. "I'm quite accustomed to my subjects moving about. My enquiry came from a place of concern for your good self."

"Oh, did it? That's very kind of you, Mr Pickwick."

"Call me Percy."

"Are you sure?"

"Of course. Now, what's bothering you, Mrs Churchill?"

"Well, there's rather a lot happening at the moment, what with the various investigations going on and that sort of thing. And I had a little fright last night."

"Goodness, what happened?"

"It was just the sexton playing a little trick on us with his friend Jake. And I've made a little boo-boo I'm not particularly proud of."

"Oh dear. What might that be, then?"

"If I tell you, will you promise to keep it a secret?"

"Absolutely."

Churchill proceeded to tell Mr Pickwick about the ring that had been found and then stolen.

"You mustn't blame yourself, Mrs Churchill."

"But I left the office door unlocked, and then advertised to the entire village in the local newspaper that I had a valuable ring in my possession! It was a crime I invited upon myself, I'm afraid."

"It's the thief who was at fault, Mrs Churchill, not you. Besides, I'm sure he'll be apprehended before long."

"But what will Inspector Mappin say about it? He isn't particularly fond of me at the best of times."

"Don't you go worrying about him. You've only followed what you considered to be the correct course of action. It would be downright unreasonable of the inspector if he chose to admonish you for it."

"Oh, thank you, Percy. That's made me feel a little better already."

He smiled. "I'm glad to hear it."

"I would dearly love to see how my portrait is coming along, won't you allow me the very sneakiest of little peeks?"

"I'm afraid not, Mrs Churchill, I have a terrible superstition about such things."

"How I wish you didn't!"

"Even if I wasn't the superstitious type, Mrs Churchill, I think works in progress tend to look rather dreadful. I often think seeing an unfinished painting is rather like coming across a lady in a state of undress."

Churchill emitted an unexpected gasping noise. "Gosh, what a comparison, Percy! Does that happen to you often?"

"Very infrequently." He gave a self-conscious cough. "Perhaps I used an impolite comparison there. I meant that one would rather see the final result. It's better to admire a lady in her evening gown than to view the undergarments used to create the silhouette, don't you agree?"

"You might find a few gentlemen who would disagree with you on that front, Percy, but I think I understand what you're saying. I must confess that all this talk of undress and undergarments has left me rather flushed. I fear it will quite ruin the shade of my complexion for the portrait."

"Please don't worry about that, Mrs Churchill. I can assure you that I have a good mix of peaches and cream on my palette."

"For my face?"

"For your fair complexion."

"You're such a flatterer, Percy."

"I merely paint what I see." He winked.

"Oh, you silly billy." Churchill felt her face flush an even deeper shade of red. She patted her cheeks and glanced out of the window to see the sun shining down on the fields.

Chapter 24

"I'm delighted to report that the postman has delivered my invitation to the garden party at Gollendale Hall," said Churchill to Pemberley as they walked down a track that led to a little white cottage.

"That is excellent news indeed. I'm so looking forward to it!"

"*You're* looking forward to it, Pembers?"

"Yes. The invitation presumably includes a guest."

"It does."

"There we go then. How exciting!"

Pemberley looked so pleased that Churchill couldn't bring herself to admit she had considered asking Mr Pickwick to be her guest. She decided this piece of news would be best left for another time. They soon reached the cottage door, which was surrounded by a pretty rose arbour.

"I sincerely hope Mrs Roseball will act as a welcome tonic after last night's ordeal," said Churchill. "I can still feel myself shaking. I was all of a tremor during my sitting with Mr Pickwick earlier, and part of me wonders if that weird sexton chap hasn't simply set us up for it."

"As some sort of practical joke?"

"Why else would he have left Jake the Skull lying there on that grave? I shouldn't wonder if he wasn't behind all the shenanigans himself."

"And possibly every other shenanigan in the village. He could also be the murderer with his dark hat and coat."

"Indeed he could!" Churchill knocked at Mrs Roseball's door. "I think we should pin it all on Grieves and take ourselves off for a few days in Weymouth, Pembers. I like the idea of sand between my toes."

"Ugh, no thank you."

"What's wrong with sand?"

"Nothing. It's toes I can't stand."

"What's wrong with toes? Oh, good morning, Mrs Roseball!"

The small, round lady squinted at them through the thick lenses of her spectacles, then welcomed them in.

"How's the weather?" she asked as they walked into her front room. "It looks sunny out there, but I suspect the temperature is a little lower than it was yesterday. The wind's coming from the north-east now; I felt it change at around seven o'clock this morning. I knew it was about to change to a north-easterly because I had a pain in my right leg most of yesterday."

"Does your right leg have the ability to predict the weather, Mrs Roseball?"

"My entire body does. It's just one of those things you're born with." She flapped a hand dismissively. "Tea?"

"Yes, thank you. I see you also have a penchant for china shepherdesses," said Churchill, eying up a line of them on the mantelpiece.

"Oh no, I'm only looking after those for Mrs Hatweed.

She hasn't space for them all, you see. They're very precious to her, so I swore to protect them with my life. Do sit. Theophilus will move for you."

A black cat coolly observed the two ladies and their dog from the settee once Mrs Roseball had left the room. Oswald hid behind Pemberley.

"Hello, puss!" said Churchill.

The cat hissed in reply.

"Mrs Roseball said he'd move for us, so I think we should take a seat." Churchill moved to sit down but the cat hissed again and bared his sharp, white teeth. "What do you think, Pembers. Should I just sit down?"

"Mrs Roseball did say he would move for us."

"Righty-ho, then." Churchill turned tentatively in readiness to place her behind on the settee. As she began to lower herself down, she felt a sharp, needle-like pain in her thigh.

"Yow!" Somehow her legs found the strength to propel her body upright again. "Did that cat just attack my leg, Pembers?"

"Yes," replied her assistant, who had backed away several feet. "Perhaps we should sit on the floor."

"By all means go ahead, but I'll never get up again if I do that. Oh look, there's a little pouffe in the bay window. I'll sit on that."

Churchill was still positioning herself on the small cushioned footstool when Mrs Roseball reappeared with the tea tray.

"What on earth are you doing over there, Mrs Churchill?"

"The cat doesn't like me, Mrs Roseball. He stuck his claws into my thigh."

"Theo would never do such a thing!" She walked over

to the cat and stroked his head before lifting him off the settee. "There you go, ladies."

"Thank you," said Pemberley, making herself comfortable on the settee with a wary Oswald on her lap. Churchill watched enviously, realising it would take more effort than she could muster to get up off the pouffe.

"Why don't you sit on the settee, Mrs Churchill?"

"I'm quite all right here, thank you, Mrs Roseball."

"But I insist."

"I'm afraid I must insist on sitting on this pouffe for now."

"Surely not! It doesn't look at all comfortable with your knees squashed up against your chest like that."

"I'm fine," she replied through gritted teeth. "Now, you're probably wondering why we've come to visit."

"There's a reason?" replied Mrs Roseball, pouring out the tea.

"Yes. We were wondering whether you had any idea who might have murdered Mr Butterfork."

"Well, there's a question."

"You knew him well, didn't you?"

"Reasonably well, yes."

"Mrs Hatweed told us you visited him on the day he died."

"I did. Although I didn't know then that he would die that day, of course." She handed Churchill a cup of tea.

"Which was probably just as well."

"I suppose if I'd known I could have warned him."

"Indeed, but that's probably not worth lamenting over."

"How differently things could have turned out, eh?" Mrs Roseball took a seat on the settee next to Pemberley.

"Well, quite."

"Although I suppose if I'd told him he was about to be murdered he wouldn't have believed me anyway."

"We're entering the realm of pure speculation now, Mrs Roseball. Do you mind me asking why you visited Mr Butterfork that day?"

"It was to ask him about this chap." She pointed at Theophilus, who now sat on the rug in the centre of the room, staring at Churchill. "He hadn't been well and I was struggling to find enough money for the veterinarian fees. My income is small, you see, as there's only so much damson jam people will buy."

"Have you thought about adding another flavour?" Pemberley asked her.

"No."

"Perhaps if you made another flavour people would buy that too, and then you would sell more jam?"

"Such as?"

"Anything really. Strawberry jam is usually quite popular."

"I don't like strawberries."

"But other people do."

"This is probably a discussion for another time," interjected Churchill, who was beginning to feel a sharp pain in her abdomen as she sat squashed up on the pouffe. "Did Mr Butterfork cough up the fees for the veterinarian?"

"Yes, and a little extra, too. If it hadn't been for Mr Butterfork, Theophilus might not have been here today!" Mrs Roseball beamed down at her pet, who continued to glare unblinkingly at Churchill.

"How wonderful that he was saved," replied Churchill, studiously avoiding the cat's malicious stare. "So you have no idea who could have stolen Mr Butterfork's money and murdered him that evening?"

"No. I hope you don't think it was me!"

"Why on earth would we think it was you, Mrs Roseball?"

"Because I'm short of money and own a gun."

"You own a gun?"

"Yes. My late husband brought it back from the war with him."

"And where is the gun now?"

"It's in the writing bureau." Mrs Roseball put down her tea, got up and walked over to the small walnut desk in the corner of the room. She opened a drawer and pulled out a revolver.

"I see," said Churchill, nervously. "I almost wish I hadn't asked now. Besides, the gun used in Mr Butterfork's murder was found in the churchyard, so we know your gun wasn't the murder weapon. You can put that back now."

Mrs Roseball peered down at the revolver in her hand. "I don't even know if it has any bullets in it."

"Why not just put it back in the drawer, Mrs Roseball?"

"Do you know how to tell if it has any bullets in it?"

"There's probably no need to determine that right now. Let's just put it away, shall we?"

"They'll be in the cylinder," said Pemberley helpfully. "Does it have a fixed cylinder, a swing-out cylinder or a break-top mechanism?"

"I have no idea," replied Mrs Roseball as she clumsily turned the gun over in her hands.

Churchill's stomach lurched uncomfortably.

"Is there a hinged loading gate at the back of the cylinder?" asked Pemberley. "Have a look on the right-hand side."

Mrs Roseball peered at it through her thick lenses and Churchill flinched as the barrel wafted precariously in her direction.

"Can we please just put the gun away?" she pleaded.

"I can't see a hinged gate thingy," said Mrs Roseball, squinting closely at it.

"Perhaps it has a break-top mechanism, then," said Pemberley. "Or it might have a swing-out cylinder."

"Can you please stop encouraging this, Miss Pemberley?" asked Churchill.

"If there are cartridges in the cylinder it would be best if Mrs Roseball were to remove them," replied Pemberley.

"I think it would be best if the pistol were put back in the drawer and a gun expert were subsequently summoned to come and remove it," said Churchill.

"I don't want the revolver taken away," protested Mrs Roseball. "I need it more than ever with a murderer on the loose!"

"Do you have a tea chest stuffed full of money, Mrs Roseball?"

"No."

"Then I think you should be all right. It really is quite dangerous for you to have such a thing in your house, you know, especially when you're not sure whether it's loaded or not."

"What nonsense, Mrs—"

The air was ripped apart by an ear-splitting bang. Mrs Roseball recoiled backwards, the gun clattered to the floor and the acrid smell of gunpowder filled the room.

"Oh, good grief!" exclaimed Mrs Roseball, clutching her chest. "What have I done?"

Pemberley sat rigid on the settee, her eyes squeezed shut and her mouth hanging open.

Oswald was nowhere to be seen.

Churchill was astonished to find that she had remained seated on the pouffe. She slowly began to check each part of her body for a bullet wound. She began to breathe a little more easily when she realised there was none.

"Oh, oh," moaned Mrs Roseball, staggering around the room, her spectacles askew. "Oh, help!" She stumbled against the wall and slid down it until she slumped onto the floor.

"I think we're all still alive," said Churchill with relief. "Miss Pemberley, can you hear us?"

Her assistant's eyes sprung open. "Is it over?" she asked.

"Yes, it's over."

Oswald's little head appeared from behind the settee.

"And Oswald's still alive, too," said Churchill. "But what about Theophilus? He was sitting on the rug just now."

Mrs Roseball pointed to the bay window, where the black cat was hanging from one of the curtains next to Churchill, his fur as bristled as a fox's tail.

"Well, I must say, Mrs Roseball," said Churchill, "that's one way to find out whether a gun is loaded or not. Where did the bullet end up?"

"There," said Pemberley, pointing straight ahead of her at the fireplace. Churchill looked to see a hole in the wall just above the mantelpiece.

"Oh no!" exclaimed Mrs Roseball, looking aghast. She rose to her feet and dashed over to the mantelpiece, picking up a china shepherdess that was missing its head. "How am I going to explain this to Hatters?"

Chapter 25

"My nerves are completely shot to pieces, Pembers," said Churchill as they staggered back to the office. "First a terrible fright in the churchyard and then Mrs Roseball almost finishing us off with her revolver."

"That was very dangerous indeed," agreed Pemberley. "We could have been killed. Poor Oswald could have been killed!"

"Oh, what a dreadful thought! We mustn't take him on our travels any more, Pembers. We can't afford to go putting him in harm's way."

"But he has to come with us. He's our detective dog!"

"And what would you do if he came to any harm?"

"The incident with Mrs Roseball was very rare. Our work is quite safe most of the time."

"I suppose it is. I'll tell you what, though, I'm going to struggle to finish off that jar of damson jam I have in my pantry."

"Why?"

"Because every time I take a mouthful, I'll be reminded

just how close we came to death today! Damson jam will never taste the same for me again. What a terrible shame."

"It is rather annoying that Mrs Roseball has ruined jam for us."

"Well, only damson jam. I think I'll be all right with other flavours."

"She's ruined all jam for me. I never want to see a jar of the stuff again."

Churchill paused as they reached the door of the office. "Do you know what I think, Pembers? I think we should take the rest of the day off. It's been an exhausting twenty-four hours and we need to prepare ourselves for a little piece of reconnaissance in Cowslip Park this evening."

"Must we? I feel as though I want to retire."

"What, now?"

"It would be rather nice, wouldn't it?"

"But what would you do with your time?"

"I've no idea."

"Well, in the meantime, let's meet in the park at a quarter to six."

A tall, bespectacled nanny strolled through Cowslip Park that evening pushing her charge in a perambulator with a large hood to protect him from the sun's dipping rays. She wore a smart apron over her long, pale blue dress, which was tied at the waist with a dark blue belt. Her hat and gloves were also dark blue. A similarly attired nanny, whose dress was of a shorter, wider fit, passed her bespectacled counterpart on the path, and the two acknowledged each other with a polite nod. Then the shorter nanny pushed her perambulator in the direction of the Masonic lodge, adopting a subtle sidelong glance as she surveyed the men arriving for their evening meeting.

The two nannies met again on the other side of Cowslip Park.

"Seen anyone you recognise yet, Pembers?" whispered the shorter nanny as she paused to peek at the bundle of blankets in her pram.

"Quite a few of them, yes. I've seen most of the men in the village, actually."

"Goodness! Are they all Freemasons?"

"So far I've seen Mr Hurricks, Mr Manners, Dr Bratchett, Farmer Drumhead, Mr Grieves, Mr Fordbridge, Mr Crumble, Mr Verney, Farmer Jagford, Mr Downs, Mr Jones Sloanes and the mayor."

"The mayor?"

"And Mr Pickwick."

Churchill felt her heart skip excitedly. "Oh, him," she added as nonchalantly as possible.

"Your gentleman friend."

"Gentleman friend? What on earth does that mean? He's merely an acquaintance."

"He's painting you."

"That's because he's a painter. Actually, I don't mean a painter, because that suggests he paints walls and fences. He's an *artist*."

"Who have you seen go in?" asked Pemberley.

"A boss-eyed chap with red hair and a stooped gentleman with exceptionally large ears."

"Mr Brunt and Mr Sergecan."

"Never heard of them." Churchill reached into her pram, unwrapped the bundle of blankets and pulled out a paper bag. "Fruit scone, Pembers?"

"No, thank you; not without jam and cream. Actually, just cream. I'll never be able to eat jam again."

"I've got some cream in here and all the relevant accoutrements, but I left the jam at home. In fact, I might take to pushing a perambulator about all the time. It's an excellent method of transporting one's eatables. I can fit so much more in here than in my handbag." She glanced over at the Masonic lodge. "A few more are making their way along the path now. Let's do another circuit and see who we can spy."

"Aren't you worried someone might recognise us?"

"I haven't seen anyone so much as glance in our direction yet, Pembers. Two mature nannies pushing prams are hardly likely to attract the attention of a bunch of gentlemen gathering to discuss their Freemason business. We're practically invisible to them!"

"But these costumes aren't a complete disguise, are they?"

"But they are, Pembers, because we're out of context. No one would expect Mrs Churchill and Miss Pemberley to be spending a summer's evening walking around the park with perambulators. Even if the brief thought occurred to someone that we seemed familiar he would immediately consider himself mistaken and dismiss the idea from his mind."

"I do hope you're right."

"Consider how many Freemasons you've spotted already. Did any of them recognise you?"

"No."

"Good." Churchill leaned into her perambulator and cut open a scone. "A nice bit of cream will be delicious on this... shame about the jam. That reminds me, Pembers. How do you know so much about revolvers and their cylinders with all that hinged-top-break-swing-gate business? You appeared to be quite the expert."

"Little good that did us!"

"How did Mrs Roseball even manage to fire it accidentally?"

"I didn't see her finger touch the trigger, so I can only guess she knocked the hammer, which hit the bullet in the chamber. It sometimes happens with those old revolvers."

"How do you know all this?" Churchill bit into her scone.

"A cowboy taught me."

"A *cowboy?*" Churchill could barely form the word around her large mouthful of scone. She hoped the keen, quizzical look on her face would encourage Pemberley to keep talking.

"Once when I was a companion to the lady of international travel, we found ourselves on the same transatlantic steam ship as Buffalo Bill's Wild West tour and a very nice cowboy showed me how to use his revolver."

"Did he indeed?"

"I learned everything I know from him."

"Golly, well perhaps you can teach me one day. I feel my gun knowledge is sadly lacking."

"Shouldn't we be keeping an eye on the time, Mrs Churchill?"

"Oh yes, we should." She checked her watch, then gulped down the remainder of her scone. "Right, let's get on with our reconnaissance. We'll have to hoof it across the park now if we're to get to those stragglers on time."

Churchill went one way and Pemberley went the other. A few minutes later they met again on the path close to the lodge. Churchill stopped.

"I don't think it's a good idea to stop here," whispered Pemberley. "It'll arouse their suspicions."

"Don't worry, Pembers, it would be quite normal for

two nannies to stop and discuss their charges during an evening stroll in the park. Now, your spectacles afford you better eyesight than me. Who do you see over there?"

"Mr Toolberry."

"Never heard of him."

"Mr Bowloak."

"I've no idea about him, either. If only I had my field glasses and could get a better look at them."

"That would give you away completely. Nannies never have field glasses with them."

"Good point well made. Keep an eye on your charge, Pembers, he's growing a little restless."

Pemberley peered into the pram. "Oh that's a shame, he's woken up. He was having a lovely nap in there."

Churchill watched nervously as Oswald peered out from beneath the pram hood. "Walk him on a bit and see if you can lull him back to sleep."

"I don't think it'll work. The baby's awake now and I expect he's hungry."

"Let's give him a scone."

"Dogs shouldn't eat scones, Mrs Churchill. You know that."

"But we need to keep him quiet!"

"He will be quiet. I've trained him not to bark."

"Since when?"

"Ever since I got him."

Churchill shook her head incredulously and glanced over at the two men, who had almost reached the steps of the Masonic lodge. She checked her watch and saw that it was a minute to six o'clock.

"Surely that's the last of them gone in now. What do you think, Pembers?"

"I can see one more making his way over."

"There's always one, isn't there?"

"It's Inspector Mappin."

"Right. Out of all the gentlemen who have turned up this evening, he's probably the most likely to recognise us."

"I thought you said we were unrecognisable out of context?"

"I did, but the inspector has a keen policeman's eye."

"Really?"

"Actually, he has nothing of the kind, but let's not risk it. I think we should make a swift departure all the same. Our job here is done!"

The two ladies quickly moved on, but Churchill had only taken a couple of steps when she heard Pemberley gasp behind her. She spun around to see Oswald out of the pram and cantering at great speed toward Inspector Mappin. The little dog had no doubt remembered the juicy bone the inspector had given him and was eagerly anticipating another.

Churchill was about to call out when she realised doing so would give them away. She reasoned it would be better to march on and pretend Oswald was nothing to do with them.

Pemberley's mind hadn't followed the same thought process, however, and she gave a loud whistle in an attempt to call the dog back.

"Ssh!" hissed Churchill. "We have to pretend he's not with us."

"I can't just leave him!"

"He won't go far. He'll jump all over Inspector Mappin and then come back to find us."

Churchill turned and pushed off with her pram as fast as she could go. She would leave her secretary to face Inspector Mappin if it came to that. After all, it was Pemberley's fault for letting Oswald escape.

Only it wasn't Pemberley's name that carried on the evening breeze.

"*Mrs Churchill!*"

Chapter 26

INSPECTOR MAPPIN SCRIBBLED something down in his note-book. "It's just as well that I carry this with me even when I'm off duty," he commented, checking his watch. "You ladies have made me five minutes late for my meeting."

"You've made yourself late for your meeting, Inspector," retorted Churchill. "There was no need for you to take down our particulars. We weren't even committing a crime."

The inspector sighed. "We've already discussed this, Mrs Churchill. You were both acting suspiciously."

"And we've already told you we were carrying out surveillance."

"Compton Poppleford Masonic Lodge will take a dim view of being spied on. That said, spying involves a certain level of sophistication, and I see no sophistication in dressing up as nannies and pushing empty perambulators about the place."

"Oh, but they're not empty, Inspector. Mine happens to contain a number of useful provisions and Pemberley's contains a dog. In fact, I'm quite impressed by the way he managed to jump back in again all by himself. I think he likes his pram. We were carrying out careful surveillance of one or more persons, and our operation has been quite ruined by you apprehending us for no reason whatsoever."

Inspector Mappin gave a despairing shake of his head. "Does this have anything to do with the ring you found in Crunkle Lane? Have you dressed up in ridiculous nanny costumes in a bid to identify the ring's owner?"

"These are bona fide uniforms, Inspector, not costumes. And we're merely here to ascertain who in the village happens to be a Freemason. We weren't expecting to discover that most of the men in the village belong to the organisation."

"I could have told you who our members were, Mrs Churchill. You didn't have to go to such elaborate lengths."

"Ah, but would you have told us?"

"No, I don't suppose I would."

"Exactly. Now, have any of your Freemason friends—"

"Masonic brothers."

"Have any of your *Masonic brothers* mentioned that they might have lost a ring?"

"No."

"Have any of them come down to the station to ask whether a lost ring has been handed in?"

"No."

"That is very interesting indeed. One has to wonder whether the gentleman in question is worried about implicating himself."

"Somewhere in the village there's a man who has lost his ring but doesn't want to admit to it because he lost it while committing a dreadful murder," added Pemberley.

"Exactly!"

"That's enough," said Inspector Mappin. "It's quite out of the question that a Freemason could have murdered Mr Butterfork. Every brother I've ever known has been an honest, law-abiding individual. Any man who was otherwise simply wouldn't be permitted to join in the first place."

"You've never arrested a Freemason before, Inspector?"

"No, and nor will I ever have to. Now, you have remembered that you're due to hand the ring over to me shortly, haven't you?"

"Yes, we haven't forgotten." Churchill said, giving Pemberley an uncomfortable sidelong glance. "I wonder if you could tell us which of your mason friends wears a dark grey overcoat, Inspector?"

"I should think a good number of them do."

"You've heard about the expert analysis Mrs Thonnings conducted on the piece of snagged fabric found in the churchyard, I presume?"

"Yes."

"It came from the dark grey overcoat the murderer was wearing as he fled through the churchyard. The murder weapon was also found close by."

"Yes, I recall all that."

"Don't you think you should be rounding up all the men around here who own dark grey overcoats, in that case?"

"You make it sound as though I'm some sort of sheepdog, Mrs Churchill."

"One of your Mason friends owns such a coat. Pemberley and I saw him the other afternoon."

"Which one?"

"We don't know, because we only saw the back of him. But if you were to check everyone's coats at the meeting this evening you could easily find out."

Inspector Mappin shook his head. "I'm off duty, Mrs Churchill, and there's no need for you to tell me how to go about my job."

"But the coat has to be an excellent lead, wouldn't you agree?"

"I'll be the judge of that."

"And if the chap with the dark grey overcoat also happened to have lost his ring, we'd have ourselves a rather firm suspect."

"But he's a Freemason, Mrs Churchill. He couldn't possibly be a murderer."

"I shall happily agree with you for the time being, Inspector, just to make our conversation run a little more smoothly. I'm sure you have no wish to detain us any further."

"You're right, I don't. But this can't go on, you know." He wagged a finger at them. "It's disruptive."

"Disruptive to what?"

"To my evening."

"You could have simply ignored us."

"My job is to keep the peace, Mrs Churchill."

"Miss Pemberley and I weren't making any noise."

"You were unnerving people."

"Such as?"

"Me, for one."

"Please do accept our apologies for unnerving you; that certainly wasn't our intention. Now you've wasted another few minutes of your time, and you could be missing out on something dreadfully important in there. What are they likely to be talking about, anyway?"

"That's the lodge's business, Mrs Churchill, not yours."

"Or yours at the moment, Inspector, given that you're still out here."

"Any more of this nonsense, Mrs Churchill, and I shall

be referring this case to my superiors." He wagged his finger again. "Now, please go home and leave all this well alone."

Chapter 27

"I THOUGHT you told Grieves you would never set foot in the churchyard again, Mrs Churchill," said Pemberley as the two ladies and Oswald walked toward St Swithun's the following morning.

"I did, but that's because it was dark and I was frightened. After giving it some careful thought, I decided I just wanted to get the case cleared up. It can't be too difficult, can it?"

"I'd say that it would be extremely difficult."

"Someone must be behind it all, and whether it's Grieves himself or someone else we just need to catch them in the act."

"Why would Grieves be behind it?"

"I don't know. Why would anyone be behind it? It's certainly one of the strangest cases I've ever come across. Anyway, our visit to Cowslip Park yesterday evening went well, don't you think?"

"I'd say it went terribly. Inspector Mappin found us out!"

"Let's forget about that part. The bit that went well

relates to the fact that we now have a nice long list of all the local Freemasons."

"It's not a written-down list," replied Pemberley. "It's still in my head."

"Get writing it down then, Pembers. We don't want to forget anybody. If we can find one with a dark grey coat and a missing ring, he'd have to be our chief suspect."

"Why hasn't the ring's owner arrived to claim it yet?" asked Pemberley.

"Because whoever it is must be the murderer! The longer he leaves it the guiltier he looks. And besides, we don't really want him to collect it now it's been stolen, do we? I really don't know what we're going to do when the time comes to hand it over to Mappin."

The two ladies noticed someone stepping out through the gate as they approached the churchyard.

"Who's that?" asked Pemberley. "I don't think I've ever seen her before."

The fair-haired lady had a trim figure and wore a well-tailored jacket and skirt in pale blue.

"It's Miss Agnes Pickwick," replied Churchill. "Mr Pickwick's sister."

Miss Pickwick, who hadn't yet seen them, paused beside the gate to remove her gloves. Then she shook each glove and dusted it off before neatly tucking the pair inside her handbag. After she had looped the handbag over her arm, Miss Pickwick started walking toward Churchill and Pemberley at a brisk pace.

"Good morning!" Churchill called out as Miss Pickwick drew near.

"Oh, good morning!" she called back. "Lovely day, isn't it?"

"Extremely. Perfect weather for visiting the churchyard."

"Oh." She gave a tentative smile and glanced behind her. "Yes, it is. I've just been there myself, actually, visiting the resting place of a dearly departed relative."

"I didn't realise you and your brother had family in this part of the country, Miss Pickwick."

"Ah well, not family, exactly. We were so close that I considered her a great-aunt, you see. Anyway, I must be off. Do enjoy your stroll, ladies!"

Churchill and Pemberley narrowed their eyes as they watched Miss Pickwick march on down the cobbled lane.

"She'll be annoyed when she notices all that mud on her perfect shoes," commented Pemberley.

"She will. And she'd clearly dirtied her gloves, too. I wonder which aged relative she was visiting."

"She looks significantly younger than Mr Pickwick," commented Pemberley. "Could she be his half-sister, do you think?"

"He didn't mention such a thing. Perhaps there are a good deal of Pickwick siblings in between. He could be the eldest and she could be the youngest. And after all, he isn't *that* old, Pembers."

"He's old enough to be of interest to you, Mrs Churchill."

"*Of interest?* What could you possibly mean by that? He's painting me, that's all there is to it. Now, come along, Miss Pemberley. We'd better go and see what she's been up to in the churchyard."

"I dread to think."

Oswald trotted on through the churchyard gate with the two ladies following behind him.

"The churchyard looks so much friendlier in the daytime, don't you think?" commented Churchill with a deep sense of relief.

"It still gives me the heebie-jeebies."

"I'm tempted to be guided by Oswald here. A recent visitor would have left a fresh scent, don't you agree? Look at his little nose; he's got it snuffling about on the ground there. It can only be the scent of Miss Pickwick he's picked up."

"Rather highly perfumed, I should think," said Pemberley. "She looks like the sort of lady who would cover herself in expensive eau-de-cologne from a fancy cut-glass perfume bottle with a long tassel. I can just imagine it sitting on her dressing table next to her silver vanity set."

"How nice for Miss Pickwick."

"It must have an enormous looking glass, of course."

"What must?"

"Her dressing table. In fact, it probably has *three* looking glasses. One in the centre and one on either side, placed at an angle so she can admire herself from whichever angle she chooses."

"I see."

"All framed with ornate gilt, of course."

"The looking glasses?"

"Yes. And the dressing table itself must also be very grand. Elegantly shaped with an inverted bow front so she doesn't knock her delicate knees on it, no doubt."

"I think we've heard enough about Miss Pickwick's bedroom furniture, Pembers."

"Bedroom? Oh no, I was merely referring to the dressing room. The bedchamber would be another matter entirely, with a Queen Anne four-poster bed—"

"Pembers, that's enough! We must concentrate on the task in hand. Now, I must say I'm growing more than a little interested in the elderly relative Miss Pickwick claimed to have been visiting. A lady she considered a great-aunt, didn't she say? I wish we'd asked her the lady's name now."

"Perhaps Miss Pickwick is the headstone cleaner."

"Now that's a thought. Perhaps her gloves had lichen on them, and that's why she dusted them off before putting them back in her handbag. Perhaps she's the one who's behind all the churchyard shenanigans."

"It's not the sort of thing ladies with elaborate dressing tables tend to do," said Pemberley. "They're usually far more interested in the wave of their hair and the shape of their lips."

"That may be a slight generalisation. Where's that dog got to? He must have sniffed something out by now."

"He's over there." Pemberley pointed out the small scruffy form of Oswald toward the rear of the church.

"Isn't that the site of Benjamin Grunchen's grave?"

"Yes."

"Oh dear, he'd better not start digging it up again. Let's get over there and stop him, Pembers."

The two ladies hurried over to where the little dog stood and found him sniffing intently at a pot of bright red carnations.

"How very interesting!" exclaimed Churchill. "These look so fresh they could only have been placed here this morning."

"By Miss Pickwick!"

"Exactly! But on Mr Grunchen's grave?"

"Maybe she considered him a great-uncle."

"We could have accepted that explanation if she'd said the word 'uncle', but she didn't, did she? She distinctly used the word 'aunt'. I think there may be something fishy going on here."

"Why would she have placed carnations on Mr Grunchen's grave?"

"I have no idea, Pembers."

Oswald sniffed excitedly around the base of the pot.

"There's certainly a smell of freshly disturbed earth here, wouldn't you say?" Churchill added. "Oswald must have got a whiff of it, too." Churchill crouched down by the flowers. "I think this pot may have been placed here as a distraction."

"A distraction from what?"

"Miss Pickwick dirtied her gloves, but I don't see why they would be dirty from placing a fresh pot of carnations on the grave of Mr Grunchen. She's been rooting about with her hands somewhere if you ask me."

"Under the pot of carnations, do you think?"

"That's the only logical explanation, wouldn't you say?"

Churchill stooped down and lifted the pot of carnations away from the grave. Beneath it was a section of flattened, yet freshly disturbed, earth.

"Ugh!" exclaimed Pemberley. "How deep did she go?"

"I dread to think, but I suppose there's only one way to find out." Churchill knelt down by the graveside, moved the pot of flowers to one side and retrieved a pair of leather gloves from her handbag.

"You're not going to dig as well, are you, Mrs Churchill?"

"Just some minor excavation work, Pembers."

"But it's a grave!"

"I realise that. I'm hardly going to go digging up poor Mr Grunchen himself, am I?" She pulled on her gloves. "I merely want to find out what that Pickwick woman has been up to. She didn't have obvious dirt on her skirt, did she? She must have hoisted it up and got her stockings grubby instead."

"It wouldn't surprise me. She seems the sort."

"I can't help but notice that you seem to be harbouring an instant dislike of Miss Pickwick."

"I don't know her personally, but I'm always suspicious of people with bright teeth and hair."

"I know what you mean. It's often a sign that there's something a little bit off about them, isn't it? And digging around in Benjamin Grunchen's grave hasn't exactly helped her cause. Right then, here goes."

"Oh, I can't bear to look!"

"I'm merely extracting the upper layer of soil, Pembers. I want to see what she's been doing down here."

"Maybe she decided to rake it over and plant some grass seed. And then she placed a pot of carnations on top of it while she's waiting for the seed to take."

"That's hardly a plausible explanation."

"I know, but I couldn't think of anything else. I can't imagine a single other reason why anyone would want to go digging about in a grave. It gives me the shivers!"

Churchill gently scooped the soil with her gloved hand and moved it into a little pile to her left. "This must be linked to the small hole dug in this same grave a week or two ago."

Pemberley tutted. "I can't understand what the woman has against the poor man. What has he ever done to her?"

"I can't imagine he ever did anything to her. He died in 1865."

"Perhaps his ghost haunted her."

"What nonsense, Pemberley! You don't believe in all that supernatural piffle, do you?"

"Of course not, but maybe she does."

"I think I've found something here."

"Ugh! What is it?"

"It's a piece of fabric, I think."

"A shroud?"

"How could it possibly be a shroud? I've only dug down a couple of inches, and I'd like to think Mr Grunchen's body is enclosed within a coffin."

Churchill continued to excavate the soil. "It looks like a bundle of something," she continued, "wrapped in sacking of some sort. Can you help me, Pembers?"

"All right then, if I must." Pemberley knelt down next to Churchill and began removing the soil. It wasn't long before the two ladies had uncovered a bundle of sacking about the size of a large fruit cake.

"I've no idea what this can be," said Churchill, "but I think we should lift it out."

"What if it's something awfully unpleasant?"

"I can't imagine Miss Pickwick handling anything awfully unpleasant, can you?"

"No, I can't."

"Come on, then. Let's haul this thing out."

Churchill wrapped her hands around the bundle and lifted it out. The sacking was tied with string, which Churchill carefully unknotted and pulled away. Then she cautiously unfolded the sacking.

"Oh, I don't like this at all!" moaned Pemberley. "What if it's another skull?"

"Why would it be a skull?"

"I don't know!"

"Don't panic yet, Pembers, there's another layer to unwrap."

"Miss Pickwick has excellent bundle-wrapping skills."

"She does, doesn't she? This looks like a layer of canvas. And there's more string here. Wait a moment... there, I've got it. And now..."

"Oh, I can't look!" Pemberley covered her face with her hands.

"Don't worry, Pembers, it's nothing scary at all."

"How do you know?"

"Because I'm looking at the contents of the bundle at this very moment."

Pemberley removed her hands, leaving traces of soil all over her face. "Money!" she exclaimed when she saw the pile of banknotes and coins lying uncovered in the bundle.

"That's right. Miss Pickwick has buried a large sum of money in the grave of Benjamin Grunchen."

"Well I never. Where did she get it from?"

"Mr Butterfork's tea chest, perhaps?"

Pemberley gasped. "You think Miss Pickwick is the murderer?"

"She must be. Where else would she have got all this money?"

"But why leave it until now to bury the cash?"

"Perhaps she was allowing a period of time to pass so nobody became suspicious. Maybe the hole Grieves spotted before was a sort of cursory, exploratory hole."

"She was digging about in an attempt to ascertain whether there would be enough space for her to bury Butterfork's money!"

"Exactly."

"But this can't be all of it. He had an enormous tea chest filled with the stuff, from what I heard."

Churchill glanced around the churchyard. "Perhaps she's buried it in a number of graves around here."

Pemberley shook her head in disbelief. "That woman has a lot to answer for. I knew I disliked her as soon as I saw her. But we can't go digging around in all the graves; it wouldn't be right."

"Of course it wouldn't, and we shan't." Churchill stood to her feet and dusted the dirt from her tweed skirt. "I'm afraid this is a matter for Inspector Mappin and his bumbling constables. We'd better go and report it to him."

Chapter 28

"Thanks to your fine work we've uncovered two more bags of money, Mrs Churchill," said Inspector Mappin. "One in the grave of Mrs Sally Fletcher and another in the final resting place of Mr Arthur Brimble."

"The other graves that had been tampered with!" she exclaimed. "This explains it all. I'm only pleased we were able to help, Inspector. I trust Miss Pickwick is firmly under lock and key in your cells."

"Not quite, Mrs Churchill."

"Why ever not?"

"We need to have more than a strong suspicion that she had something to do with it."

"But we saw her coming out of the churchyard!"

"Does that prove she buried the money in Mr Grunchen's grave?"

"Someone had just done so, as the flowers were fresh and the earth had been freshly dug over."

"It could have been someone who visited the churchyard earlier in the morning."

"But she had dirty gloves! She brushed them off and

hid them away in her handbag, didn't she, Miss Pemberley? Ask to see her dirty gloves, Inspector!"

"Dirty gloves would not provide sufficient proof that she buried the money in Mr Grunchen's grave, I'm sorry to say."

"But her shoes were muddy."

"Which suggests she may have walked through some mud in the churchyard, but we still can't be sure she went anywhere near Mr Grunchen's grave."

"I know what you need to do, Inspector. You should ask her which grave she visited this morning. She gave us a vague explanation about some old dead aunt who wasn't really an aunt or something, didn't she, Miss Pemberley? I got the distinct impression she was spinning a tall tale at the time. If she's unable to name the deceased 'relative', that would surely prove she was up to no good."

"It would certainly arouse our suspicions, but it still wouldn't prove she buried the money in the grave."

"Oh fie, Inspector! She was clearly up to no good when we saw her. Miss Pemberley here was instantly suspicious of her, and that's rather uncommon, wouldn't you say, Miss Pemberley? She's usually quite content to give people the benefit of the doubt."

"I'm not sure I am, actually," replied Pemberley. "I'm often rather suspicious of people."

"Not a particularly helpful reply, Miss Pemberley, I must say."

"Never mind that," said Inspector Mappin. "The fact of the matter is there's simply no evidence to suggest Miss Pickwick buried the money in the graves. And when you also consider how respectable the lady is, I think it highly unlikely she had anything to do with it. Extremely unlikely, I'd say."

"Respectable people don't commit crimes then, Inspector?"

"Not as a rule."

"Perhaps some people are merely pretending to be respectable."

"It's possible. But that's rather an unwarranted accusation to throw at Miss Pickwick, don't you think? Especially given that she's the sister of your gentleman companion."

"*Companion?* He's nothing of the kind, Inspector! He simply happens to be painting me at the moment."

"I see."

"Perhaps you'd like to buy the portrait once it's finished, Inspector," suggested Pemberley. "You could hang it above your fireplace."

The inspector gave an astonished cough. "I don't think that would do," he said, looking flustered. "And besides, Mrs Mappin has firm ideas about the pictures we hang on our walls."

"I must say I'm a little offended you didn't jump at the opportunity to hang my portrait in your home, Inspector," said Churchill.

"I'm sure your companion Pickwick will gladly hang it above his fireplace."

Churchill's face reddened. "I don't see why he should, and why are we even discussing my portrait, anyway?"

"You brought it up," said Pemberley.

"I don't think I did. And besides, I've lost track of our conversation now. Where were we?"

"We had reached the point in the conversation at which I told you I couldn't possibly arrest Miss Pickwick because there simply isn't any evidence," replied Inspector Mappin.

"Couldn't you interview her as a witness? I'd be interested to hear her replies. I'd like to know how she'd go about explaining the muddy gloves and which deceased almost family member she was supposedly visiting in the churchyard."

"I could interview her as a witness, I suppose."

"Good. Because if you can find who buried Mr Butterfork's money in the churchyard you'll have found his murderer."

"What makes you think it's Mr Butterfork's money?"

"Oh, come on, Inspector. It's quite obvious, wouldn't you say?"

"It could be his money, but we can't be certain of that."

"Surely that's the most likely explanation?"

"I'd say that it's likely, yes, but there can be no complete certainty about it."

Churchill sighed and helped herself to a ginger snap biscuit.

"This is how one considers these matters when one is an experienced member of the police force, Mrs Churchill," he continued. "Working theories are useful, but assumptions cannot be made. Now, has anyone visited you to claim the ring yet?"

"Not yet."

"How interesting."

"It is rather, isn't it? You'd think someone would be missing it. Have you asked your fellow Masons about it?"

"I have, actually, but no one appears to be missing a ring."

"That is most perplexing. And it also suggests someone is lying."

"Masons don't lie, Mrs Churchill!"

"Hear me out, Inspector. That ring belongs to someone, and he lost it while he was on Crunkle Lane, close to the scene of Mr Butterfork's murder. Now if he'd been in the locality on entirely innocent business, he would have admitted to losing the ring and come forward to collect it, don't you think?"

"I suppose so."

"The fact that he hasn't admitted to losing the ring or come by to collect it suggests he's the guilty party, wouldn't you say? By coming forward to collect the ring he would risk implicating himself!"

"Unless he's scared," added Pemberley.

"What do you mean by that?"

"Perhaps he lost the ring while he was in the locality on innocent business, but then it just so happened that the murder was committed at around the same time. Now he feels wary about coming forward because he thinks everyone will assume he was involved in the murder."

"There is that to consider, I suppose, but it seems unlikely. Have you checked the hands of your Masonic brothers, Inspector?"

"To check whether they're all wearing their rings?"

"Yes."

"No, I haven't."

"Why ever not?"

"Because that would place me on an investigative footing, Mrs Churchill, and I don't want to be an officer of the law when I attend Masonic meetings. I'm merely Mr Mappin when I go there. And besides, Masons don't always wear their rings."

"So you refuse to investigate any Masons at all, even if they may have committed the crime?"

"Masons simply aren't criminals, Mrs Churchill!"

"So why doesn't the chap who lost his ring in Crunkle Lane want to admit he was there?"

"Perhaps he hasn't realised the ring is lost yet."

"How ridiculous! Of course he would have noticed by

now. I'm quite amazed you haven't taken a peek at your friends' hands to see if anyone is missing one, Inspector."

"I'm not on duty when I go to Masonic meetings, Mrs Churchill."

"You turn a blind eye, you mean? I suppose there's at least one good reason for becoming a Freemason in that case."

"A moment ago you were trying to suggest Miss Pickwick was the guilty party," said the inspector. "You really need to make up your mind, Mrs Churchill."

"Perhaps it's both."

"Both of whom?"

"The Freemason who wears a dark grey coat and lost his ring and Miss Pickwick. Perhaps they're in it together."

The inspector tutted and placed his hat back on his head. "I've never heard such nonsense in all my life. I may as well take the ring off your hands while I'm here."

"It'll have to be tomorrow, Inspector."

"Tomorrow?"

"Yes, it'll have been three days by tomorrow, and that's when we're due to hand it over to you."

"I see. Well, thank you again for your assistance in recovering the bags of money, Mrs Churchill, but you really must leave the rest up to me."

"Oh, darn it," said Churchill once the inspector had left. "Miss Pickwick's clearly up to no good, but that fool Mappin has no interest in arresting her."

"He might be right, you know."

"When has that dunderhead ever been right about anything, Pembers? He called her respectable. Pfft! She's clearly fooled him with her smart clothes and winning smile. But she doesn't fool us, does she? We'll have to find out exactly what she was doing in the churchyard. I'm pretty certain she wasn't visiting Great-Auntie Betty."

"How do you know her name?"

"I don't, I just made it up.

"Perhaps Miss Pickwick is completely innocent."

"What do you mean? I thought you were particularly suspicious of her."

"Maybe I was wrong."

"Oh dear, Pembers. I don't know what to think now. Actually, I do, because I like to think I have a good hunch about these things. Perhaps Miss Pickwick didn't bury that money in the churchyard, but either way she was up to no good."

"That means Mr Pickwick may also be involved."

"Nonsense! If anyone around here is genuinely respectable it's him."

"Perhaps he's hoodwinked you, Mrs Churchill."

"I would never allow myself to be hoodwinked, Miss Pemberley."

"If you say so."

"Mr Pickwick is as innocent as the day is long, and Miss Pickwick is as guilty as sin." Even as Churchill spoke these words a seed of doubt began to settle itself in her mind.

Chapter 29

"You must be missing your studio, Percy," said Churchill during her sitting the following day. "Has it been repaired yet?"

"Almost. It's not a fancy studio, however; just an adapted summerhouse, really."

"I recall you telling me now, but it's nice to have one all the same. You must have fairly large grounds to accommodate a summerhouse."

"Oh, nothing too extravagant."

"And a suitably large house to go with them, no doubt."

"It suffices," he said with a smile. "I can't complain."

"Is it in the village or close by?"

"Close by. Near Triddledon Lane, in fact."

"I've never heard of it."

"Just east of here."

"I'm not fishing for the exact address in case you're worried about me paying you a surprise visit, Percy!"

"Oh, that wouldn't worry me at all!"

"Would it not? Gosh." Churchill felt an excitable flip in

her stomach and decided to change the subject. "That buried money was rather a funny old business, don't you think?"

"A very funny business indeed. I can't understand it at all. Why on earth would someone want to bury money in a churchyard?"

"It's all terribly strange."

"Just hold your position there for a moment, Mrs Churchill. The light is falling on you in the most beautiful way, and I simply must capture it."

"Oh, must you? How delightful." Churchill sat as still as possible and listened to the soft, soothing sound of bristles against canvas. "How I wish I could see how my portrait is coming along."

"No, no. Naughty, naughty!" Mr Pickwick grinned and wagged his paintbrush at her in mock admonishment.

"But surely it must remain in view while you're not working on it."

"Not at all. I always keep any works in progress covered with a sheet. Your portrait has its own special place behind the counter in my gallery."

"Does it really?"

"It certainly does."

"I'll have to sneak in one day and take a little look now you've told me that!"

"Then I'd have to give you a little rap over the knuckles with my paintbrush."

"Oh, you wouldn't dare!"

"We'll see about that, shall we?" he said with a wink.

Churchill did all she could to stop herself grinning from ear to ear. "Actually, I have a little admission to make," she ventured once she had regained her composure. "I'm aware that you're a Freemason, Percy, so I hope you don't mind me mentioning this."

"Why should I?"

"It's rather a personal, private matter, you see."

"I'm entirely comfortable about discussing my personal, private matters with you, Mrs Churchill."

"Oh goodness, really?" She gave a nervous giggle. "Well I never!" She patted her warm brow with a clean white handkerchief. "Call me Annabel, by the way."

"Here's my ring, Annabel," he said, holding up his hand so she could see the band of gold, "and I wear it with pride. Have you discovered who the owner of the missing ring is yet?"

"Sadly no, nor have we recovered the ring itself. It's all a bit of a sorry mess. I don't suppose you know whether one of your Masonic brothers happens to have lost a ring?"

"I'm afraid not. I do wish I could be more helpful, Mrs Churchill, but I think you'd better report the theft to Inspector Mappin."

"Oh, I couldn't possibly do that! He'll be terribly cross if he finds out it's been stolen."

"But it's not your fault."

"Well, I may have accidentally left the door unlocked."

"It's still not your fault. You didn't invite anyone in to steal it, did you?"

"I didn't. You're quite right there, Percy."

"Then tell him it was stolen so he can track down the culprit."

"I'm not convinced he's capable of that. And besides, he'd already asked to keep it safe down at the police station."

"Do you know what I think?"

"What's that?"

"I think it'll turn up one way or another."

"What makes you say that?"

"These things always do. The moment you stop looking for something, there it is right in front of you. I've experienced this strange phenomenon with so many things during my lifetime."

"Oh, I see."

Churchill was about to ask what he was referring to when he interrupted her thoughts.

"There's the light again, it's simply divine! Just hold still for me, Annabel."

Mr Pickwick's charming demeanour was making it difficult for Churchill to broach the topic of his sister. After a few minutes of quiet she decided there was no more time to waste. "I hear the police are asking all those who have visited the churchyard in recent days whether they happened to see anything unusual. Have they spoken to your sister yet, do you know?"

"My sister?" He paused, his paintbrush poised.

"Yes, Miss Pickwick."

"I know her name all right, but why would they want to speak to Agnes?"

"She was in the churchyard yesterday; the day the money was discovered, in fact. Miss Pemberley and I saw her leaving, and she told us she'd just visited the grave of an elderly aunt. Well, not a real aunt, but a friend she considered an aunt."

"Ah, yes. I know she often likes to visit old Mrs Longhorn's final resting place."

"Perhaps while she was visiting old Mrs Longhorn, she caught sight of someone desecrating old Mr Grunchen."

"She didn't mention that she had."

"I don't suppose you know whether Mrs Longhorn's resting place is anywhere near Mr Grunchen's, do you?"

"I've no idea at all, I'm afraid."

"Have you ever visited Mrs Longhorn yourself?"

"Oh yes, many a time. We were so close that I considered her a great-aunt."

"Just as your sister did."

"Exactly."

"Whereabouts is she buried in the churchyard?"

"My sister?"

"No, Mrs Longhorn."

"Oh, yes!" He gave a chuckle. "I get a little confused sometimes, it must be my age!"

"You're not so very old, Percy."

"I'm afraid I am."

"I'm sure there's plenty of life left in those old bones yet."

"There might be if there was someone around to keep them lively."

"Is that so? And is there?"

"There might be... or there might not be, Annabel." His neat moustache gave a playful twitch.

"I see. Well, I'm not entirely sure what this conversation is about now. Let's return to the subject of the money in the graveyard."

"Must we?"

"I do like a good mystery, Percy! Surely you've learnt that about me by now."

"I suppose that's why you're a private detective."

"Absolutely. Now, can you roughly recall where Mrs Longhorn's final resting place is?"

"Yes, I think so. When the churchyard path forks you take the left path, which wends its way round in a little loop. If I recall correctly, she's just on the right after the little loop."

"I see." Churchill narrowed her eyes as she tried to picture the location in her mind. "Not enormously far from Mr Grunchen, then. Are you quite sure your sister saw no one suspicious lurking around there? Someone with a fresh bunch of red carnations, perhaps?"

"She didn't mention that she had seen anyone. Perhaps you could ask her yourself."

"I suppose I could. She might take it the wrong way, though, don't you think?"

"Why would she?"

"If I start asking your dear sister probing questions about Mr Grunchen's grave she might mistakenly think that I suspect her of something."

"Why would she think that?"

"People often put their defences up when they feel as if they're being probed."

"I'm quite sure my sister wouldn't mind at all. She's quite an affable sort."

"I see. Well, thank you, Percy. I might just speak to her in that case."

"Hold it there!"

"What is it?"

"Freeze!"

"Pardon?"

"It's the light, Annabel."

"Again?"

"Did you notice it change just then? The way it's falling upon you now is simply wonderful. Ethereal, even. Let me just capture it."

Chapter 30

"Where would Miss Pickwick have bought a bunch of red carnations from, Pembers?"

"If she did buy them, that is."

"That's what we need to find out, isn't it? If we can find the florist who sold Miss Pickwick those red carnations, we'll know for sure that she was up to no good at Benjamin Grunchen's graveside."

"There's only one florist in Compton Poppleford and that's Mrs Crackleby."

"That should make it relatively straightforward, then. She has a stall on the high street, doesn't she?"

"Yes, but we can't possibly go and speak to her or she'll sell us all her flowers."

Churchill gave a laugh. "She might manage that with more susceptible types, but I'm sure I'll be able to resist her cut-throat sales tactics when I encounter them."

The two ladies and Oswald made their way along the high street toward the red awning of Mrs Crackleby's flower stall.

"Mr Pickwick suggested I ask his sister directly about the red carnations, but I can't imagine her taking kindly to that, can you?"

"Not at all," replied Pemberley. "Ladies of her sort do not like to be questioned. And she'll immediately assume you suspect her of something, which will bring out the very worst in her."

"Maybe we're judging her a little too harshly. Mr Pickwick described her as an 'affable sort'."

"Does she look the affable sort to you?"

"No, she doesn't."

"Nor to me."

"But perhaps we shouldn't judge the woman on her appearance. Maybe we should take some time to acquaint ourselves with her a little better first."

"And how would we do that?"

"I really don't know."

"Perhaps your friendship with Mr Pickwick could grow a little warmer. That way you might encounter her more frequently."

"Pembers! What a scandalous suggestion!"

"It may be the only way."

"If we discover that she didn't buy any red carnations from Mrs Crackleby we can forget all about her."

"And if she did?"

"We'll cross that bridge when we come to it. But I must say all this talk of a warm friendship makes me sound like some sort of floozy. It's quite disgraceful!"

Churchill and Pemberley walked up to the florist's stall to find buckets and baskets of colourful blooms arranged neatly beneath the awning.

"Good morning, Mrs Crackleby."

"Oh, how lovely to have some customers at last! Mrs Churchill and Miss Pemberley, isn't it? Compton Poppleford's private detectives. I could have sworn everyone who walked past me this morning was quite determined not to notice me standing here trying to sell my wares. These poor chrysanthemums are quite bereft without a pretty vase to sit in atop an occasional table."

"I didn't realise they were sentient," said Pemberley.

"No, they're chrysanthemums, as I just said. And as for the poor peonies, they crave nothing more than a pleasant, well-lit spot beside the window. Not full sunlight, mind you, but a place where they'll be noticed and admired. Visitors never fail to be impressed by a vase of beautiful peonies. They lift a room, wouldn't you say?"

"Indeed," responded Churchill, resolutely determined that she wouldn't be purchasing any.

"It's usually a shilling for a bunch but I'll give you two for a shilling and sixpence."

"Perhaps later, Mrs Crackleby. We've come to have a word with you about one of your customers."

"Ah, yes. Who would that be, then?"

"Miss Pickwick. She's the sister of Mr Pickwick the gallery owner."

"I've never heard of her."

"We have reason to believe she may have bought a bunch of red carnations from you."

"I can't say that I remember."

"Have you sold a bunch of red carnations to anyone recently?"

"Yes, I have."

"May we ask who you sold it to?"

"I'm afraid my memory's a little hazy, Mrs Churchill."

"You can't remember the name of a single customer to whom you sold a bunch of red carnations over the past few days?"

"I find my memory improves significantly whenever I sell a few bunches of flowers."

"A few? How many is a few?"

Churchill and Pemberley returned to their office half an hour later completely weighed down with fresh flowers.

"*Seven shillings!*" fumed Churchill. "That woman had us wrapped around her little finger!"

"But it wasn't all for nothing," replied Pemberley, setting two bunches of chrysanthemums, a display of gladioli and an arrangement of lilies down on her desk. "We have all these lovely flowers to show for it. Don't they smell delightful?"

"We only have two vases," replied Churchill. "What else can we put them in?"

Pemberley looked around the room. "The teapot?"

"But we need that for our tea!"

"We could take them out whenever we have tea and put them back in afterwards. Same with the milk jug."

"They'll have to do for now, I suppose. I think I have a few old vases rattling around at home that I can bring in tomorrow."

"I suppose we can fit all the chrysanthemums together in the milk jug. There! They look quite lovely, don't they?"

"I see what you mean about Mrs Crackleby. It's no wonder people avoid her like the plague when they're walking along the high street."

"If you so much as stray within three yards of her flower stall you're in for it."

"I can appreciate that now. However, she did reveal something rather interesting, didn't she? We now have confirmation that Miss Pickwick purchased a bunch of red carnations on the very same day we saw a fresh bunch on Mr Grunchen's grave. She must have put them there, just as we suspected."

"It could be a coincidence."

"If it is a coincidence it's one of such a colossal size that it would be practically improbable."

"But we still can't prove, without a doubt, that Miss Pickwick put the vase of red carnations on Mr Grunchen's grave."

"I'd say that it was incredibly likely, wouldn't you?"

"But that wouldn't be enough to stand up in a court of law."

"Oh, Pembers, you sound like one of those boring barrister types who ruin everybody's fun."

"We'll just have to carry out a little more detective work to prove it."

"But how?"

"I don't know."

"Tsk!" said Churchill dejectedly.

"Coo-ee! Anybody home?" A red-haired lady poked her head through the door.

"This isn't our home, Mrs Thonnings. It's our place of work."

"Yes, of course. I only said it because you spend so much time here." Once she had stepped inside the room, she paused to survey the blooms. "I see you got caught by Mrs Crackleby."

"Indeed we did," replied Churchill.

"I give her a wide berth whenever I walk along the high street. I once strayed a little too close to her stall while stepping sideways to avoid Inspector Mappin on his bicycle and ended up with three bunches of freesias."

"You should have billed Inspector Mappin for them."

"I tried, but he wouldn't hear of it."

"That doesn't surprise me in the least. He charges around on that bicycle expecting everyone to leap out of his way."

"It's about to get even worse, you know."

"How so?"

"He's on the waiting list for a motorcycle, apparently."

"Oh no! That'll give him an enormously big head."

"He says it's essential so he can respond to emergencies quickly."

Churchill snorted. "Since when did Inspector Mappin respond quickly to emergencies? What a joke!"

"He presumably needs the motorcycle because he's currently unable to," Pemberley chipped in.

"Whose side are you on, Pembers?"

"No one's. I'm merely trying to view the situation objectively."

"Pah! He'll be a total menace on that motorcycle, there's no doubt about it. Is that what you came to tell us, Mrs Thonnings? About Mappin's motorcycle?"

"No, actually it was... Oh dear, do excuse me." She pulled a handkerchief from her sleeve and sneezed into it.

"Bless you!"

"Thank you. I came here to ask about. Oh dear..." She sneezed again.

"Bless you again."

"Thank you. I've heard all about your portrait, Mrs Churchill."

"Have you indeed?"

"Achoo!"

"Bless you."

"Thank you. Yes, and I was wondering whether you thought... Achoo!"

"Bless you."

"Thank you. I think it's the flowers."

"What were you wondering?"

"I was wondering whether you thought Mr Pickwick might be interested in painting me."

"He's quite busy painting me at the moment."

"I realise that. But perhaps once he's finished your portrait, he might consider doing mine."

"I have no idea, Mrs Thonnings, I'm afraid you'd need to ask him yourself. But I imagine he looks for certain characteristics when choosing a sitter."

"Such as?"

"Only Mr Pickwick would know that, but I sensed when he asked me to sit for him that he felt I possessed certain qualities which conveyed a particular mood. You only have to look at his portrait of Viscountess Bathshire to get an idea of what I mean."

"I'm not sure I know what you mean, Mrs Churchill," said Pemberley.

"Well you should, Miss Pemberley. You've seen the painting of Viscountess Bathshire, have you not?"

"Yes, but I still don't know what you mean when you say the subject is in possession of certain qualities."

"It's a sort of bearing; call it class, if you like, or even elegance. A sort of... *je ne sais quoi*." Churchill observed Pemberley's baffled expression and sighed. "The fact of the matter is that Mr Pickwick cannot simply go around painting everyone in the village. Can you imagine the size of the queue outside his door? It's something that has to be by invitation only."

"Achoo!"

"Bless you yet again, Mrs Thonnings."

"Thank you. Achoo!"

"And again."

"Thank you. Perhaps I'll ask Mr Pickwick if he'd like to invite me to be painted."

"Ask away, Mrs Thonnings, but—"

"Achoo! Oh dear, it's definitely the flowers."

"Oh, good grief, Mrs Thonnings! Perhaps you could take your sneezing somewhere else for the time being!"

Chapter 31

"I DON'T KNOW what poor Mr Pickwick will think when he discovers his sister is a criminal," said Churchill as she and Pemberley walked down to the police station.

"There may still be a tiny element of doubt, but I certainly think she's guilty," replied Pemberley. "It's quite apparent to me that she's been hiding Mr Butterfork's money in the churchyard graves. What a despicable thing to do."

"Awful! She must have planned it carefully, with several visits to the churchyard carried out. During each visit she made some sort of mark on the headstone of any grave she deemed suitable. Whether it was cleaning the headstone a little, leaving a rose or digging an exploratory hole, these were all methods of marking the graves so she could return to bury her haul. Mr Grieves the sexton will be very interested to hear all this once we've spoken to Inspector Mappin. I told you we'd solve it, didn't I? In fact, we've solved both cases at the same time. Fancy Miss Pickwick being a murderer! I despair for her poor brother, I really do. He's such a gentleman. I can't understand how he should have turned out so nicely and she so evil!"

"They do seem to be very different in character."

"They do indeed!"

"Not like brother and sister at all."

"Not at all. Wait a minute, what are you implying, Pembers?"

"Nothing. It was just an observation."

"Well, I still feel terribly sorry for him. His sister must be the black sheep of the family."

"But what about the dark figure?" asked Pemberley. "And the Freemason's ring? And the dark grey overcoat?"

"The dark figure must have been her," said Churchill. "It's no stretch of the imagination to suggest that she possesses a dark grey overcoat."

"And the ring?"

"Perhaps she dropped it there to mislead the police."

"It's possible."

"Or maybe it has nothing to do with the murder at all."

"Maybe it doesn't. That would be a good thing, given that we still don't know where it is."

Churchill and Pemberley reached the small white police station at the bottom of the high street and stepped inside.

"Flowers?" queried Inspector Mappin.

"We thought you might like a nice bunch of chrysanthemums, Inspector." He eyed the pink blooms warily as Churchill placed them on his desk.

"We don't have flowers in the police station as a rule."

"Then why don't you make a new rule? They certainly brighten this drab place up a little." Churchill noticed something small and gold on the inspector's leather desk mat. "That's not a Freemason ring, is it?"

"As a matter of fact, it is. Another one! I need to have a word with my Masonic brothers about taking better care of their belongings. Has anyone claimed the ring you found yet, Mrs Churchill?"

"Erm, not yet, Inspector. In fact, the one you have there on your desk may well be the ring in question."

"This one?"

"Yes, I think so."

"But I caught one of the Flatboots trying to flog it down at the Wagon and Carrot."

"Well, I should probably confess now that the ring has gone missing from our office, Inspector. Someone broke in and stole it."

"Who? When?"

"We don't know who, but it was shortly after we placed the notice in the *Gazette*."

"Why didn't you tell me?"

"Because I'd given you every assurance that the drawer in my desk was perfectly safe, only it turned out not to be."

Inspector Mappin tutted. "At least we've recovered it now. I'm surprised no one has laid claim to it yet."

"Have you arrested the relevant Flatboot for breaking into our office?"

"No, because I didn't realise he had. And besides, we can't be sure who broke into your office. The Flatboots have a reputation for fencing stolen goods, but some other scallywag may have carried out the robbery itself. If you'd reported it to me at the time, I could have done some proper investigating."

"I see. Well, it's all water under the bridge now, Inspector. In the meantime, you'd better get your hand-cuffs ready, as we've an unquestionable arrest for you to make."

"Really? Have you solved a case, Mrs Churchill? You

usually make some sort of grand announcement at a large gathering in these instances."

"I think this one needs to be handled rather quietly. There's a certain gentleman I'd prefer not to embarrass, you see."

"Ah. Would the suspect happen to be Miss Pickwick, by any chance?"

"I've no idea how you came to such a swift conclusion, Inspector, but yes."

Churchill spent the next few minutes explaining why Miss Pickwick was undoubtedly guilty of Mr Butterfork's murder.

Inspector Mappin listened intently, then sat back in his chair and folded his arms. "It's a compelling story, Mrs Churchill, but not completely convincing... yet."

"What do you mean? How can it not be?"

"I said *yet*, Mrs Churchill. That means I'll need to do a little more detailed investigating myself."

"Oh, fiddlesticks, Inspector! It's quite clear the woman should be behind bars."

"I'd like to interview Miss Pickwick first."

"You haven't even done that yet?"

"No, but her name is on my list." He opened his note-book and consulted it. "Yes, there she is all right. She's about four people down, but I suppose I could move her up to the top." He drew a little arrow on the page. "There, I shall speak to her this afternoon."

"Merely *speak* to her, Inspector?"

"And make some further enquiries."

"But Miss Pemberley and I have already made plenty of enquiries."

"I'm sure you have, Mrs Churchill. It's quite impressive really, given that you weren't even meant to be working on this case."

Chapter 32

CHURCHILL SPOTTED a small crowd on the high street as she made her way to the office the following morning. Intrigued, she walked past her premises and up to the group standing outside the bank.

It wasn't long before she spotted the tall, slender frame of her trusty assistant Pemberley standing next to the shorter, red-haired figure of Mrs Thonnings.

"Goodness, what's happened here?" she asked the two ladies.

"It's Mr Burbage," replied Pemberley.

"Oh crikey, how awful!"

"He's in a bad way," added Mrs Thonnings.

"I should think he would be."

"He didn't deserve it."

"Absolutely not," agreed Churchill shaking her head sadly. "Mr Burbage was nothing but a harmless bank manager. I used to enjoy my little chats with him while I was making my deposits and withdrawals. I can't pretend he was a terribly exciting man, but he was a bank manager after all. And as bank managers go, he was one of the most proficient I've ever known. It's so terribly sad."

"I can see him talking to Inspector Mappin now," said Pemberley, standing on her tiptoes and craning her neck to see over the heads of the onlookers standing in front of her.

"Talking to Mappin?" asked Churchill incredulously. "How can he be talking when he's dead?"

"Who's dead?" asked Mrs Thonnings.

"Mr Burbage! You just told me he'd been murdered!"

"He hasn't been murdered," corrected Mrs Thonnings, "he's been robbed! The *bank* has been robbed."

"Oh." Churchill felt a surprising sense of deflation. "The pair of you can be incredibly misleading at times."

From the corner of her eye she spotted the large form of Mrs Hatweed and instantly wondered whether the housekeeper had any further details about the robbery.

"Oh hello, Mrs Churchill," said Mrs Hatweed as the portly detective nudged up alongside her.

"Good morning, Mrs Hatweed. I don't suppose you've heard any whispers of what's been occurring at the bank?"

"Apparently they'd been digging the tunnel for two weeks."

"Tunnel? What tunnel?"

"That's how they got into the bank; they dug a tunnel. Then last night they dug the final bit, which brought them out right in the middle of the vault!" She chuckled. "Clever really, don't you think?"

"I'm afraid I still don't quite understand. The robbers dug a tunnel into the vault?"

"Yes."

"But where did it begin?"

"In their basement."

"Whose basement?"

"The building next door." She pointed a finger at it.

"But that's Pickwick's Gallery!"

"Exactly."

"The robbers dug a tunnel to the bank from Mr Pickwick's basement?"

"Yes. It went down into the ground, beneath the dividing wall and up into the bank. Then they emptied out the vault and carried it all back through to the basement of the gallery."

"All without his knowledge? How terribly sneaky. Poor Mr Pickwick!"

Mrs Hatweed gave a hearty laugh that made her curls bounce. "Oh, Mrs Churchill, you are funny!"

Churchill felt confused by this response. "It's terribly unfortunate for Mr Pickwick. How will he convince the police that he had nothing to do with it?"

Mrs Hatweed laughed even louder. "I'd say he was rather conspicuous by his absence, wouldn't you?"

"Absence? Has he gone somewhere?"

"Yes. He's taken off with that woman who was supposed to be his sister."

"But Miss Pickwick *is* his sister."

Mrs Hatweed responded with another laugh, which riled Churchill further. "That's what he told you, wasn't it?"

Churchill glared at the red, mirth-filled face of Mrs Hatweed as several realisations settled themselves in her mind.

"Are you suggesting Mr Pickwick robbed the bank?" she asked.

"Yes! Pickwick and his lady friend – a gangster's moll if ever I saw one – along with some young ruffian they'd employed to do the digging. I saw that young Flatboot hanging around the gallery a few times and wondered what on earth his business could have been there. You don't usually see someone with heavily stained trousers frequenting the local art gallery."

"They've just upped and left? Taken the money and vanished?"

"Yep."

"I refuse to believe it!"

"Refuse all you like, Mrs Churchill, but it's the truth."

Churchill's thoughts turned to her portrait. "It can't be true," she muttered beneath her breath, pushing her way through the crowd until she reached the door of Pickwick's Gallery. The door was locked but she saw two constables loitering inside: one with a brown moustache and the other wearing spectacles. Churchill recognised them as Constable Russell and Constable Dawkins, the two officers she had encountered in the churchyard. She hammered repeatedly on the door until Russell answered it.

"You can't come in here," he said.

"Oh hello, Constable Russell. Remember me?"

"Yes, but you still can't come in."

"I've come for something that belongs to me."

"What might that be?"

"There's a painting over there behind the counter. It's covered with a piece of cloth, but it's a portrait of me."

"I'm afraid I can't let you inside, Mrs Churchill."

"You've told me that already. Could you just bring the painting over to me?"

"I can't allow you to remove anything from the scene."

"Fine, but can I at least take a look at it?"

"Hmm, I don't know." He turned and looked over at Constable Dawkins. "Mrs Churchill wants to look at that painting behind the counter."

"Why?"

"She says it's hers."

"It'll only take a minute of your time, Constables," she pleaded.

Constable Dawkins gave a shrug and sauntered over to the counter. He peered behind it before retrieving the painting, which was still covered with a sheet, and brought it over to her.

"Thank you," she said. "I won't even touch it, and you can pop it back exactly where you found it, but I'd like to look at it, please."

"Why?"

"Just to check it's the right one. Can you lift the sheet?"

The constable did as he was told and lifted the cover from the painting.

Churchill gasped, as if winded from a blow to the stomach. She took a step back, closed her eyes, reopened them, then gasped again.

On the canvas in front of her was the crudely painted form of a person wearing blue. There was nothing to suggest the person was female, let alone Mrs Churchill. Countless layers of paint had been daubed carelessly on top of one another, creating a work resembling that of a young child let loose with a paintbrush.

"That's not very good, is it?" commented Constable Russell. "Are you sure it's yours?"

"No, it's not mine," replied Churchill, steadily backing away. "I was mistaken... Thank you for your time, Constable."

"Are you all right, Mrs Churchill?" he asked. "You look rather pale."

"I am, I..." Her legs began to feel a little unsteady. "I think I'd feel a lot better if I just sat down here for a moment." A strange buzzing sensation filled Churchill's head as she lowered herself onto the cobbles.

"Assistance, please!" Constable Russell called out.

"Does anyone have a chair? A blanket? Smelling salts? A glass of water?"

"There's no need to fuss, Constable, I'm quite all right. I just need a moment to recover myself."

Churchill pushed her handbag behind her head and used it as a pillow as a group of concerned faces gathered around and peered down at her. She closed her eyes as the faces began to swim and swirl.

"Mrs Churchill!" shrilled Pemberley. "Whatever's the matter?"

"Just a little shock to the system, Pembers. Nothing to worry about. I'll be quite all right in a moment."

Pemberley knelt beside her. "Oh, Mrs Churchill! Stay with us!"

"I'm not dying, Pembers, I'm absolutely fine. Just a little... overwrought."

A heavy sense of shame and dismay lay upon her as she realised Mr Pickwick had fooled her; that he was nothing more than a common crook and she had well and truly fallen for his charms. Her chest ached as though she'd been kicked in the ribs by a horse.

"What a bitter blow," she murmured. "What an utter betrayal. How was I so easily fooled, Pembers?"

Then she felt a swell of anger surge through her body. The man had lied to her repeatedly and abused her trust. Her teeth clenched and she balled her fists. "What I wouldn't give right now to find that man and give him a darn good talking to! If I ever, *ever*, see him again, I will not be responsible for the violence I wreak upon his person!"

Oswald began to lick her face as she shook her fist at the blue sky above her head.

"Now that tickles," she said, trying to push him off. "Please remove your dog from my face, Pembers."

"He's trying to revive you, Mrs Churchill. He's like one of those St Bernard rescue dogs in the Alps."

"They're a little more useful because they happen to carry brandy."

"They don't, actually, that's just a myth."

"Right, well I could certainly do with a tot of restorative brandy about now." Churchill pushed herself up and tried to stand. She finally did so with the help of Pemberley and two other members of the crowd.

"Let's get you down to the Wagon and Carrot," said Pemberley, holding her arm. "I'm sure we can find something restorative in there."

Chapter 33

"Call me a silly old fool, Pembers, but I once considered that accursed Pickwick fellow to be almost on an equal footing with the late, great Detective Chief Inspector Churchill."

The two ladies were seated in a dingy corner of the Wagon and Carrot public house. Oswald lay beneath the table, chewing on something he had found beside the fireplace.

"You're a silly old fool," Pemberley replied obediently.

Churchill took a gulp of her third brandy. "Why, oh why, was I charmed by him? I believed every word he told me!"

"He was a charming man. These confidence tricksters often are. In fact they have to be, otherwise they wouldn't be very good confidence tricksters, would they?"

"But he was more than that, Pembers. He was a bank robber! What an utter disgrace. A gentleman like him!"

"A gentleman *criminal*."

"Only he isn't a gentleman; he's a scoundrel. And as

for his sister, we knew there was something up with *her*, didn't we?"

"I'm not convinced she was even his sister."

Churchill took another gulp of brandy and sighed. "I suppose there wasn't a very strong family resemblance, was there? There isn't always one, of course, but there was really no resemblance there whatsoever. What a horrible man. A horrible, horrible man!"

"And woman."

"Yes! The pair of them are just as bad as each other. Why didn't I see it sooner, Pembers? I should have realised. I'm a private detective, for goodness' sake, I'm supposed to spot these things! Oh, where's my brandy gone? Did you drink it?"

"You did, Mrs Churchill."

"Then it's only right that I should have another."

"We only came here for something restorative. I'd say you were more than restored by now. Perhaps even a little over-restored."

"Just one more, Pembers, and then we can resume our normal day's work."

"Will you be capable of a normal day's work after drinking four brandies, Mrs Churchill?"

"Of course I will! I'm quite sure my day will be even more productive than usual."

"Really?"

"Yes! Now I'll have a fourth whatnot, and then we can get on with it. Are you having a fourth, Pembers?"

"No. I've only had the one, and that suited me just fine."

"Well, if you're sure, then, but if you ask me I think you should have another."

. . .

"Gosh it's bright out here," commented Churchill as the two ladies and Oswald emerged from the Wagon and Carrot. "And what's happened to the cobbles?"

"What's wrong with them?"

"I don't know, that's what I asked you. They seem a little bumpier than usual."

"I see. Would you like to take my arm?"

"Yes, I will, thank you. Bumpier and lumpier."

The two ladies began to walk along the high street toward their office.

"Lumpier and bumpier. What am I talking about, Pembers?"

"The cobbles, I think."

"That's right! Lumpy, bumpy cobbles. I have to say I'm completely heartbroken about that scoundrel Pickwick. Dastardly, that's what he is! You should have seen the picture he painted of me. Actually, I'm glad you didn't; I've seen better-looking dogs' dinners! He was merely pretending to paint me, Pembers. *Pretending!* All that talk of '*Hark, see how the light falls upon you, Mrs Churchill.*' I've never heard so much baloney in all my days, and yet I fell for it. I completely fell for it!"

"So you've said, Mrs Churchill."

"It's not the cobbles, you know. It's my shoes."

"Your shoes?"

"Yes, they're the lumpy, bumpy things. I'd better take them off."

"I wouldn't do that if I were you, Mrs Churchill."

"I would." She bent down and removed her shoes. "There. Don't toes look funny in stockings?"

"Please put your shoes back on, Mrs Churchill."

"Why? I like the feel of these cobbles without shoes. They feel all... cobbly."

"You'll hurt your feet."

"Nonsense. My feet are as tough as old boots." Churchill opened her handbag and attempted to shove her shoes inside.

"Your feet will hurt once the brandy's worn off."

"Worn off? I didn't have that much."

"You had five in the end."

"I thought it was four."

"You had 'one for the road', as you put it."

"Ah yes, but that's still only four. One never counts the one for the road. Darn it, I can't quite fit these shoes inside my handbag. I'll have to leave it unfastened."

Churchill looped her arm through Pemberley's and leaned against her trusty assistant as they made their way back to the office. As the inebriated detective stumbled along, she noticed a shiny motor car pull up outside the town hall. An elegant lady dressed in mint green stepped out, and Oswald ran up to greet her.

"Oh look, it's Lady Darby!" exclaimed Churchill. "My favourite lady in Dorset!"

"I think we should cross the street," said Pemberley, tugging at Churchill's arm.

"Why? I'd very much like to speak to Lady Darby!"

"I really don't think you should at this moment in time."

"But she's my great friend!"

"And if you want to remain her friend, we should cross the street so she doesn't see you while you're tipsy."

"Tipsy? What nonsense, Pambers."

"*Pem*bers."

"I prefer Pambers. I'm not tipsy, Pambers, and how dare you suggest such a thing. Anyway, I insist on speaking to my friend."

"You'll embarrass yourself, Mrs Churchill, and she'll uninvite you to her garden party."

"Embarrass myself? Since when have I ever done such a thing?" Churchill pulled away from Pemberley. "Yoo-hoo! Lady Darby!" she trilled, waving at the lady who was just about to step inside the town hall.

Churchill woke later that afternoon to find herself lying on the settee in her front room. Sunlight was filtering in through the window and she felt a strange weight on her chest.

"Oh dear, what time is it?" she moaned as a dull pain throbbed in her head. "What day is it even? And where did this fur blanket come from?"

The fur blanket raised its head and yawned.

"Oh, it's you, Oswald! I've a vague memory of Miss Pemberley accompanying me here, though why she had to do that I'll never know... I recall drinking a brandy or two at the Wagon and Carrot, and then..."

"Tea!" announced Pemberley as she brought in a tray complete with a teapot, cups and a plate of sandwiches.

"Thank you, Pembers. I don't think I've ever seen such a welcome sight in my life!"

Oswald jumped down onto the floor as Churchill raised herself up into a sitting position.

"How did I end up falling asleep?" she asked. "I don't even remember lying down. I was just trying to recall what happened, in fact. We went to the Wagon and Carrot, and then we left and... Why did we come here?"

"You were rather tired and emotional, Mrs Churchill."

"Well yes, and it's all the fault of that darned Pickwick fellow. Took me for a complete fool, he did. Did you see the 'portrait' he painted of me? Oh, such wicked deceit!"

"You must forget all about him now, Mrs Churchill.

Thinking about everything he did will cause you nothing but further pain."

"You're right. I'll push him out of my mind completely, and when he and his… sister, or lady friend or whatever she is, are finally caught and stand trial for their misdemeanours I shall sit on the public benches in the court-room and jeer at him."

"I think that might place you in contempt of court, Mrs Churchill."

"I don't care about that, Pembers! Frankly, I care not a jot. They can throw me out as soon as I've shown him exactly what I think of him."

"It's probably best if you get a little more rest," added Pemberley, pouring out the tea and handing Churchill a cup and saucer.

"Thank you, Pembers, you're a treasure. Goodness, what a day! How lovely it is to just sit down and be calm for a moment. Those sandwiches look quite delicious. Is that ham?"

"Yes, with a little of the lettuce I found growing in your cold frame."

"Thank you, Pembers. What would I do without you?"

A cloudy memory began to materialise into something a little more distinct as Churchill sipped at her tea. Then an uncomfortable sense of dread started swimming in her stomach. "Did we see Lady Darby after we left the Wagon and Carrot, Pembers?"

"Erm… Yes we did, actually."

"You didn't allow me to speak to her, did you?"

"I tried to stop you."

"Did you succeed?"

"Not quite."

The sense of dread increased into a sharp pang of

alarm, and Churchill's tea slopped into her saucer. "Did I speak to her?"

"Yes."

"Oh dear. What did I say, exactly?"

"It's rather difficult to summarise, Mrs Churchill."

"At least give me a hint, Pembers. Did I embarrass myself?"

"That's rather subjective, isn't it?"

"What on earth did I say?"

"You recounted the morning's events to her."

"The robbery at the bank, you mean?"

"Yes."

"Well, that's all right, I suppose. Was I polite about it?"

"Most of the time."

"What do you mean?"

"There were a few choice words."

"Choice?"

"I consider them quite unrepeatable."

"Oh no! That bad?"

"They were mainly adjectives... and a few nouns. All of them used to describe Mr Pickwick in one way or another."

"Oh." Churchill shook her head in shame.

"You also told Lady Darby you had been looking forward to having Mr Pickwick accompany you to her garden party, which was news to me."

"Oh no. I didn't say that, did I?"

"Yes. I didn't realise you'd been harbouring such warm feelings toward him."

"I hadn't! I liked the man, of course, but not in that sense. I can hardly believe I told her such a thing! Oh dear, how shameful."

"Had you asked him to accompany you?"

"Heavens, no!"

"But you must have considered it."

"Not at all!" Churchill took a sip of tea. "Well, I may have considered it for a minute or two, but then I dismissed the idea from my mind. There was, perhaps, a fleeting moment when he was painting me during which I might have thought about it, but I certainly had no intention of asking him, and I'm quite ashamed that I mentioned it to Lady Darby. I trust I didn't detain her for too long."

"No, not long at all. She made an excuse that she was late for a meeting with the mayor."

"Ah."

"That was just after you shared Mrs Thonnings's joke with her."

"Oh no… which one? I do hope it wasn't the one about the butler, the cook and the pumpkin!"

"I'm afraid it was."

"I told Lady Darby the joke about the butler, the cook and the pumpkin? Oh goodness, what a travesty! That's my fate sealed. There'll be no hope of me going to Lord and Lady Darby's garden party now." Churchill set her cup and saucer down and rested her head in her hands. "The next time I ask for a nice restorative brandy you must flatly refuse, Pembers."

"I'll do my best."

"I don't suppose Lady Darby laughed at the joke, by any chance?" she asked hopefully, raising her head a little.

"No, she didn't."

"Oh dear, then I suppose I shall have to accept that our budding friendship is at an end." She picked up her tea again. "I actually think that joke is quite funny. Members of the upper classes often lack a decent sense of humour, don't you find?"

Chapter 34

"Turns out you were right about Miss Pickwick, Mrs Churchill," said Inspector Mappin when he paid a visit to the office the following day.

"It's just a shame I was so wrong about *Mr* Pickwick," she replied sullenly.

"He fooled us all," said the inspector, "but only until I received an interesting telephone call from a detective from the Metropolitan Police. He informed me that three seasoned criminals – Mr James 'Gentleman Jim' Snareskin, Mr Alf 'Ratface' Rudgepole and Miss Molly 'Cutpurse' Fennel – were known to be frequenting the Compton Poppleford area."

"Gosh, they sound like quite the motley crew. Any sign of them, Inspector?"

"Very much so. A police messenger made the journey down from London yesterday with photographs of the trio. When I saw the photographs of these three individuals, I recognised them all immediately. Mr Snareskin had renamed himself Mr Percival Pickwick and Miss Fennel had posed as his sister, Miss Agnes Pickwick."

"Snareskin? That's his real name?"

"Yes."

"Ugh, what a horrible name! No wonder he was so keen to change it to Pickwick."

"And what about Ratface Rudgepole?" asked Pemberley. "Who's he?"

"You'll never guess," replied the inspector.

"In that case you'd better tell us," responded Churchill dryly.

"None other than…"

"Yes?"

"Mr Butterfork!"

"Mr Butterfork was Ratface Rudgepole?" exclaimed Churchill. "And Pickwick, I mean Gentleman Jim Snareskin, knew him?"

"They were criminal associates."

"Well I never! So they never worked for the same insurance company after all. The convoluted talk about insurance salesmen, underwriting and all that other baloney was also a lie! Have Gentleman Jim Snareskin and Cutpurse Fennel been arrested yet?"

"Not yet. They were last seen travelling along the road between Salisbury and Andover, so my colleagues in Hampshire are keeping a keen lookout for them. We believe Gentleman Jim may be heading for his lair in Dartford, Kent."

Churchill struggled to associate the bank robbery and the lair in Dartford with the man she had known as Percy Pickwick.

"The Kent constabulary will be awaiting him in Dartford, of course," continued Inspector Mappin. "He'll struggle to escape our clutches."

"And what of the men who dug the tunnel?" Pemberley asked. "Have you caught them yet?"

"Gentleman Jim appears to have paid off one of the Flatboots, who has since fled to Wales."

"That'll be who I saw coming out of the gallery with a wheelbarrow the other day," said Pemberley. "I thought it a bit odd at the time."

"I'm sure the Welsh police will catch up with him soon enough, but it's Gentleman Jim everyone wants."

"What a scoundrel," replied Churchill. "And you only learnt of his true identity after the robbery?"

"Yes, and I now have a sneaking suspicion there's a mole within the Metropolitan Police."

"How clever!" commented Churchill.

"What's so clever about that?"

"Well, we pride ourselves on our detective dog, but a mole operating as a police officer is something else altogether. I didn't realise you could train them to do your job, Inspector."

"He means a spy," said Pemberley.

"Oh, silly me," replied Churchill with a twinkle in her eye. "A spy in the Metropolitan Police, you say? Never!"

"I suspect that someone in the force alerted Gentleman Jim to the fact we were to be warned about him," said Inspector Mappin. "And that prompted him to strike quickly so he could get away from here as quickly as possible. The tunnel was clearly ready to go, with just one last little bit waiting to be dug out at the right moment."

"Since you put it like that, Inspector, it does seem rather too coincidental he carried out his plan with immediate effect after you received the telephone call."

"Communications with colleagues in Hampshire and Wiltshire confirmed that several robberies have taken place at country houses recently. Artworks were taken, and I suspect they were the very ones Gentleman Jim used to fill his gallery."

"Golly, what a charlatan."

"And I think there can also be little doubt that Gentleman Jim isn't just a robber, but also a murderer."

A chill ran down Churchill's spine. "Oh dear me. Do you really think so? Do you think he murdered Mr Butterfork?"

"You mean Ratface Rudgepole," said Pemberley.

"Yes, him," said the inspector. "It makes sense, wouldn't you say? The men were old acquaintances from London's criminal underworld and Rudgepole was in possession of rather a lot of money. Ill-gotten gains, I suspect. Perhaps Gentleman Jim felt he was entitled to some of it. He clearly decided to murder his former associate over it, and in a horrific manner at that."

"And he accidentally lost his Mason's ring in Crunkle Lane," said Churchill. "No wonder he never tried to claim it. But then, come to think of it, I saw a ring on his hand. Perhaps he swiftly acquired another."

"Perhaps he did," replied the inspector. "It's terribly disappointing to discover that the Freemasons admitted two crooks into their ranks."

"It is indeed," replied Churchill. "You should have checks in place for that sort of thing. I struggle to believe Percy might be capable of murder, though. If you ask me, that Fennel woman did it."

"*Cutpurse* Fennel," added Pemberley.

"I did a little probing about her," said Inspector Mappin, "and she couldn't have murdered Ratface Rudgepole. She had an alibi for that night."

"Which was?"

"She was attending a literary event at the local library."

Churchill gave a snort. "I think that would be most unlikely. It isn't even open at that hour!"

"Not usually, no, but once a month Mrs Higginbath hosts a literary event and invites an author in to read their work."

"Pah! Did you know about this, Miss Pemberley?"

"Yes."

"Why haven't you ever mentioned it?"

"I didn't think you would have any interest in it whatsoever, Mrs Churchill. Firstly, you don't like Mrs Higginbath, secondly, you're prohibited from holding a reading ticket at the library, and, thirdly, you don't like bicycling."

"What's bicycling got to do with it?"

"The reading was given by Mrs Esmerelda Kitchen, who wrote a book called *Scenic Bicycling Routes for Dorset Ladies*."

"How dull! I'd much rather read something by that Jane Austen lady."

"That's why I didn't mention the evening at the library to you."

"Did you attend, Miss Pemberley?"

"No, Oswald and I were busy."

"I see. And that Fennel woman had an interest in bicycling through Dorset, did she? A woman of highly criminal character?"

"She probably attended to cultivate the image of herself as a well-heeled lady about town," said the inspector.

"By visiting Mrs Higginbath's library and listening to some woman drone on about bicycles?"

"It was a literary event."

Churchill snorted again.

"The whys and the wherefores matter very little," said Inspector Mappin. "The fact of the matter is that a number of people can vouch for Cutpurse Fennel's presence at the literary evening. Therefore, she can't have had anything to do with the murder of Ratface Rudgepole."

"But she had a hand in burying their ill-gotten gains in the churchyard, didn't she?"

"It certainly seems that way. But all this can only mean that Gentleman Jim Snareskin is the murderer."

"Golly, what a thought. There's no doubt the man is a miscreant and a dastard, but a murderer?"

Churchill returned to her cottage that evening to find an envelope lying on her doormat. As she picked it up to examine the sloped black handwriting, she saw that the letter bore a postmark from Andover.

Inside was a short note:

My dear Mrs Annabel Churchill,
I know you won't ever forgive me, but I'm so terribly sorry.
Gentleman Jim ('Percy')

Chapter 35

A GAGGLE of gossiping locals gathered outside the bakery for a confab the following morning. Churchill spotted the red hair of Mrs Thonnings, the bespectacled Mrs Roseball and the large form of Mrs Hatweed, among others.

"I'm still in total disbelief about the news," Churchill heard Mrs Hatweed say. "To me he was, and always will be, Mr Butterfork. Alf 'Ratface' Rudgepole sounds so terribly wrong."

"I can't understand the rat face bit at all," added Mrs Roseball. "He didn't have a face like a rat at all, did he?"

"Perhaps he did when he was younger," suggested Mrs Thonnings. "Ah, good morning, Mrs Churchill! We're just discussing recent events."

"So I hear."

"Did he finish painting your picture before he took off?"

"No, he didn't."

"What a shame."

"He didn't really start it, if truth be told."

"Oh dear. He must have been one of those slow

painters, like Vermeer," commented Mrs Hatweed. "It took him ages to finish his paintings."

"He wasn't a painter, though, was he?" said Mrs Strawbanks, joining the group. "He was pretending all along. Those paintings he claimed were his handiwork in that spartan place he called a gallery weren't his at all! They were probably stolen, if you ask me. He and Butterfork had us all fooled, didn't they? Are you all right, Mrs Churchill? You don't seem your usual self today."

"I'm fine, thank you."

Mr Pickwick's note had left Churchill in a thoughtful mood. The events and conversations of the past few weeks had begun to blend together in her mind. She tried to figure out whether there was something she had missed and came to the conclusion that there was. She eyed the display in the bakery window.

"A few fruit buns will see me right," she added.

"Let me treat you, Mrs Churchill," said Mrs Thonnings. "You've had a difficult few days."

"That's very kind of you, Mrs Thonnings, thank you."

The two ladies walked into the bakery together.

"This must all have come as a terrible shock. After all, you were quite friendly with Mr Pickwick, weren't you? Really quite friendly. I suppose we should call him James Snareskin now. Or Gentleman Jim. Funny how he has so many names, isn't it? I only hope they can find and arrest him on the road to London. It's dreadful to think of all the terrible things he's done—"

"Mrs Fingle!" interrupted Churchill. "Does that name mean anything to you, Mrs Thonnings?"

The haberdasher considered this for a moment. "The lady who fell into the river?"

"That's what I heard. She drowned during a midnight swim, isn't that right?"

"Yes, we were all very sad to hear about that, especially as it was the first time she'd ever gone for a midnight swim."

"Was she on her own?"

"Yes. If someone had been with her they'd have pulled her out, wouldn't they?"

Churchill began rearranging the incident board as soon as she returned to the office with the fruit buns.

"What are you doing, Mrs Churchill?" asked Pemberley. "The case is solved."

"No it isn't," she retorted. "It's all been muddled, that's what. Did Atkins ever investigate the death of Mrs Fingle?"

"I think he considered it, yes, but there was no case to answer for, as the inquest recorded it as an accidental death."

"Did he create a file?"

"He probably did, yes. He created a file for everything, which is why we have so many filing cabinets in here. Let me see if I can find it." She got up from her desk and wandered over to the cabinets. "What did you find in the bakery?"

"Fruit buns."

"And you haven't even sampled one yet? Are you all right, Mrs Churchill? You seem a little out of sorts."

"I'm fine, thank you." She paused beside the incident board. "I really am. I received something in the post yesterday." Churchill walked over to her handbag, which she had placed on her desk, and pulled out Gentleman Jim's letter. She handed it to Pemberley.

"Gosh," said her assistant once she had read it. "I wonder why that stinker sent you this?"

"I think he must be feeling a little regretful."

"He's only got himself to blame."

"Well yes, he has."

"Odd that he feels the need to apologise for pretending to paint you when he's quite happy to go around shooting people dead and stealing their money."

"That's just it, Pembers. This letter suggests the chap has some sort of conscience. There's no doubt he's a scoundrel, a fraudster and a good-for-nothing rogue, but he does seem to feel a tiny measure of guilt for fooling me."

"You mustn't make excuses for him, Mrs Churchill."

"Oh, I'm not, and if I ever see the man again I'll pick that useless portrait up and wrap it round his neck. But I just can't see him being a murderer."

"What are you basing that on, Mrs Churchill? A hunch?"

"Yes." Churchill went back to her handbag and looped it over her wrist. "While you're busy digging out Mrs Fingle's file, Pembers, I must pay someone a quick visit."

"Pay whom a visit?"

"Mrs Harris."

"Why on earth would you need to visit Mrs Harris?"

"I've just remembered something from the summer fete."

"What about the fruit buns?" Pemberley asked as Churchill headed toward the door.

"Oh, you have them, Pembers."

Churchill returned to the office a short while later with a bag of chocolate eclairs.

"If I'd known you were coming back with those, I

wouldn't have eaten the fruit buns," said Pemberley bitterly. "I'm full up now. How was Mrs Harris?"

"Interesting."

"In what sense?"

"I'll explain shortly." Churchill took a seat at her desk. "Thank you for fetching me Mrs Fingle's file. I'll have a read through while I eat these eclairs."

"With a drop of tea, perhaps?"

"That'll do very nicely, indeed, thank you."

Churchill spent a busy hour examining Mr Atkins's notes and sketches in Mrs Fingle's case file. Then she sat back in her chair and ruminated, surreptitiously dropping half an eclair onto the floor for Oswald as she did so.

"He's not allowed chocolate eclairs, Mrs Churchill."

"Who said I gave him an eclair?"

"No one. I just know that you did."

"Even though you're sitting over on the other side of the room?"

"I have an eye for these things."

"I understand Mrs Fingle was Mr Butterfork's housekeeper."

"Yes, that's right."

"And she went for a midnight swim one winter evening."

"Yes."

"In *winter*."

"Yes."

"And no one thought that strange?"

"She was quite a strange lady."

"And because she was a strange lady, everyone expected her to do strange things."

"Yes, when you put it like that, I suppose that was the case."

"Therefore, no one questioned her decision to go for a midnight swim in winter."

"No, they didn't. From the sound of things, she simply took herself off and went for it. I don't think anyone had the opportunity to question her decision."

"I meant afterwards. Didn't anyone think it odd after the event?"

"Of course they did, but——"

"But she was a strange lady, so they didn't dwell on it. I see our conversation has come full circle." Churchill bit into another eclair and gave this some further thought. "I suppose a strange person would be an easy target for someone who wished to cause mischief."

"To Mrs Fingle?"

"Indeed. Someone may have deliberately caused her harm."

"Now you're beginning to sound like Atkins."

"Good. I can see from the file that my predecessor spent a bit of time on this case but was met with general indifference. Someone with malicious intent exploited the fact that Mrs Fingle was considered rather strange."

"But whom?"

"Whom indeed. That's the question I've been asking myself."

"Do you think someone pushed her into the river?"

"It's a distinct possibility. There's no evidence to say they didn't."

"Or to say they did. And besides, there was no motive."

"Ah, but I think there was a motive."

"Really? Atkins couldn't find one. That's one of the main reasons why he abandoned the case in the end."

"Well, I think I may have found one, but I'll be more certain after I've spoken to an old, old friend."

"And who might that be?"

"A retired detective superintendent named DS Dickie Harlow who worked for many years with the esteemed Detective Chief Inspector Churchill of the Metropolitan Police."

"He worked in London?"

"Yes."

"Then what would he know of Mrs Fingle?"

"Hopefully a little more than you might think, Pembers." Churchill rummaged around in her handbag for her address book. "I shall telephone him to find out."

Chapter 36

"DICKIE'S AGREED to make a few enquiries for me," said Churchill as she replaced the telephone receiver.

"About what?"

"A few pertinent matters, including the Great Plumstead Bank Heist," replied Churchill. "Gentleman Jim was also involved in that, apparently."

"Goodness! He's been up to all sorts, hasn't he?"

"He certainly has, and by the sound of things a number of police forces from around the country would like to speak to him. I suppose I should show Inspector Mappin the letter he sent me, he'll be interested to see that it was posted in Andover."

"He'll already have moved on from there."

"I'm sure he will have, but I'd better share it with the local constabulary all the same. Would you care to join me, Pembers?"

They found Inspector Mappin at his desk, which was decorated with a vase of pink chrysanthemums.

"They've lasted well, Inspector."

"They have, Mrs Churchill. I've grown quite accustomed to them now; so much so that Mrs Mappin has promised me a new bunch when these are past it."

"How lovely. We're here because I thought you might like to see this note I received from the fugitive. You'll be interested to see it because the postmark confirms he was recently in Andover."

"Very interesting," said the inspector as he first examined the envelope and then the letter. "I'll let the Hampshire and Metropolitan police forces know. Would you like this back, Mrs Churchill?"

"No thank you. You can keep it."

"While you're here, you might be interested to hear about a few developments in the case."

"Oh yes. What might they be?"

"We've been searching Gentleman Jim's accommodation above the gallery."

"Above the gallery? But he told me he lived in a house near Triddledon Lane, and that he had a summerhouse in the grounds that he used as a studio. Oh, wait…"

"Lying again," Pemberley piped up.

"Indeed."

"He was living above that place he called a gallery," continued Inspector Mappin, "presumably to enable the gang to keep working on their tunnel at night-time. Anyway, I'm pleased to say that Constable Dawkins found a dark grey overcoat with a hole in it during the search. The hole appears to have been snagged on something; no doubt the piece of hawthorn in the churchyard. We've compared it with the piece of snagged fabric you found in the churchyard."

"Miss Pemberley found it, actually."

"Oh yes. Thank you, Miss Pemberley. We found that the snagged piece of fabric matches the overcoat exactly."

"Oh goodness, really?"

"It's not terribly surprising, is it?" commented Pemberley.

"No, I suppose not," said Churchill.

"But there is a little anomaly," added the inspector, sitting back in his chair. "The gun found in the churchyard was not used in the murder of Ratface Rudgepole."

"It wasn't?" exclaimed Churchill.

"No. The ballistics chap at Bovington looked it over and decided the spent bullets found at the scene of the murder could not have come from that gun."

"But how could he know such a thing?"

"It simply doesn't fire that particular type of bullet."

"How odd."

"It suggests that Gentleman Jim kept the murder weapon on his person and somebody else left the pistol in the churchyard for some unknown reason. I suppose it could have been sitting there for a good while before your dog found it, but it turns out to be completely unconnected to the case."

"And the ring?"

"It must be Gentleman Jim's."

"But he still had his Mason's ring. He showed it to me."

"Perhaps he replaced it after losing the original in the lane while fleeing the murder scene?"

"It's possible, I suppose."

"I've made extensive enquiries at the lodge but found no one else who had lost a ring."

"Then I suppose it must be Gentleman Jim's."

"If he bought a replacement he could only have done so from a particular jeweller's in Dorchester. I'll make some enquiries there to confirm the purchase, although it really isn't necessary, as we already have all the evidence we need."

"You're absolutely certain Gentleman Jim murdered Ratface Rudgepole, are you?"

"Absolutely, Mrs Churchill. The motive and evidence is all there. We just need to catch him now."

"I'm still not convinced, Pembers," said Churchill as the two ladies walked back to the office.

"How can you not be convinced that Gentleman Jim is the murderer? You heard what Mappin said. There's motive and plenty of evidence. In fact, I quite enjoyed our conversation with him just then. There was no bickering at all, and no one accused anyone of meddling or being inept. Inspector Mappin can be quite amiable at times, can't he? I understand now why Mrs Thonnings mentioned him doing nice things behind closed doors."

"That's a thought I'd rather not dwell on. On reflection, I'm beginning to think there are several things we've missed during the course of our investigation. It's easy to assume that a career criminal is capable of murder, but one shouldn't tar them all with the same brush."

"It's rather difficult not to."

"Perhaps I'll have a clearer idea once DS Dickie Harlow has telephoned me back. Oh look, there's Lady Darby. Oh dear, I've just remembered my tongue was a little loose the last time I spoke to her."

Lady Darby, dressed from head to toe in lilac, paused beside the shiny motor car she was about to step into. "Oh, good morning, Mrs Churchill." Her mouth smiled, but her eyes didn't follow suit. "I was planning to call on you."

"Were you? That would have been lovely, Lady Darby. How's Lord Darby's foot?"

"It's on the mend, thank you. He's managing to get out into the gardens and is able to do a circuit of the parterre quite comfortably now."

"Is he indeed? How marvellous."

"I was hoping to speak to you about the garden party, actually."

"Ah, yes."

"There's a been a slight change of plan—"

"Let me make this quick and easy for you, Lady Darby, as I have a busy day ahead of me. I assume you're uninviting me."

"Uninviting you? Oh goodness, no. I never uninvite people, Mrs Churchill. It's just that we've had to change our plans a little and revise down the number of attendees, you see. Most embarrassing, I know, but—"

"It's quite all right, Lady Darby, I understand. If it was the joke about the butler, the cook and the pumpkin that offended, I'm really very not sorry."

"There's no need to apologise about that... Oh, *not* sorry, did you say?"

"Have a wonderful day, Lady Darby."

Chapter 37

"WELL, THAT WAS VERY INTERESTING INDEED," said Churchill as she replaced the telephone receiver.

"What did Dickie Harlow say?"

"Not a great deal, Pembers, but just about enough." Churchill began scribbling furiously on a piece of paper. "Take a look at this."

Pemberley walked over to the desk and looked down at what Churchill had written. "Do you recognise it?"

"No."

"Ah, I get it!"

"Get what, Mrs Churchill? I don't understand."

Churchill scribbled some more. "It's an anagram, don't you see?"

"No." Pemberley stared some more, then her eyes widened and a grin spread across her face. "Actually, I do see it now. Very clearly indeed!"

"I think it's time we arranged a little gathering in St Swithun's churchyard, don't you?"

"Must it really be in the churchyard, Mrs Churchill?"

"Yes."

Chapter 38

A BRIEF RAIN shower had left the churchyard smelling of fresh foliage. Small furls of mist curled up from the headstones and wet grass, giving the churchyard an eerie feel, despite the sunny afternoon.

"What's this all about, Mrs Churchill?" asked the sexton, his wide-brimmed hat and black coat smelling of damp, musty wool.

"You'll see soon enough, Mr Grieves. Look, everyone's arriving now."

Churchill, Pemberley and the sexton watched as a steady stream of people filed in through the church gate and up the path. Oswald sniffed each new arrival and happily accepted several pats on the head. Mrs Thonnings walked in with Mr Burbage the bank manager, Mrs Crackleby stood chatting to Mr Jones Sloanes, Mrs Roseball and Mrs Hatweed walked alongside Farmer Drumhead, and Mr Simpkins the baker followed close behind. Next came Lady Darby, Mrs Higginbath, Mrs Strawbanks and Mrs Harris. Inspector Mappin appeared to be scolding Constables Dawkins and Russell about something as they entered the churchyard. Several members of the Flatboot family clambered over the wall to survey the proceedings while chewing on pieces of straw.

"Is everybody here?" Churchill called out as the group gathered around her.

"How would we know?" replied Mrs Thonnings.

"That's a good question. I think most of you are here, perhaps with the exception of one or two, so I'll begin." Churchill leafed through the papers in her hand and cleared her throat.

"Will this take long?" someone called out.

"It will if you keep interrupting me." She cleared her throat again.

"No one interrupt her," someone else hollered, "or it'll take even longer."

"Are there any chairs?" asked Lady Darby.

"No chairs allowed in the churchyard," responded the sexton.

"I'd like to begin now," said Churchill, rustling her papers impatiently. "Now, you're all well aware that a terrible murder occurred in Crunkle Lane a week ago. Someone shot the gentleman we had all come to know as Mr Butterfork before stealing the money he kept in his tea chest."

Churchill paused for effect, carefully scanning the faces before her.

"And?" Mrs Crackleby called out.

"And that brings me on to my next point."

"Mr Pickwick did it," said Mrs Strawbanks, "and some of his coat got ripped off in the churchyard."

"Yes, I'm coming to that part, Mrs Strawbanks," replied Churchill. "Shortly after the gunshot was heard, the culprit was seen running down Crunkle Lane and vaulting over the churchyard wall. He landed close to the grave of Barnabus Byers just over there."

Faces followed the direction of Churchill's pointed finger.

"Then he leapt over the grave of Betsy Wolfwell and snagged his coat on a hawthorn branch. We have no idea where the dark figure went after that."

"Only we do, because it was Mr Pickwick," said Mrs Strawbanks.

Churchill glared at her and continued. "In the meantime, Miss Pemberley and I were consulted by the sexton, Mr Grieves, who had noticed that some of the graves in the churchyard had been tampered with. Our surveillance of the grounds revealed that a lady calling herself Miss Pickwick had placed a posy of carnations beside one of these graves. The grave in question was that of Benjamin Grunchen just over there."

Faces turned again in the direction Churchill was indicating.

"Beneath the posy of carnations was a patch of disturbed earth."

"Ugh!" said Mrs Roseball.

"And when we excavated the disturbed earth, we found a quantity of money buried there. Further investigations carried out by Inspector Mappin and his men resulted in two more bags of money being recovered. It seems the proceeds of a crime had been buried within the graves; the same graves that had been tampered with."

"Why would someone tamper with the graves?" asked Lady Darby.

"I believe the person who was planning to bury the money there did so," replied Churchill. "The guilty party paid several visits to this churchyard and deliberately marked the graves they deemed most suitable for burying the money in. Perhaps it was a reminder for him or herself, or maybe it was a signal for someone else. Either way, the graves were undoubtedly singled out in this manner."

"So Mr Pickwick leapt over the wall and buried the money in the graves?" asked Farmer Drumhead.

"Not immediately, as there was no time for that on the night of the murder. He would have taken the money with him. My guess is that he took it back to his lair above the pretend art gallery he had opened on the high street. The money couldn't remain there for long in case it was found, so 'Miss Pickwick', supposedly his sister, helped bury it in the graves over the course of the next few days. After all, who would look for money inside a grave? They clearly hadn't reckoned on the keen eye of Mr Grieves!"

The sexton gave a rare, appreciative smile.

"And now my story moves to Plumstead," announced Churchill.

"Where's that?" asked Mrs Thonnings.

"London."

"Why London?"

"Will you please allow me to explain?"

"But what's London got to do with it?"

"The Great Plumstead Bank Heist," stated Churchill, soldiering on as best she could, "occurred about eighteen months ago in the southern suburb of Plumstead. An old friend of mine, now retired from the Metropolitan Police, informs me that a gang robbed a bank on the high street by tunnelling into its vault."

"Just as Mr Pickwick did with his art gallery," said Mrs Strawbanks.

"Exactly. Only, his name was Mr McGovern when he was over in Plumstead, and he ran a sparsely stocked gentleman's outfitters. His accomplice was a man who called himself Mr Crewe. Now, these two gentleman were actually seasoned criminals called Mr James 'Gentleman Jim' Snareskin and Mr Alf 'Ratface' Rudgepole. There were other members of the gang too, and after the heist some were caught while others escaped. Among the escapees were Gentleman Jim and Ratface. They went on the run together and a manhunt ensued. Despite the best efforts of the police, the two thieves always seemed to be a step ahead. Witnesses saw Gentleman Jim and Ratface having a disagreement at a public house in Slough a few weeks after the heist. Rumour has it they fell out over the division of spoils, which resulted in Ratface fleeing in the dead of night with all the money."

"And he came here?" asked Mrs Hatweed.

"After a while," responded Churchill. "He appears to have spent some time searching for the ideal hideaway before deciding that the obscure little village of Compton Poppleford in deepest, darkest Dorset would be the perfect hideaway. Once here, he referred to himself as Mr Butterfork. The story he told was that he had left his insurance job to nurse his rich, elderly aunt in Benton Thurstock."

"Dreadful place," muttered Mrs Hatweed.

"Mr Butterfork presumably hoped no one from his criminal past would ever find him," added Churchill.

"Only Mr Pickwick followed him here, shot him dead and took the money back," said Mrs Strawbanks.

"Thank you for that, Mrs Strawbanks."

"Why didn't he keep his money a secret?" asked Mrs Harris.

"I can only guess that he had so much he didn't know where to hide it or what to do with it," replied Churchill. "So he established himself as some sort of Lord Bountiful and shared his wealth with the villagers. It was also a way of ingratiating himself with his new friends."

"It certainly worked," commented Mrs Thonnings. "He was very popular indeed."

"Ratface Rudgepole had four visitors on the day he died," said Churchill. "Mrs Thonnings, Mrs Roseball, Mrs Strawbanks and Mr Pickwick."

Faces turned and necks craned as the group looked round at the three women mentioned.

"I didn't murder him, if that's what you think!" protested Mrs Thonnings.

"Me neither!" Mrs Roseball piped up.

"Nor me!" added Mrs Strawbanks.

"Calm down, ladies, we already know it was Mr Pickwick," said Mrs Hatweed.

"But hold on a minute," said Lady Darby. "You said Mr Pickwick visited Ratface on the day he died, but the two men already knew each other, didn't they?"

"That's right, Lady Darby. Gentleman Jim was obviously keen to find his former partner in crime because he wanted his share of the money from the Great Plumstead Bank Heist. He eventually tracked him down to this village and decided to have a little extra fun while he was here. Now, I'm no expert on career criminals, but I do recall some of the stories my dearly departed husband, Detective Chief Inspector Churchill, used to tell me about them. It seems gangsters can never resist another job. Having pulled off the heist in Plumstead, Gentleman Jim decided to carry out another crime in our sweet little village. When Mr Borridge's barber shop closed he clearly saw an opportunity to open a commercial establishment in its place and tunnel into the bank's vault next door. He recruited one of the Flatboots for this task, and if anyone happened to overhear any tunnelling noises, Gentleman

Jim's explanation was that he was having a leak fixed in the basement."

"Very clever," said Mr Simpkin with a nod.

"It still hasn't been filled in," Mr Burbage complained.

"What hasn't?" asked Churchill.

"The tunnel under my bank. Who's going to fill it back in?"

"That's a very good question, Mr Burbage, but it's something that must be resolved elsewhere."

"When?"

"Shush, let her get on with it!" someone called out.

"To assist with his plan, Gentleman Jim stole a number of artworks from various country houses," continued Churchill. "And, lo and behold, Pickwick's Gallery opened. Somewhere along the way he recruited a seasoned gangster, Miss Molly 'Cutpurse' Fennel, who agreed to pose as his sister."

"Was she his lover?" asked Mrs Thonnings.

"Probably," interjected Pemberley.

"We have no way of knowing." Churchill took a breath, then continued. "Ratface had managed to establish himself as a reputable member of the community, and Gentleman Jim set about doing the same thing. Both men joined the Masonic lodge and their respectability was never questioned.

"We don't know what Ratface's response was when he realised Gentleman Jim had found him; however, with both men clearly determined that their pasts should remain hidden, they must have reached an uneasy agreement to maintain their secret identities and keep the peace. Perhaps gentlemanly negotiations about money took place behind the scenes. I suspect they did, as we know the pair of them met once a week under the guise of playing cards. Perhaps Gentleman Jim merely pretended to reach an agreement with Ratface to lull him into a false sense of security."

"I would imagine so," said Mrs Strawbanks with a nod.

"And then there's Mrs Fingle," announced Churchill.

"What? Where did she come from?" asked Lady Darby.

"She died," someone said.

"Ratface recruited Mrs Fingle as his housekeeper when he first arrived in the village," said Churchill, "but she drowned during a mysterious midnight swim. I have reason to suspect that she was murdered."

"Oh no. Not that silly rumour again," said Inspector Mappin. "It was an accident."

"My predecessor, Mr Atkins, also suspected she was murdered," continued Churchill. "He suggested someone had lured her to her death on the bank of the river one winter's evening." She paused to allow time for gasps and mutterings, then continued. "After Mrs Fingle died, Mrs Hatweed became Ratface's housekeeper."

"Why are you all looking at me?" the housekeeper asked those who had turned to look at her. "I haven't done anything wrong!"

"Mrs Hatweed was very keen indeed to become Ratface's housekeeper, weren't you, Mrs Hatweed?" said Churchill.

"Not at all!" She gave an awkward laugh, which made her curls bounce. "It was just an ordinary housekeeper job as far as I was concerned."

"Are you saying Mrs Hatweed pushed Mrs Fingle into the river so she could become Ratface's housekeeper?" asked Mrs Thonnings.

"Never!" called out Mrs Harris. "That's impossible."

"I refuse to believe it," said Mr Burbage, shaking his head.

"It wasn't me!" protested Mrs Hatweed.

Churchill waited for the mutterings to subside, then continued. "Mr Atkins's file also revealed a terrible falling out," she announced, "between Mrs Fingle and Mrs Strawbanks."

Chapter 39

"ME?" The beads on Mrs Strawbanks's jewellery rattled as she glanced around.

"Mrs Fingle grew tired of your prying from the house on the opposite side of the street, Mrs Strawbanks," said Churchill. "She confronted you about it a number of times, didn't she?"

"Well yes, she did, but… I didn't murder her over it! What would the use in that have been?"

"There could have been a lot of use in it if everyone believed the murder to be an accident," said Churchill. "Which they did."

"I did *not* murder Mrs Fingle!" protested Mrs Strawbanks.

"Perhaps Ratface took her side in the disagreement."

"He may well have done. He did, in fact, but only because she was his housekeeper. He was biased!"

"Perhaps you wished to be rid of the pair of them."

"No! I… Mrs Churchill! Please, everyone. You must believe me!"

"I don't know what to believe now," said Mrs Roseball sadly.

Mrs Churchill continued. "I mentioned earlier that several members of the gang which carried out the Great Plumstead Bank Heist were caught, while others escaped."

"What about Mrs Strawbanks?" asked Mr Grieves.

"All will become clear once I've finished, Mr Grieves. I discovered from my retired Metropolitan Police friend that Ratface Rudgepole was apprehended after he scarpered from Slough with all the money."

"He was arrested?" someone called out.

"Almost."

"What?" came another voice.

"He played his trump card," stated Churchill. "Having been a criminal for most of his life, he possessed a considerable amount of information that he knew would prove invaluable to the constabulary. He struck a bargain with the police and gave them a series of names, and in return his most recent misdemeanour was overlooked. Ratface Rudgepole became an informer."

"And they just let him off?"

"That shouldn't be allowed!"

"As a result of the information Ratface provided, a number of men were arrested, stood trial and were imprisoned," said Churchill. "One of them, a young man named Mr Ernest Wethead, was the getaway driver in the Great Plumstead Bank Heist."

"Golly! Ratface must have made a lot of people angry," commented Mrs Harris.

"Indeed he did," said Churchill. "A number of people sought revenge, including Mr Wethead's mother."

"And who might she have been?"

"Well, she's changed her surname slightly. She made an

anagram of it, in fact, so Ratface wouldn't suspect anything. I'm talking, of course, about Mrs Hatweed."

"No!" shouted Mrs Harris.

Astonished gasps followed.

Mrs Hatweed opened her mouth to speak but seemed to think better of it.

"Mrs Hatweed pushed Mrs Fingle into the river so she could become Ratface Rudgepole's housekeeper and carefully plot his murder!" announced Churchill.

Loud mutterings replaced the gasps.

"But that's impossible," protested Mrs Strawbanks. "Mrs Hatweed wasn't even there when Ratface was shot; she was asleep. I had to call at her house to wake her! There's simply no way she could have shot him and run home in time!"

"Did I say she murdered Ratface?"

"Yes!"

"I merely said she *plotted* his murder. She had already done away with Mrs Fingle, and no doubt decided she would be pushing her luck if she tried to get away with it a second time. Now this next part is pure speculation, but I think I have a pretty good idea as to who fired that fatal shot."

"She asked someone else to murder him?" asked Mrs Higginbath.

"Yes."

"A *hitman?*"

"Of sorts. The person she hired wasn't a professional but was certainly in need of money. This someone I speak of went to astonishing lengths to demonstrate an apparent ineptness with guns. You ran the rifle range stall at the summer fete, Mrs Harris. Perhaps you can remind us who won the prize that day."

"Why, it was Mrs Roseball. She achieved an impressive score of forty-eight points."

"Thank you, Mrs Harris," said Churchill. "I remember the mayor announcing Mrs Roseball's name at the prize-giving ceremony, yet when Miss Pemberley and I visited she pretended to know so little about guns that she fired her own revolver in apparent error."

The round, bespectacled lady rose to her feet. "I've never heard so much nonsense! This is lies, all of it!"

"Then how do you explain your prowess on the rifle range and the bullet hole in your wall... and the headless china shepherdess? One of the shepherdesses your good friend, Mrs Hatweed, asked you to look after for her?"

"Everyone knows it was Gentleman Jim who shot Ratface. You're still trying to protect him, Mrs Churchill, even after everything he's done!"

"You mishandled the revolver so badly it was almost comical, Mrs Roseball. Someone who knew nothing about guns would have left it well alone, feeling too scared to touch it. But a certain confidence lay behind your inepti-tude. You knew what you were doing all along, and you managed to frighten the living daylights out of Miss Pemberley and my good self in the process."

"What rubbish!"

"But I thought Gentleman Jim took the money and fled over the churchyard wall with it?" queried Mrs Thonnings.

"He did," replied Churchill. "At some point he must have learned of Mrs Hatweed's plan or maybe she learned of his. I think there had to have been some collusion between the two, as they were both seeking vengeance. Mrs Hatweed wasn't interested in Ratface's money; she was only interested in exacting revenge on behalf of her imprisoned son. Perhaps she agreed that Gentleman Jim could take off with the money once a portion had been left to Mrs Roseball as payment for the assassination. It must have been a temptingly large sum for Mrs Roseball. As she says herself, she receives only a meagre income from her damson jam."

"I find it hard to believe that Ratface would have let Mrs Roseball into his home late that evening while he was in his nightwear," commented Mrs Strawbanks.

"So do I," agreed Churchill, "and for that very reason I suspect Mrs Hatweed secretly let her friend into the house before she left that evening. Mrs Roseball must have hidden somewhere until Gentleman Jim turned up."

"But how can we be sure it was Mrs Roseball who pulled the trigger?" asked Mrs Strawbanks. "Perhaps Gentleman Jim did it after all."

"I never considered him to be the murdering type," replied Churchill. "I like to think he took the money and left the room before Mrs Roseball carried out the deed, but we shall only ever know the true events of that evening if Mrs Roseball chooses to share them with us. Inspector Mappin, I last saw the revolver in Mrs Roseball's writing bureau. Hopefully it's still there, so your ballistics chap at Bovington should be able to confirm that it was used in the murder of Mr Rudgepole."

Inspector Mappin nodded. "My men will get down there at once."

Mrs Roseball made a move to leave but the inspector got to her first and clipped a pair of handcuffs around her wrists. Constable Russell did the same with Mrs Hatweed.

"I don't regret it, you know," said Mrs Hatweed, her curls bouncing defiantly. "It was all for my Ernie. An innocent boy locked up because of that wretched Ratface! I wish Ernie had never met him. I told him to stay away from that public house they all frequented, but he wouldn't listen. I warned him he would fall in with the wrong sorts. Ratface bullied my poor Ernie into being the gang's getaway driver. Ernie was afraid for his very life if he didn't do what that bully asked!

"I worked out who Mr Pickwick really was when I overheard his and Ratface's conversations while they played cards," continued the housekeeper. "I took Gentleman Jim to one side and told him I could help him get his hands on the money. I knew Mrs Roseball was always in need of a few bob and the three of us hatched our plan together. We agreed that Mrs Roseball would hold Ratface at gunpoint while Gentleman Jim took his share of the money. He left a good amount for her and went on his way. He didn't know what our final plan for Ratface was."

"You did well to track Ratface down, Hatters," commented Mrs Strawbanks. "I'd have done the same if it was my son."

"You'd have murdered someone?" Churchill asked.

"I'd have stopped short of that, but I'd have tracked him down all right. Hatters should be shown some leniency."

"Ratface was an unpleasant man," said Churchill, "but poor Mrs Fingle was entirely innocent, and pushing her into that freezing river was unforgivable."

"Oh yes, that's true," agreed Mrs Strawbanks. "I wouldn't have done that."

"How did the gun find its way into the churchyard?" asked Mrs Thonnings. "Could Mrs Roseball have given it to Gentleman Jim, who then threw it away?"

"An excellent question, Mrs Thonnings," replied Churchill. "It transpires the gun we found wasn't actually used in Ratface's murder. My theory is that someone planted it there to confuse the investigation. I'd hazard a guess it was Mrs Hatweed. However, the gun found here in the churchyard was a pistol and Mrs Roseball owns a revolver."

"It was a revolver that killed Ratface Rudgepole," confirmed Inspector Mappin.

"Not very clever clue-planting work in that case," commented Mr Grieves.

Inspector Mappin and Constable Russell began to lead the two prisoners toward the churchyard gate.

"And the Freemason's ring?" asked Pemberley. "Was that relevant to the investigation?"

"I don't think we'll ever be completely sure of that, my trusty assistant. Perhaps it was lost accidentally on Crunkle Lane, but I suspect it was left there deliberately so that whoever was investigating would find it and waste time trying to discover its rightful owner. Maybe it was another attempt on Mrs Hatweed's part to confuse us. I believe a number of obstacles were thrown across our path during the course of our investigation, including Gentleman Jim eating up sizeable chunks of my time by claiming to paint me. And I'll admit that I fell for it completely."

"All that time he spent painting you was valuable time you could have spent working on the case, Mrs Churchill," said Mrs Thonnings.

"I couldn't have put it better myself," replied Churchill.

Chapter 40

"Impressive work, Mrs Churchill," said Mr Grieves as the crowd began to disperse, "but you're not quite finished yet."

"Oh yes I am. I'm spent! Miss Pemberley and I need a little holiday after all that."

"The incidents in the churchyard still haven't been fully explained. Follow me."

He led them over to the dingy corner of the churchyard shaded by the giant yew tree.

Churchill gave a shiver as they surveyed the grave of Saul Mollikin, the man who had been cursed by the witch on Grindledown Hill.

"Well?" asked the sexton. "How do you explain that?"

The crop of fresh green grass was denser than before.

"I don't know, Mr Grieves, but I'm quite sure this grave had nothing to do with the buried money. It's obvious that the earth here hasn't been disturbed for a while."

Pemberley and Oswald walked over to the yew tree.

"When did this branch come down?" asked Pemberley, pointing to a jagged scar on the trunk of the yew tree.

"A few weeks ago," replied the sexton, "during that night of heavy wind we had."

"It was a large branch, from the looks of things," said Pemberley.

"It was. Took me most of the next day to cut it up and cart it away."

"So there's your answer," said Pemberley.

"What do you mean?" asked Churchill.

"This tree blocks most of the light to Saul Mollikin's grave. When the branch came down the sunlight managed to get through. That's why grass is beginning to grow there."

"What wonderful insight, Miss Pemberley!" beamed Churchill. "That explains it!"

"Possibly," replied the sexton. He glanced at the yew tree, then down at the grave, then back at the tree again.

"There you go, Mr Grieves, all solved. We'll be on our way now. I feel the need for some of that fruit cake I could smell Mr Simpkin baking yesterday afternoon. I hope he has some left."

Churchill, Pemberley and Oswald walked along the high street toward the bakery.

"Mrs Churchill!" a voice called out from behind them.

"Oh, what is it now?" she muttered. "I can't muster the energy to speak to anyone else. Can you, Pembers?"

Her assistant had already turned to see who was trying to attract their attention. "It's Constable Russell," she said.

Churchill turned to see the moustachioed young man jogging toward her. "I have some good news that you might like to hear," he said. "We've just received word from the Surrey police force that Gentleman Jim and

Cutpurse Fennel have been apprehended on the road between Camberley and Bagshot."

"They've got them? That's excellent news."

"Thank goodness," said Pemberley. "Let's hope he doesn't become an informer and get away with it, though."

"If he's a proper gentleman he'll serve his time," said Churchill. "Come along, Miss Pemberley. Let's go and get some of that delicious fruit cake."

Chapter 41

A FEW DAYS LATER, Churchill and Pemberley noticed a large van parked outside Pickwick's Gallery. As they approached, they saw several men loading pictures into it under the watchful eye of Inspector Mappin.

"The corner's torn on that one," he said, pointing to a hole in the brown paper that had been carefully wrapped around a painting. "It'll need to be redone."

The man he addressed turned around resignedly and carried the package back inside the gallery.

"Are the paintings being returned to their rightful owners, Inspector?" asked Churchill.

"They certainly are. Gentleman Jim had built up quite a collection. All stolen, of course."

A stout, puffy-faced man in smart tweed strode out of the gallery. He wore a monocle and was carrying a clipboard and pencil.

"Is everything in order now, Mr Botfield-Cripps?" asked the inspector.

"I think so. It's a great shame some of the artworks have been defaced. The ignoramus scrawled the name

'Pickwick' over all the signatures, but a little restoration work should fix that quite easily."

"Mr Botfield-Cripps is an art expert," explained Mappin. "He helps us identify artworks of value and ensures that they're safely transported back to their homes."

"The discovery of these paintings has brought great relief to their owners," said Mr Botfield-Cripps. "Lord Ashby, in particular. He told me he's missed the Duke of Marlborough terribly. He's looking forward to having the old chap watch him from above the mantelpiece again when he dines."

"How creepy," commented Pemberley.

"I beg your pardon?" replied the art expert.

"It's just a practice the aristocracy is used to, Miss Pemberley," interjected Churchill. "From the moment they lie in their cribs they must grow accustomed to their ancestors staring down at them from the walls."

Pemberley grimaced.

"Gentleman Jim will be facing a long list of charges when he appears at the Dorchester Assizes," said Inspector Mappin. "I must say I'm quite looking forward to the proceedings," he added with a grin.

Mr Botfield-Cripps gave a nod. "He's a prolific thief, there's no doubt about it. One piece of artwork has left me rather confused, however."

"Why's that then?" asked Mappin.

"It's not on the list of paintings reported as stolen," said Mr Botfield-Cripps, consulting his clipboard, "and its style couldn't be more different from the other works we've recovered here. There's a distinct lack of accuracy in the painting. The representation of the figure is quite obscure."

"Eh?" The inspector raised a puzzled eyebrow.

"But quite pleasingly obscure, I should add," continued Botfield-Cripps. "And I noticed the strong symbolism present, despite the use of a limited palette. The work seems somewhat improvised, but that's fairly common in abstract art."

Churchill realised which painting the art expert was referring to. She had planned to speak, but decided to keep listening, as Mr Botfield-Cripps seemed amusingly intrigued by it.

"Wassily Wassilyevich Kandinsky," he announced.

"Whatty what?" asked the incredulous inspector.

"A Russian artist, very prominent in the abstract art movement. A number of his works have been displayed over here in recent years, in fact I recall a particularly large exhibition up north in Leeds. I wonder if anything went astray during that time. The work is unsigned, of course, but it could simply be a preliminary sketch. I think some further consultation with a colleague of mine at the prestigious Leeds College of Art is required."

"You see to that, Mr Botfield-Cripps," said Churchill with a smile on her face. "I think we would all be quite interested to hear what your colleague has to say."

"Do you really think it was painted by a famous Russian artist?" asked Inspector Mappin.

"Kandinsky, yes. It could have been."

"I think I recall seeing it now," said Churchill. "I may even recall Gentleman Jim telling me its title. It was called *Winsome Lady Blue* or something like that." She laughed. "Come along, Miss Pemberley. Let's take Oswald for his walk."

"But just a moment," said her secretary. "I think I know which painting it is. Couldn't it be the one he——"

"Let's leave the men to get on with their work."

Churchill took her secretary by the arm. "We've had a busy few days, haven't we? I fancy a relaxing stroll by the river."

The End

Thank you

~

Thank you for reading *Trouble in the Churchyard*, I really hope you enjoyed it!

Would you like to know when I release new books? Here are some ways to stay updated:

- Join my mailing list and receive the short story *A Troublesome Case*: emilyorgan.com/a-troublesome-case
- Like my Facebook page: facebook.com/emilyorganwriter
- Follow me on Goodreads: goodreads.com/emily_organ
- Follow me on BookBub: bookbub.com/authors/emily-organ
- View my other books here: emilyorgan.com

And if you have a moment, I would be very grateful if you would leave a quick review of *Trouble in the Churchyard* online. Honest reviews of my books help other readers discover them too!

Get a free short mystery

~

Want more of Churchill & Pemberley? Get a copy of my free short mystery *A Troublesome Case* and sit down to enjoy a thirty minute read.

Churchill and Pemberley are on the train home from a shopping trip when they're caught up with a theft from a suitcase. Inspector Mappin accuses them of stealing the valuables, but in an unusual twist of fate the elderly sleuths are forced to come to his aid!

Visit my website to claim your FREE copy:
emilyorgan.com/a-troublesome-case

Wheels of Peril

A Churchill & Pemberley Mystery Book 5

A bicycle brake cable cutting killer is on the loose.

When Mrs Mildred Cobnut of Compton Poppleford Ladies' Bicycling Club suffers a fatal accident, hapless Inspector Mappin begins a murder investigation. As luck would have it, world-renowned Swiss detective, Monsieur Pascal Legrand, is staying in the village; with such sleuthing expertise on hand, the case will surely be swiftly solved.

Meanwhile, Churchill and Pemberley have another case to worry about: Ramsay the missing goat. But with Churchill having crossed swords with Mrs Cobnut, the elderly detectives soon become embroiled in the murder investigation.

Who is the mystery man who calls on Mrs Twig? What causes Farmer Glossop's horse to bolt down the high street? Will Churchill ever finish a slice of Pemberley's prune cake? There are many questions for the detective duo to answer before they can hope to beat the famous Monsieur Legrand at his own game.

Find out more at: emilyorgan.com/wheels-peril

The Penny Green Series

~

Also by Emily Organ. A series of mysteries set in Victorian London featuring the intrepid Fleet Street reporter, Penny Green.

What readers are saying:

"A Victorian Delight!"

"Good clean mystery in an enjoyable historical setting"

"If you are unfamiliar with the Penny Green Series, acquaint yourselves immediately!"

Books in the Penny Green Series:
Limelight
The Rookery
The Maid's Secret
The Inventor
Curse of the Poppy
The Bermondsey Poisoner

The Penny Green Series

An Unwelcome Guest
Death at the Workhouse
The Gang of St Bride's
Murder in Ratcliffe

Printed in Great Britain
by Amazon